No Word
  for the Sea

No Word
for the Sea

A Professor
and His Wife
Face Alzheimer's

Diane Glancy

RESOURCE *Publications* · Eugene, Oregon

NO WORD FOR THE SEA
A Professor and His Wife Face Alzheimer's

Resource Publications
An Imprint of Wipf and Stock Publishers
199 W. 8th Ave., Suite 3
Eugene, OR 97401

www.wipfandstock.com

PAPERBACK ISBN: 978-1-5326-3252-5
HARDCOVER ISBN: 978-1-5326-3254-9
EBOOK ISBN: 978-1-5326-3253-2

Manufactured in the U.S.A.   07/19/17

The excerpt from "Paterson," Part II, Book Two, William Carlos Williams, is from The Collected Poems, Volume I, 1909-1939, copyright @1938 by New Directions Publishing Corp. Reprinted by permission of New Directions Publishing Corp.

The excerpt from Of Salome is reprinted by permission of the author.

Acknowledgment also to St. Paul, Minnesota
The Minnesota History Center
Kristi Wheeler and the cabin on Crane Lake
Various faculty travel and research grants, Macalester College

Memory is a kind
of accomplishment
        a sort of renewal
                even
an initiation, since the spaces it opens are new
places
        inhabited by hordes
                heretofore unrealized,
of new kinds–
        since their movements
                are toward new objectives
(even though formerly they were abandoned)

—William Carlos William
"Paterson," Part II, Book Two

The next evening
Mary Magdalene and Salome
went out and purchased embalming spices.

—Mark 16:1

I was not, in the beginning of time, a head on a plate.

—"Of Salome: On Death and Beauty"
from *Journal of the Posthumous Present*
Marvin Bell

Stephen Savard

What did I do with my cell phone? What would I do for dinner? Where was Solome? Did she leave a note? Something in the fridge? I fixed myself a sandwich. Sometimes she was helping our daughter, Soos, with the baby. Or she was at a meeting. I opened the front door. I went for a walk.

Solome Savard

Wear warm clothes.

Those were the words she heard from the next table. She had nothing but warm clothes in her closet. Winter was most of the year in Minnesota. Sweaters and trousers in logging-camp brown. Kerosene yellow. Lumber-jack check. Wood-stove black. She could push the restaurant voices away, but she listened to them as she watched for Stephen.

The thought of Crane Lake and their cabin five hours north of St. Paul rested a moment in her thoughts. She remembered thinking Stephen would be president of Cobson College. The thought returned like small waves lapping the shore. Her husband, Stephen Savard, was provost of the college, and could become president when the current president left or retired. But Stephen had been depressed. It happened suddenly, but with certainty. He had been a history professor, chair of his department, dean of his division— then provost— still going where he was going. What was bothering him? They had worked all their married life for their children and their place in St. Paul among friends and colleagues. Why had she never looked beyond possibilities? What was this cut back she felt cornered in her thoughts?

She read the menu in the restaurant.

Imagine tables close as clothes in a closet. Two women at the next table talking. Imagine someone's mind wiped clean as the next table in front of her. With a chill she remembered Stephen's mother saying she found her father's work-tools in the dining-room drawer. Solome remembered his distance at family gatherings.

In the restaurant, the conversations were unrelated to one another, yet all sounded together. Imagine the conversations lifted above the knives and forks like rigging in an inland harbor. Imagine seeing no one she knew in the downtown St. Paul restaurant that overlooked the Mississippi River. She thought of the miles the water traveled from Itasca, its headwaters, to the gulf in New Orleans. At least she didn't have to explain Stephen's absence to anyone.

Imagine a country without its own language. Well, it had a language. It just wasn't its own. It came from across the ocean, tossing boats, stirring waves. It was itself made of other languages, bits and pieces meshing over history, reverberating in the restaurant.

She tried again to call, but Stephen must have turned off his cell phone, or left it in his office. No one answered at the house. Where was he?

When had Stephen begun? Begun what? A journey into forgetfulness. A journey into his own language, into words that did not follow their order.

Solome looked at the menu again. Should she leave or stay?

Sometimes she asked Stephen about something and it was as if he was already separated from the land. It angered him when she caught him like that. When did Stephen fall into his roily language? What did that mean? She didn't know. Or he would repeat the same question. Where was the shore he was headed? It was as if he spoke behind a seawall.

They had been married thirty years. They had three children. One daughter, Gretchen, was working toward a Ph.D. at Columbia. The other, Susanna, was married and had a baby. Mark Stephen, their son, born twelve years into their marriage, was a freshman at Cobson College. Solome and Stephen had a resonance and a history. They shared a family. A people. A country. They shared a language, broken as it was.

She sat in the restaurant a while longer. She called Stephen again, but there was no answer at the office, or the house, or on his cell. Finally she ordered. She would eat by herself if Stephen didn't show. She remembered in school, she had been called, Solo.

Solome had had a name from the Bible. But her mother had misspelled it. In the Bible, it was Salome, the mother of James and John. But there was another Salome, the daughter of Herodias, who had asked her mother what she should ask from Herod after she had danced for him. Herodias told her, ask for the head of John the Baptist. There were reasons— Herodias had left her husband for his brother, and John said a man should not take his brother's wife. Herodias held a grudge, and had an answer ready for her daughter.

Why had Solome's mother named her that? She had like the sound of it, she said. The word meant, *clothed.* But she felt clothed with two different women.

In the Bible, Salome had asked her mother what she should wish for, but Solome decided what she wanted. She hadn't asked anyone. She wanted a husband, children. Then a job. What she got was a longing for something more.

When the meal came, she ate by herself in the restaurant. When she finished, she paid for it and left.

Stephen was walking along the street, several blocks from their house, when she drove up. She braked and pulled to the curb. When he didn't notice, she honked.

"What are you doing?" She asked. "You were supposed to meet me at the restaurant."

Imagine a language that could absorb all the shipwrecks, all the landings, all the changes, the disruptions and upsets. Imagine a language that could reach anywhere with its sound and meaning. If Stephen could just speak, he could cover his absence in the restaurant, which he now remembered. He could explain it, make it understandable or acceptable or tolerable. He wanted a language with boundaries that were never settled, as if the language were water, both changing the shore, as it was changed by it.

"Didn't you wonder where I was?" She asked. "What did you do for dinner?"

Stephen could say he had amnesia. He could make light of his forgetfulness, but that wouldn't work.

He hadn't even remembered to take Brown, the dog. Solome would have to walk him later.

Did Stephen want to ride?

He'd rather walk, he told her, and Solome drove on. Stephen followed, crossing the street, walking toward their cul-de-sac, the houses circling like a squall.

Stephen Savard

I was walking when Solome drove up, angry. The next morning, I wondered about my oversight. Why hadn't I been at the restaurant? What was I thinking when I left my office? I didn't know. Had I written it on my calendar and forgot to look? Why hadn't Jan, my secretary, reminded me, as she often did? Somehow it slipped away. What had I done that day? I felt stupid. It was a feeling I felt more often. There was a clear space in my mind. A place where nothing came. No thoughts. No ideas. I was in meetings— finance and long range planning. Further cut-backs were necessary. I had to re-member the numbers. The reasoning. I had lunch with a board-of-trustees member. Tenure review. Allocations. More policy decisions. I could list them. Often I felt irritable. My job frustrated me. It was going by fast. I had trouble keeping up. I didn't always have time to give my family the attention they needed. Jan, my secretary, told me that Mark Stephen was protesting something on the commons. Didn't Mark know his father was provost?

What was the name of those bushes on campus I liked to smell? They bloomed purple in the spring.

"Lilacs," Jan said.

"Of course," I answered.

"It will be a while before they bloom."

I sat in my office with the door closed. No, I had given my family everything I could. I felt angry over their demands. What were they demanding? Their weight on my shoulders. Yet I liked them. I felt pleasure with my family. How could there be contradictions? Confusion. I also thought of the presidency of the college. But the president wouldn't retire for years. I felt it slip past me, though Solome wouldn't give up. No, she wouldn't. Not because of anything or anyone I could blame. But because of something within myself. I could retire— be through with this, though I would like to teach one last history course. I was on the spot. What would I say next? They were looking at me in the meeting. Sometimes I saw impatience in faculty members.

There was a frustration. A fuzz. I wrote out the report I would give at the faculty meeting at the end of the day. It took me longer than I thought. My calls were backed-up. My e-mails. My appointments.

That evening, on a walk with the dog in Hill Park near our house, I watched a plane turning on the horizon until it was gone. Solome mentioned a recent plane crash that had been in the news.

I couldn't remember. I was thinking of something else, long ago, but I didn't tell my wife. The little black box I carried was my childhood. It would survive a crash. What was I thinking? What crash? I worried about my memory. I didn't want to think about it, but I knew something was happening. I felt like I was experiencing something I didn't know. I felt a darkness in my thinking. A panic. Or a dread with a panic behind it. The feeling sat on me with its weight. I couldn't move out from under it. I didn't know what it was. I grew more sullen. Quiet. Sometimes I caught Solome looking at me. But it was the black box— the memory of my early years. The repeating without knowing.

"You've said that Stephen," I heard Solome say.

One evening, the word, "Alzheimer's" struck me. Where had it come from? I remembered my mother wondering if her father, my grandfather, had died of Alzheimer's before anyone recognized what it was. I suddenly thought of a day that would come when I would be in a small room looking from a window waiting for someone, and I wouldn't know who they were, nor recognize them when they arrived. The word and the thought that followed didn't often come, but once in a while, as I sat in my office, or in a meeting, the dread came over me again. Was I slipping as my grandfather had slipped and died before anyone knew the word, "Alzheimer's?" What had my father died of? Heart attack. He had been young. Maybe it hadn't had time to show. Maybe the thought of it had crushed him.

Solome Savard

Imagine speaking someone else's words. A mother's. A husband's.

She was on the phone calling members of the Faculty Wives Club when the past rolled into her memory again. She was telling the wives about one of the other wives, who had just had surgery. She was ordering flowers, making conciliatory comments. The college had turned a corner toward downsizing. She was the provost's wife. She was a diplomat smoothing the way.

Solome stood in Stephen's study. Jan had called. Had he left his briefcase by his desk? No. She couldn't find it. Had he left it in the car?

She looked at the photos on the shelf. There was the family lined up in front of the Depot Museum in Duluth: Stephen, Solome, Gretchen, Susanna, Mark Stephen. There they were in front of an antique store in Stillwater. In front of Paul Bunyan in Brainerd. Was that the trip Stephen was supposed to leave with them, but some meeting had come up at the college, and she had driven ahead with the children? Later, Stephen had taken the bus to Brainerd. He had gotten off the bus with a confused look on his face, but she was there to meet him.

"Here we are," she had called him. She remembered the relieved look on his face as he walked toward us.

There was the family at the Black Hills and Mount Rushmore on their South Dakota trip. There were the photos of the family at her parents' cabin on Crane Lake; her father with a fishing pole in his hand. Sometimes his absence still caught her off guard.

There was Brown, the dog, with snow on his nose.

The wedding of Susanna and Brian, their son-in-law.

The baby Susan. Her first birthday party.

The photo of Solome and Jane Mead, a friend since high school, who was like a sister.

The photos of New York on their visits to Gretchen.

There were photos of several trips Solome and Stephen took to Europe. There they were in Madrid.

Stephen Savard

It came in waves. The forgetting. The remembering.

Over the summer, work began on a new student center. It would be completed in a year. I could see a piling for the corner of the building from my window. I could hear the cement trucks.

I was functioning. Completing my work for the day. Knowing where my briefcase was. My car keys.

Then the pot hole.

What was that game in which a woman pushed something like a tea-kettle on the floor and two other women rushed ahead of it, sweeping the ice clean and slick? Shot put came to mind, but that wasn't the name. Ask Solome—

Why did I care about it anyway? I thought as I got in my car.

Sometimes men played the game also.

Most days, I was myself. Then papers jumbled on my desk. Moved by themselves. A forecast— What was there wasn't there any longer. Looking at something what was it?— what did I have to do? Think of the word I needed but couldn't find. Everything tumbling. Get a grip. Keep it buried. Don't let them see. Get ready for the meeting. Where's the briefcase? Call Solome. Look in the car. Not there. Not here. Can't go to the meeting without papers. Secretary— print out minutes again. Get lunch bring to me. I don't have— I'll eat while I prepare for the meeting. Then the candidates for sociology and religious studies departments. Get their resumes. Jan— they're in briefcase.

Solome Savard

Imagine an American memory. Minnesota winters. Sledding. Ice skating. Shoveling after a blizzard. Then summer baseball. Hot dogs. Paul Bunyan.

Imagine a woman's black gabardine evening bag. A daughter looking at it. Imagine earrings in a dresser drawer. Two mounds of sequins like the sun on an afternoon lake. Why would Solome remember the mound of sequins that were her mother's earrings? Why did those images stay in her mind at times? How often did she think of the past? And who was she with a misspelled name, Solome, a name different from others? It all harbored in her memory, that gift she wanted to name again and again.

Solome purchased a chest-of-drawers. After it was delivered, she found a stain mark down the edge. She wrote a letter to the company. A man came from the furniture store in the afternoon, and decided there was nothing wrong. He didn't offer to repair or replace it.

Imagine an American house. An American dog.

A husband confused about the day. In need of his briefcase.

Money paid for a flawed piece of furniture.

Imagine wanting something and wanting something. The feeling never stopped barking; gnawing like a squirrel in the attic, like our dog, Brown, that didn't stop barking.

Solome lived in America, yet the neighbors acted like they were in a country where they turned each other in. What could she do? It was as if part of her crossed through the walls of the house and settled in the dog, and she called out for someone and called out for someone in the dog's bark.

What could she do with a dog that stayed chained in the backyard? She asked her Thursday afternoon discussion group. Jane Mead suggested putting him to sleep. Brown had dug a trench along the back of the house in frustration, uprooting a flower bed and an old toy buried long ago by one of the children. The yard man would fill it in again.

The dog didn't bark while Solome was there. Once, in a dream, during a nap, she'd heard barking. She woke and knew what the neighbors meant. But why had they called the police? Who was it? Not the Grunswald's. They were friends. Possibly the Morgan's. More probably the Bernard's whom she hardly knew. Or someone on the next street.

What did she want? Her business was the house and children, but now the walls were moving and she was unable to hold them back.

Solome e-mailed their oldest daughter, Gretchen, in New York about the neighbors who had called the police about their dog, Brown, because he barked when she left. She didn't mention who she thought it was, and Gretchen didn't ask.

Once Solome wrote that she was worried about Stephen.

She heard the yard man raking leaves in the back yard. Brown was yapping and jumping at him. Solome yelled from the back door for Brown to be quiet. She finally closed him in the garage.

At noon, Soos stopped by the house with the baby. Solome made sandwiches for their lunch. Then Soos put Susan down for a nap and ran errands while Solome watched her. Soos had started a romper for Susan. Solome finished it on the sewing machine while Soos was gone.

Stephen Savard

Our son, Mark Stephen, wanted to develop his own course of study at the college. He joined some students who formed a protest group. I was embarrassed that my son's name was in the college newspaper. I knew my colleagues talked about it behind my back.

The students had sit-ins. They had marches. They chalked the sidewalks. There were demands for multiculturalism.

"You don't know what you need to know," I said to Mark, irritated that he dropped by my office without notice. He walked by Jan with a sense of entitlement, though she told him I was on the phone.

Sometimes Mark stopped by the house on weekends. His returns were nothing more than a meal for Solome to serve, his clothes to wash, his room to clean after he left, and a few sharp words between us as I was becoming more and more, what was the word he used— irascible?

"Why do you stay at Cobson and embarrass your father?" Solome confronted Mark one evening at dinner. "You could go to another college if you want to act like that."

"I want to go to Cobson," Mark snapped back. "I like the climate there. My friends are there."

"What you do reflects on your father."

"Ideas change. I can't be your boy scout any longer," Mark said and left.

"What's gotten into you, Solome?" I asked. "You've never snapped at him like that."

"What's gotten into you?" She returned.

Solome Savard

When she was in high school, her parents bought a small cabin on Crane Lake, five hours north of St. Paul, near the boundary waters on the border of Canada. The shore was eroding, though they didn't know it at the time. "Fitting," her mother said. She kept the cabin after Solome's father died, though she seldom went there. "It's probably overrun by mosquitoes or fallen into the lake."

But the cabin had not fallen into the lake. Solome went there when she needed solitude. Sometimes Stephen came with her. Her mother wasn't interested in the cabin any longer, nor the children, though Mark would go occasionally with some friends. Her mother thought of selling it, but Solome asked if they could hold onto it when her mother mentioned selling.

Solome belonged to the Faculty Wives Club. She had a small job. On Wednesdays and Fridays she worked at the Minnesota Historical Society. She volunteered, actually. She worked in retrieval in the research library, going into the stacks, bringing back requested material. Sometimes she looked through the books, reading about subjects such as Ojibway winter spirits. She liked the cool, gray metal stairs, the battleship gray floors. The orderliness. The fire-proofed structure. But she felt nothing she wanted to feel. She could plug the longing now and then. Dream of an actual job with responsibility and satisfaction. That was the American dream.

There was Stephen's briefcase— in his closet again. She called him at Cobson. Did he want her to drive it there? Yes. She was used to delivering forgotten things.

Solome had raised three children. She had served in PTA and Brownie troops. She had made some of the girls' clothes. She took risks. She chose yellow wallpaper with turquoise flowers for the dining room. Maybe garish was the word for my risk, in that case. She was present with Stephen at dinners and social gatherings. She was the visible wife of the provost of Cobson College. She knew what to say to others.

Salome, the mother of the disciples, James and John, had been at the tomb of Jesus with Susanna, Joanna, who was the wife of Chuzas, Herod's steward, and other women who had been healed of spirits and demons, including Mary Magdalene. What were demons? Was that what was pursuing Stephen?

But Solome's ordinary American life was blessed. She didn't need to worry about demons. There were no tanks in the street. No gunshots in the neighborhood. No fear for her children's lives, though American cities were not safe, and at night she hurried toward her house along the lighted sidewalk with the dog. She wished sometimes they lived farther out in the suburbs, but Stephen liked being close to the college. They'd been in the same house nearly twenty-five years.

Where did the mind go when the circuits shut down?

Solome looked through the photo albums of trips and outings, birthdays, scouting and school programs, the high school graduations of their three children.

What was missing? God, what was it? God? Late one evening when she was waiting for Stephen to come back on a plane after a conference on retaining faculty, before she started to the airport to get him, she was passing through the t.v. channels and saw an evangelist on television. He preached a sermon and said she needed Jesus in her life. There was a woman listening who needed to be saved. Accept Jesus as your Savior. She sat in the chair and repeated after the evangelist, Lord Jesus Christ, you died for my sins, I accept you as my Savior.

Now she had an American religion.

While Salome had asked Jesus if her sons, James and John, could sit by his side in heaven, Solome asked Jesus to be by her side. Well, now she had Jesus. What next?

The sin would disappear from her life, the minister on television said. What was her sin? She was faithful. Punctual. Conscientious. Consistent. What had she done that Jesus had to die on the cross?

When she picked Stephen up from the airport, she said nothing to him about her television evangelistic experience.

Stephen Savard

In the airport forgot which gate looked at pass again again. Had trouble sleeping in hotel. Pillow hard. These— episodes turmoil. Thought of meeting. Disinterested. Only wanted to leave. Why didn't I care about this? Always careful in meetings and information dissemination.

There were episodes? Our lives running through. Keys with Soos' car. A call when. Have it towed. There clear up. I'll take care I'm on my way back.

I could hear the baby cry.

Solome Savard

Solome was used to *upward mobility*, but now she sensed a collision with life as she knew it. No, life as she knew it was colliding with what she didn't know. Didn't want to know. She hardly was aware of it, but Stephen was stepping off a continental shelf. Maybe it was a recognition that moved in her sleep, deep in her dreams. Could Solome continue without Stephen? What had she ever done without him? Could she face herself before God alone? Oh God, what could she do? There was a landscape like a Salvador Dali painting in her head when she opened the Bible. "The Lord shall descend from heaven with a shout; and the dead in Christ shall rise first; then we who are alive shall be caught up together with them in the clouds to meet the Lord in the air. Wherefore, comfort one another with these words."— I Thessalonians 4:16–18. What comfort was that? Solome thought— Being yanked through the sky when she didn't want to go. She closed the Bible.

Sometimes she numbered her duties to herself. Her book of numbers. Cordiality was part of Solome's fabric, her veil. She remembered her line of duties. Her children always had been ready for school. She had been at home when the children returned from school. She oversaw homework. She *got them ahead*. She hosted parties when her husband was chair of the history department at Cobson College. She hosted more parties when he was division dean, and when he became provost. Once, she had planned to continue to host parties when Stephen was president.

Sometimes everything numbed her. She called Reverend Croft, her minister, and made an appointment. "I need to know about faith." She wanted more from church. How could she tell him that? What was she doing? After their talk, a woman with the last name of Forman called Solome and asked her to their Bible study group. What conspiracy was in the church? Solome agreed to come before she knew it. She would go just once to see who these strange people were.

It wasn't church, but the Bible and the reading of it. Maybe that was the barking dog. There were words that demanded to be heard, to be paid attention. She was a Christian in a Christian nation. But she didn't know what that meant. She was a nominal Christian in a nominal nation. What was it like to be a believer who walked in faith? Was she in or out? Hot or cold? Maybe that's what Brown wanted. Meaning in his life. The dog was part of Solome out there in the yard. Digging trenches as if for war. Did soldiers even dig trenches anymore?

Two of her children, Gretchen and Mark, were in college. One daughter, Susanna, whom they called Soos, returned home after her marriage and the birth of a daughter, Solome and Stephen's only grandchild. But after a few months, Soos had reconciled with her husband. Sometimes when Stephen worked late, or had meetings, she began to feel her life was her own.

What if, in the middle of this new feeling of self-direction, her life turned a corner where she didn't want to go? What if the walls of her house were pinching together? Slowly, of course, so slowly she hardly noticed. What if her outward course reversed? The fear gripped her. What if her direction changed to downward mobility? She couldn't stand the thought. It was not what she wanted. What if it was some sinister force? Solome realized she was sweating.

On Monday evenings, Solome went to Bible study. She wanted to grow stronger in her faith. What did that mean? She would rely on what the Bible said, rather than on her circumstances?

Stephen Savard

Gretchen and Dennis were coming. No— they had called they might be coming but it wasn't settled yet. What was his last name? Solome tried to remember.

"Dennis something."

"Yes I know but what?"

"I don't know, Stephen," Solome said. "We'll find out soon enough."

What would I say to him? Why was he coming?

In the end, they postponed.

Solome Savard

Solome took the dog for a walk. She would stop to talk with Hetty Grunswald, her neighbor. Later, she would talk with her friends on the phone. She called Soos everyday, or stopped by her house. She talked to her mother nearly every day on the phone. Sometimes, on Wednesdays and Fridays, her mother met her at the Historical Society for lunch and they spent time in the exhibits. Sometimes Soos and Susan came also. Then there were the calls to Gretchen in New York of an evening while Stephen sat in his chair. Sometimes it seemed as if Stephen was purposely disengaging, losing interest in their lives. She could sense him preparing to leave, not her as his wife, but leaving his own life; not dying yet, but slowly taking his hands off the wheel. It couldn't be time for the end yet.

Solome lived in America where there was a heaven and an earth. But there was something coming for Stephen. They both felt it in the night. It was a new territory neither of them wanted to enter.

She remembered once at her parents' place at Crane Lake, a large boat docked. A woman in a black swimming suit ran toward her parents' cabin where Stephen worked with her father to screen the porch. She watched the woman run toward her husband like a dream that followed sleep into waking. Soon the woman realized she was running toward the wrong house, and turned to the house next door.

"Who was that?" Solome asked her mother.

"She's the daughter of a woman who looked in on the old couple," her mother said.

Yes, the people who lived in the next cabin with their retarded daughter.

Solome watched Stephen return to his screening after a woman in black ran toward him in the afternoon, a black butterfly, ready to carry him away, to unthread him from her.

Once there had been a common Indo-European language with words for winter and horse, but no word for the sea.

Wear warm clothes, Solome remembered.

Once she had taken a course on language. She still remembered it, or some of it. After the common language, there had been closely related Germanic languages that formed the basis of English, which formed the basis of her American language. There had been links to Sanskrit, Greek, Latin. There was a Norman conquest; there were the Anglo Saxons. Imagine a language that could move over, make room for others. Imagine new words joined to the old ones, crossing to other worlds, spreading like the sea.

The English and American language wasn't as rigid as other languages. New ideas were given new words, maybe new words were given new ideas. There were openings for possibilities: abstractions and complex thought.

Christianity also had added words: cedars of Lebanon, camels, myrrh. Even language had been converted by Christianity. There also was the story of the Tower of Babel in the Bible, where language was purposely mixed.

Solome felt the piles of language like laundry yet to be folded. She felt cardboard. Artificial. What was her language telling her? She didn't like herself. No, that wasn't it.

Where were all the facts she had once memorized?

Where was all the *wood* she had chopped? *Chores* she had done?

What if she had had the opportunity to develop a career the way Stephen had? What if she hadn't been clamped off? Was that how she saw her life?

On Monday evening, the Bible study group met at her house. The members took turns hosting the group. Solome decided to make a dessert. There were three couples, two unmarried sisters named Forman, and a man who came without his wife. The minister and his wife also sometimes attended.

The group was amazed at the Savard's house. Solome could tell by the way they looked at the room. Didn't they know she was the wife of a provost? She wished it were something she could hide. The man who came without his wife was the only one who didn't seem impressed.

Mrs. Croft, the minister's wife, thought Solome could do everything as she tasted her dessert. Flattery should have been her name.

The Bible study group was a fast-paced crowd, Stephen told her with irritation when they left.

"Do you want me to quit?" Solome asked.

"Do what you want."

The minister's wife had a drifty presence. She could be everything to nearly everyone. Solome admired her resistance to getting stuck in one place— Her wide berth.

Solome was who she was. But who was she? And why did she have the feeling she was on the swift current of a river moving toward a sea from which there was no return? Or sometimes she felt like she was on a river with a steep waterfall ahead. Would the river just stop, and she would find herself mid-air?

On Sunday morning at church, the group studied the travels of Paul in Acts. In the old class, the one Stephen and Solome had attended for years, the Fidelis class, they had speakers, and not much talk about the Bible.

Stephen Savard

"Brian and Soos need a small loan," Solome told me at lunch on Sunday.

"Let them go to the bank," I answered. I wanted to change the subject. I wanted to tell her I was embarrassed I had forgotten a colleague's name as we left church. But Solome wanted to talk to me about their youngest daughter.

"Soos called yesterday— She has enough pressure in her marriage."

"They weren't in church," I said. "They said they would be there."

Solome looked at me. "Maybe the baby wasn't well."

"Maybe they spend too much money."

"It takes a lot of money, Stephen. Susanna doesn't work so she can take care of Susan. I don't see why we can't help them."

"Because they're dependent enough as it is."

"No, they're not," Solome argued. "They handle their finances."

"Then why are they asking for money?"

"The interest they have to pay on their Visa card— "

"Tell them not to buy so much," I offered.

"I think they buy what is necessary."

"Solome— "

I knew she could hear my impatience.

" — that's their problem."

"But you give Mark what he wants— " Solome protested.

"Didn't we just help Brian and Soos?"

"That was Gretchen," Solome said. "And when did you talk to Susanna— when did she say they'd be in church?"

I looked at her. "When she called."

"I talked to her yesterday," Solome said. "You weren't here— "

"She called later— " I got up from the table. "You give them the money they're asking for," I said angrily, and left the dining room and went to my study.

Solome couldn't let go of the fact that I wasn't responsible for my forgetfulness. I knew she thought my forgetfulness was to spite her. Why would I do that?

Solome Savard

The radio station was full of static, fading in and out. Solome listened to it at night as she fell asleep, so Stephen's snoring wouldn't keep her awake. Solome remembered when she had returned with her parents Sunday nights from Crane Lake or after visiting her grandparents in Hastings, Minnesota, and they would hear a station in Mexico.

When she first had the children, Solome couldn't handle the feedings, changings, spills, colic, erratic sleep patterns, the predictability of the messes. She worked all through the day and ended up at the same place each evening, exhausted, frayed, with another pile of laundry, another pile of toys scattered over the house. Stephen's voice had pulled her through. He had called during the day, sometimes leaving between his history classes at Cobson College to eat lunch with them. Her mother helped too. But it was Stephen who talked her through the crises.

Jane Mead, her friend since high school, was always going through a crisis of her own making. Most of the time, it was Solome who listened to Jane.

In the years that followed, Solome often thought about how long it took to raise the children. Fifteen more years before they were grown. Ten more. Five more. She felt the long haul of cooking, cleaning, car-pooling. The school activities. But again, it was Stephen's voice she heard. Now Solome was on a smooth course. Hadn't she earned it with her responsible life? But what if Stephen's signal was fading? NO!

She felt the thought of losing Stephen. It was a tremor in her bedrock. Was she like one of those animals who could foresee an earthquake? Whose erratic behavior gave a signal it was going to happen?

Sometimes Solome remembered the tumult of their family history. How children tore up expectations, went their own way, stretched the family into territories the parents wouldn't have gone. But now it was Stephen who was slipping. He could remember fifty years ago, but where was yesterday? He was not yet 60 years old. How could this happen? It still seemed like they were just beginning. Was the end already here? Did it all pass that quickly?

Sometimes he stood in the kitchen while she fixed supper. Sometimes she looked at him. "Do you know where you are?" Solome asked.

"Of course, I'm in the kitchen."

"What are you standing there for?"

"I don't know."

"Sit down. Look at the paper. I'll have supper ready soon."

Sometimes she could hear his childhood when he shared an old memory with her. Sometimes he struggled for the words he wanted. It was Stephen who first mentioned the word, "Alzheimer's." What would she do if their light went out? What would she do without marriage? What if their language together fractured and shut down?

Often, her husband stumbled over his words. Trickster language. Taking as it had once given. Full of fractured words broken off from other languages, making new words that then joined with others. Wasn't it Noah Webster who imposed uniformity of spelling on words? Otherwise, her American language would be more like water, which it was. How often she thought of Crane Lake.

"We could move to a smaller house," Stephen told her at supper. But where would the children stay when they came for a visit? Solome asked. Where would someone stay if she needed help with Stephen? When she needed help with Stephen, she thought.

What was she thinking? Maybe Stephen was just overworked. Yes. There were financial and political decisions at Cobson. A department to be eliminated. There was tension between faculty members. There was a starkness in academia, despite the festive caps and robes the professors wore during convocations and graduations and official events. Maybe that was the reason for the robes. There was student unrest and editorials protesting college policies in the student newspaper. Didn't pressure cause forgetfulness? Yes, it did. Maybe Stephen needed to rest. Then he'd pull out of it.

Stephen Savard

I was in a meeting with the president and several faculty members who were protesting a change— opposing it— the elimination of their department. Arguing for their case. After the meeting, the president asked me to stay in his office. He said he felt I was gliding through meetings, not catching what was said, not adding my thoughts as I always had. My opinions were listened to— they were needed. Often, I took heat for the president. What was wrong? The president asked. Was I feeling all right?— Was there some problem he should be aware of? Was it family? Was Mark Stephen the problem? No. No. I was thinking we could eliminate a section of a department, instead of the whole department. It would be easier. In language, for instance, Russian has had a diminished enrollment for several years. Yes, the president said he could consider that. I returned to my office and closed my door. I put my head in my hands. I shut my eyes and swam in the darkness there. It was the first time I'd been called on my forgetfulness— my absence of mind in meetings. They had noticed. I'd been discovered. What could I do to cover my loss before they told me to leave?

"I don't want to go to church this morning," I told Solome. "I know there'll be people I should know, but won't remember their names. My memory doesn't work like it did." There— I had told her. But she let it slip without comment.

If Solome walked into church walked first, and said their name— she explained to me— then I would know. But I couldn't rely on her every moment. Sometimes she stopped and talked to someone and left me standing in the open. Someone else I should know would approach and speak as though I remembered who they were, and what they did. Often I knew that I knew them, but didn't see them often enough to remember.

"I don't want to go to church," I said again. But she didn't let it slip.

"I could go alone, Stephen. Students and other faculty would wonder where you were. We belong to that church because it's close to campus and you could be with colleagues and students. What if they no longer saw you? What would they think?"

Solome was right. Was I losing the ability to reason? I went upstairs and put on my suit.

Solome Savard

Solome's Bible Study group became a small, tight-knit group, despite their differences. The man who came without his wife— what was his name? John Everett?— was the only one not solicitous to her.

What did Solome want? She questioned herself in times of introspection with the group. What did she hear in the bark of the dog? What longing? What? She wanted recognition of herself. She wanted Stephen to see her for who she was.

No, it was more than that. She wanted to know who she was. It seemed to her that Stephen had been himself all his life. He was his own authority. He knew what he was doing. She knew also, or had known once, but it had been pushed aside while she raised her family and thought of herself as Stephen's wife. It was hard for her to put in words. She wanted to feel her whole being. She wanted to feel the whole of being.

Solome had lunch with Jane Mead whom she'd known most of her life. After high school, Jane had married, had been Jane Harrison for a while, but took back her name after her divorce, and kept her name when she married again. She had since divorced a second time.

"I don't know how you stay married to one man. I don't have the stamina it must take. I just want out when I'm not happy. Then I'm single again and all I think about is the next man I'll meet. I look for him at the grocery, when I'm with my friends, laughing as though being with other women is what I wanted, when all the time I'm looking for a man in the crowd who's looking at me."

"It feels like we're in high school again." Solome said.

"I see our girls starting down the same path."

"Soos wants to stay married to Brian. It's Brian who's not sure. I want to shake him sometimes for the pain he's causing her. I think the baby picks it up too."

"What else do men cause?" Jane asked.

"You haven't been this bitter."

"I'm just tired of disappointment."

"I'm reading a book about the daughter of Galileo," Solome said. "We should use it in our discussion group."

Stephen Savard

Different pieces of conversation overheard. That's what I was experiencing. All the conversations I'd had. The words circled, crossed over from the past, mixed into one another. I felt like I was flying over my life with nowhere to land, or I'd forgotten where the airport was. *And where was the pilot? Wasn't that his job?* Solome and I picked up Gretchen and Dennis from the airport. *What's his name?* I still didn't know. I stayed in my room until Solome called me down. What's wrong dad? Gretchen asked. His mind on something, I heard Solome say. Changes at the college. Mark Stephen at the house. Susanna and Brian and the baby. They looked at me like they did at college. *Why did they look?* That night I called out something to Solome. She woke and held me, quieted me.

It didn't do any good to ask for help. My colleagues didn't know what was happening. I saw it clearly sometimes. I had to stay where I was. Not ask for help from them. It only confused and frustrated my secretary. I wouldn't call out again to Solome at night when I heard someone. I knew the voice came from the past, from someone already in another world.

I think Solome wanted to say something to me, but she swallowed the words. She wouldn't ask anything of me.

At times, we had a language of politeness when meaning had gone.

It was deflection when there was something I wanted to hide.

It was imagination. Imagination was an ocean. I was trying to wash my words in it. I was trying to be shaped by language, or maybe it was language that would shape me— if I kept talking like I always had.

Solome Savard

Imagine a borrowed language. Changing. Unreliable. Imagine a language in flux, the dynamics of change and redefining the meaning of words, their messages and migrations, the different ways they could mean in combinations with other words.

Imagine spring after seven months of winter. A summer passing quickly.

On Friday, Solome had lunch with her mother at the Historical Society across the atrium from the museum shop. Her mother pushed her tray slowly. Others went around them. Afterwards, they walked through the rooms, looking at the paintings of Minnesota history and the artifacts, as they often did, until her mother tired.

"There's an opening for an assistant in acquisitions," Solome told her mother. "Part-time. I heard about it this morning. The Historical Society needs someone to research facts for the news releases and reviews of exhibits and programs."

"Can you take the time to work?" Her mother asked.

"I don't know," Solome answered. "It sounds like something I would like."

Later that afternoon, in the research library, Solome retrieved material on the Birch Coulee Battlefield Historical Site: the Battle from both U.S. and the Dakota perspectives for a change. She came across the native word for Minnesota, *Mni Shota*, turning it over and over, thinking of the changes to language. The word meant something about many waters— or something about clouds in the waters— or turbid white-edge water. When Solome wasn't retrieving materials, she looked through other books, stopping here and there in the stacks. She turned down a Minnesota Public Radio program on the radio that was left playing in the stacks for some reason. It interfered with her reading. When Solome looked at the clock, it was nearly five.

Stephen was frustrated when she got home. She was late. He couldn't find anything to eat. The dog was barking. Where was she? How could she be someplace else when he needed her? Solome didn't want Stephen's anger. Did she wish her marriage was over? She suddenly thought as she listened to him. Would she marry again? Was there anyone else she wanted to marry? How could she be thinking that? Where did those thoughts come from? The name of the Salome who asked for the head of John the Baptist was not actually mentioned in the Bible, but by other records, her name was known. Maybe that Salome was part of Solome also, a part that was veiled, hidden. If Solome wanted to be whole, she would have to look at her also.

Stephen couldn't find a shirt he wanted. He had started getting out what he wanted to wear the next day so he wouldn't have to face the decision in the morning. Solome was in the kitchen when she heard him yell for her. Would she become his caretaker for the rest of her life?

No, Solome couldn't handle a job at the Minnesota Historical Society, not even part-time. Not for a while.

For a moment, Solome wanted Stephen's head on a platter.

That's why Jesus had to die for her on the cross.

Stephen Savard

In the fall, when the yellow leaves were shining through my window, I made a doctor's appointment.

Solome went with me.

"If Stephen has Alzheimer's, it will take years for him to become incapacitated," the doctor told us.

The conversation seemed to move too fast. If Stephen had the disease, the diagnosis was still inconclusive. He talked past me. I wanted to wave my hand in his face and tell him that Stephen was sitting before him.

We left town after the appointment, not saying much to each other in the car.

We drove to the cabin on Crane Lake, past Ely, Minnesota, and Buyck, near the Boundary Waters, just under the Canadian border. I woke in the night. I couldn't remember where I was for a moment. I had to think. There was nothing solid to hold onto. There were chunks and pieces of memories of the day's events. I had driven somewhere. I was struggling with my thoughts. I didn't know what was happening. I had to fight an urge to bolt from the room and run as far as I could. There were crossed signals. Nothing was clear. There were parts of a road. Trees rushing past. A sky looking through the trees. A wedge of light. A fighting not to drown in the absence of thought. The lake! That was it. Was a mosquito humming? No. A dog barking?— No. We had left Brown in St. Paul. Mark would feed him.

It was as if consciousness was a briefcase I carried and had to pay attention to and not leave it behind. I constantly had to think until I knew what it was. Where were the keys to the car? What if we needed to leave? I had to remember again where I was and what I was there for.

That weekend, Solome and I painted a corner of the cabin ceiling to cover a watermark above the door. I thought of all the winter ice on the roof hanging into the rainspout, leaking into the cabin as it melted. It gave me something to do.

Maybe I had become like the moon that shined through the trees at the lake at night, full and whole only part of the time. Maybe I felt I was never in the same place often, yet somehow there was a return to the same places. Maybe that's the way I felt.

I thought of the frozen lake in winter, compacted, cracked, one edge lifting on another, groaning at night with ice slabs sticking up, the winter spirit near. What if Alzheimer's was like that?

The next morning, we pulled the motorboat from the water for the winter. Then we went out in the rowboat. The water did not cry. What were those thought that visited me? Where did they come from?

I had been a map maker, but it was a map of history. As I talked to Solome, I felt the currents of words. I could handle language. It was the water over which I rowed back toward the land. But the language I knew now started with something other and continued to change with words from other places, until it had become a new language of images, slippages and memories. My life felt like a card-table with collapsible legs. The legs were not locked in place. What if my illness would clip the table and it would fall, taking my life with it, and therefore Solome's? There were wars and rumors of war. Economic instability in the stock market. Wildfires. Drought. Heat. Storms. How fragile life was.

As we closed the cabin for the winter, I heard the wind high in the trees, especially the old, tall tree by the cabin next door. I felt a chill in the air. A dampness. I told Solome I thought it could snow before we returned to St. Paul. But it was the coming storm inside me.

Solome Savard

Stephen was talking to someone. Solome could hear it, and he knew she heard it, and he covered what he was saying.

"There's someone here. I can feel it." She thought he said.

When Stephen could speak about his forgetfulness, and his feelings about his forgetfulness, which wasn't often, he waited until they were at some event at the college, then said to Solome, "I know him— His name is hard to remember— He's looking at me. I have to say something."

But Solome didn't always know all his college associates, especially the new ones. She couldn't always help, though she tried as quickly as she could to learn the names. She had Jan send her a list of faculty and their photos.

"Just speak like you know him," she would say.

But to speak would let the man know Stephen didn't know him. "I have the feeling I'm only part here," he said to Solome under his breath.

Solome waited for him to talk more about his forgetfulness. She looked at him in the car.

"My world is small each day I feel it smaller," Stephen finally said.

She wondered if he knew he'd even said it.

Maybe some Alzheimer's patients didn't know what was happening to them. But Stephen would, Solome thought. Whatever was ahead, they would face it with dignity.

Stephen Savard

The history I had studied was rearranging its chronological order. To me, all the pictures in the house were crooked on the walls. I mentioned it to Solome, but she said they looked straight to her. The whole nation of myself was a history turned down like a radio.

I crossed swollen rivers, the wilderness, the buffalo herds, the Indians encampments. At last, I stood in the cul-de-sac, the houses circling like Conestogas.

Diane Glancy

Solome Savard

It snowed more that winter than it had in a long time. Solome heard the neighbors shoveling as she read the newspaper. She heard the yard man with his snow blower on their walk. She heard the snow plow late at night. Each morning, she called her mother and then Soos to see how they were doing. The snow took on a new meaning for Solome. It was the term, *white out*, she heard on the news. It described road conditions in a snow storm. Solome knew part of the world was being erased before Stephen too. How could she bring it back?

She was still awake one night when she heard Mark come in. She knew the familiar noise of his car. She thought she heard another voice. Probably a friend. Sometimes Mark tired of the noise in the dormitory at the college and came back to his room. They would want breakfast late in the morning.

There were great piles of snow in the street. Some of it they hauled off in trucks and dumped in the Mississippi River at night. Solome thought of the Christmas cards she had to send. The shopping she had to do. The party at the college to host. She had to send invitations to the smaller Christmas party they would have at their house for close colleagues and friends. She thought of the preparation she had to do for it. There was the Faculty Wives Club Christmas luncheon. The Historical Society luncheon. The party for her Discussion Group. A dinner at the house of the president of Cobson College. Other parties to which they were invited. Solome went over her shopping list again for gifts for the children and grandchild. Finally she slept.

The next morning, Stephen stood at the front window. He was leaving. Slowly leaving. He knew it, and so did she. Where was the language for that?

Stephen Savard

Solome and I sat with Soos and the baby, Susan, at the Christmas program. The church was filled with poinsettias and candles, the smell of fir and cedar. Soos hoped that Brian would meet us after work. She hoped he would attend church with her, or want Susan raised in church, or find help for their marriage. But Brian didn't come. I watched the program with Solome and Soos. The children were shepherds, angels, Mary, Joseph, the animals. The sheep were in white dresses. One lamb had a cap with ears. One said, *baa,* and when everyone laughed, decided not to say it again. Caesar Augustus had decided to take a census. Joseph had to go to Bethlehem. Mary went with him. The children didn't know what to do. They all had Alzheimer's, I thought. One child was crying. Now his father was coming for him, picking him up, carrying him up the aisle.

My thoughts came back to the sanctuary when the children were leaving— the angels with their cardboard wings and halos, the sheep and a lamb, the cows and a donkey in a brown jumper with a tail. Where had I been in my thoughts? Was I also in a *recessional*?

Some of our friends told us they'd noticed our absence in the Sunday school class we'd attended for years.

"Where have you been?" They asked. "We've missed you in the Fidelis class."

"I'm going to another class." Solome said. "I am examining my Christianity— the heat has been turned up."

Solome Savard

The Christmas season was busy with parties. Gretchen came home from school for three days. She spent most of the time e-mailing or on the phone with Dennis who lived in Connecticut and didn't come with her. Soos and Brian seemed happy. Solome's mother was cheerful. Things were hopeful.

The bleakness of January hit after the holidays. Solome fell into the sub-zero weather. She sat in the chair and imagined she sat in a room in which there was nothing. That's the way she felt. She rarely thought about herself as a person without Stephen and the children. When she did, it was a snow-covered field without any tracks. Solome's volunteer job at the Historical Society was not a consideration. Two days a week. Nothing that demanded much of her. And if it did, she could let go.

Solome was too tired to go to the Monday night Bible study after Christmas. She wanted the nothingness of her thoughts a while longer. But nothing did not stay nothing. Something always began to form. A fallen hair. Dust from the air. They settled on the floor. Were drawn to each other. They formed a gray fuzz which was the beginning. More dust from the air settled on the floor. It came up in the air from the furnace. It sifted down through the ceiling and in through the insulation and the windows. She used her hand as a broom. She was on her knees on the floor. She swept the fuzz as though her hand was a broom. She swept the holy, living dust mites.

Diane Glancy

Stephen Savard

Forgot to put ice cream back in freezer. Left on counter. Ran down into drawers. Solome angry then sorry she was angry. It's all right all right— it happens to everyone no don't say anything— don't.

I had another appointment with the doctor. He imaged my brain to have a map to measure its future journeys.

I *could* be in the early stages of Alzheimer's, though it was *not certain* how soon the disease would develop, or *if* it would. There were several things that could look like Alzheimer's. Maybe it was a phase— an adjustment a little more jarring than normal. Maybe I was unconsciously backing out of responsibility I didn't want. Or felt no longer wanted. His words seem to cross. Was he crossing me? I felt anger. Solome put her hand on my arm. Was he blaming me for the blame I already felt? Was I hearing him or imagining what I heard?

"How do you know for sure?" I heard Solome ask.

"Usually the only way is an autopsy."

We were shocked into silence. The doctor must have realized he spoke hastily. We had not gone that far in our thoughts yet.

The doctor apologized.

We returned home silently in the car.

"I thought we could travel," Solome said as we ate supper that evening.

"We've been to Europe several times," I answered. "I wouldn't mind going back to Germany."

"I was thinking of someplace farther— why not China?"

I met a colleague in Germany— at a conference— at the university in Freiburg— a man named Siceloff. There— I had remembered his name precisely. His wife was Johanna.

"Remember?— we ate with them at a table in a restaurant on the square— alfresco—" I told Solome. "Afterwards we traveled."

"I've always liked the Chinese rooms at the Minneapolis Art Institute," Solome continued.

"I remember nearly missing the plane in Frankfurt," I said.

"We wouldn't go on our own," Solome told me. "We'd take one of those faculty tours that guide us along. We get their brochures in the mail all the time."

I knew Solome was high on responsibility. She was low on the feeling of loss. She would face her worries. She had run at first because she was frightened. Maybe horrified was more like it. But she came back. She would go on as she always had.

Solome Savard

Wear warm clothes, she remembered. Those warm clothes would have to be faith. What else did she have to wear? She dragged herself back to Bible study, though her discussion group was reading a book that numbed faith.

Imagine a language not your own. Imagine a Monday night Bible study where a little group studied the book of Hebrews. They were Else and Bill Renke, Elaine and Harold Franklin, Charlotte and Ralph Steward, the Forman sisters, sometimes Pastor and Mrs. Croft, and of course, John Everett, the man without his wife. Solome listened to John Everett read the list of men who had lived by faith— Gideon, Barak, Samson, Jephthah, David, Samuel.

"Faith is evidence of things not seen. Faith is the substance of things not seen," Reverend Croft concluded. Solome would have to think about that.

Solome lived in a country founded by pilgrims. The Indians had been pushed out of the way, their languages nearly extinguished. The continent had been cleared of buffalo. Their history was kept neatly in exhibits and in the stacks of the Historical Society. Refugees and immigrants still arrived, but the new wave of immigrants was non-European from Somalia and Mexico and all parts of Asia. The whole world seemed to be coming.

Stephen continued to manage his work with small lapses. It was as if being in the office, he could do office work. He also still traveled to meetings. Sometimes Solome went to conferences with him, when wives were invited. Otherwise, she kept busy with shopping, working on Wednesdays and Fridays, lunching with the Faculty Wives Club, or with Soos or her mother. She had her discussion group on Thursday afternoon, church on Sunday mornings and the Bible study on Monday evenings. She walked the dog, visited with Hetty Grunswald, and other neighbors and friends. She looked forward to trips to Crane Lake.

Solome still felt like two different women, divided between the responsibility to her husband and children, and doing what her mother wanted. But there was another Solome. One who wanted to do what she wanted. But what was it she wanted?

When a friend died suddenly in late February, Solome saw his widow grieving in a side row of the church. Solome thought of the loss of Stephen, who sat beside her. Her mother on the other side. She remembered her father's funeral. The smell of flowers. The words summing up her father's life. At least, the end of those two lives were known. The anxiety of the journey to the end was over for them. Now their work of grief began.

Stephen Savard

Solome and I lived on Upper St. John Street in St. Paul.

Did she think there were enough saints in their address? I had asked.

Soos and her daughter, Susan Anna Stiple, and Soos' husband, Brian Stiple, the son-in-law, came for supper one night in March. Solome had e-mailed Gretchen that she was planning a family dinner for Friday evening, if there wasn't another heavy snow, which was forecast. They would miss her.

But the snow wasn't heavy, and I picked up Solome's mother after work. We had settled at the table. The food was served. I felt like myself. The evening felt solid. Yet Solome seemed nervous, as if at any moment we could topple off the earth.

Mark often brought home friends from the college. They seemed in awe of being in the provost's house. Mark always had a different girl. Tonight he said he was bringing Jill, but showed up with Jean.

After dinner, on that Friday evening, the phone rang. It was Gretchen.

She was getting married. That was the news. Gretchen and Dennis were going to marry. Strange, I thought— when Gretchen called or wrote, it often seemed they weren't together.

"What's his last name?" Solome asked.

"Dennis' last name is Kamrar."

"What nationality is he?" I asked on the phone. "What religion?"

"What difference does it make?" Gretchen said to me. "I'm going to marry him. Do you have something against the name?"

"Are you pregnant?" Soos asked.

There were four phones in house. Solome, her mother, Soos and I could talk at once.

As long as Dennis was her boyfriend, and they were getting married, it didn't matter. Gretchen had several boyfriends during her long college career, which began at the University of Minnesota in Minneapolis and ended in New York. Solome said she knew Gretchen probably lived with them at one time or another. She left that thought in the category of things she didn't want to consider.

"Are you going to be Gretchen Kamrar?" Soos asked when her first question wasn't answered.

"No, I'm not pregnant. And yes, I will keep Savard as my name."

Would Solome call the church first thing tomorrow morning and find a date in June when they could have the wedding? Gretchen also wanted the reception at the St. Paul Club.

"What's wrong with the University Club?" I asked, but my question went unanswered.

"June?" Solome asked. "Gretchen, it's the first of March. You can't prepare for a wedding in three months. Especially with you out of town."

But Gretchen insisted it could be done.

"It took six months for Soos' wedding."

"I'll help you, mother," Soos said on the phone from the other room.

Soos stayed on the phone after Solome and I returned to the table. Brian was holding Susan on his lap. Mark and the girl he brought with him, Jean, were gone.

Solome told Brian that Gretchen was getting married.

"I heard," he answered.

Solome's mother brought coffee from the kitchen when she hung up the phone.

"Did Mark leave?" Solome asked.

"They're standing outside," her mother answered. "Jean is smoking."

When everyone returned to the dining room, Solome served dessert. As we ate, I saw Solome look at the yellow wallpaper with turquoise flowers.

"The risk you took with the paper is beside the point, isn't it?" I said.

They looked at me, not asking what I meant.

Solome Savard

Solome called Jane Mead the next day. They had raised their children together, though Jane had only one daughter, Soos' age. They attended birthday parties and dance recitals. But the girls had gone to different schools and hardly knew one another any longer.

"Gretchen is the one I thought would remain single," Jane said. "I'll tell Cathy. She's one who would like to get married."

On Saturday morning, Solome called the church. Every Friday and Saturday evening in June was taken for weddings. The St. Paul Club was booked too. Solome called Gretchen who flew into a panic. She would not settle for that.

"Try Saturday afternoon. Saturday morning. We'll have a picnic on the lawn of the club, if necessary."

"There was a reception at the Historical Society last year." Solome told her.

"I don't want my reception at a museum." Gretchen said flatly. "I want the club."

"The St. Paul Club is booked. The University Club?"

"No."

On Monday Solome called the church again. There was no time. She asked Reverend Croft to review his calendar in June.

"Do you have any afternoons?" She finished.

"I have a wedding at 2:00 every Saturday afternoon."

"Early on Friday evening? A 6:00 wedding?"

"I'll give you to Martha."

Solome would regret a 6:00 wedding. An early wedding meant a sit-down dinner at the reception. You couldn't have people for a light buffet until after 8:00.

"No, 6:00 is too late," the secretary said. "He has an 8:00 wedding on June 21st."

"Why is that too late?" Solome asked.

"The wedding parties come to the church at least two hours before the wedding. They want time to get ready. The photographer takes pictures. You can't overlap weddings." Martha explained. "You can't have one party arriving as the other is leaving." Solome heard her impatience too. She knew it was true.

"5:30. 5:00?"

"There's a possibility on Friday, June 6th."

"June 6th is too soon. Is there a Saturday morning later in June? 11:00?"

"I have an opening on Saturday morning the 28th, though I've already had another inquiry—"

"We'll take it," Solome said.

Gretchen was not happy about a Saturday morning wedding.

They could postpone the wedding, Solome suggested to her. They could have it at another church.

No, Gretchen wanted to be married in the church she'd attended as a girl. She wasn't getting married in a church she'd never attended.

No, she wanted the wedding in June and not August because they would be interviewing for jobs and she would be writing her dissertation. Dennis already was teaching at New York University, though his job was not permanent. They wouldn't hire her, Gretchen said. The same institution usually didn't place both husband and wife.

Solome tried to persuade Gretchen that June was too soon for a wedding. It would be too much of a strain. Impossible, really. They could have a July wedding.

"No," Gretchen said.

Soos' wedding had been large. Solome had planned most of it. Soos was struggling in school at Cobson and didn't care about the details. Solome always felt that Soos married Brian in a fit of desperation. Maybe it wasn't true, but there was an impatience in Soos to move onto something else. A marriage, for instance.

Gretchen, on the other hand, knew how she wanted the wedding. She was busy with her studies, but she would take time to plan it. Solome would help her. Dennis' parents would take care of the flowers, the rehearsal dinner, but Solome would have to make arrangements with the florist and decide on the restaurant. Solome and Stephen would pay for the wedding, the music, the reception, the invitations and stamps. Then there was Gretchen's dress, veil, shoes, and a hundred things they hadn't thought of yet.

"Just find a place for the reception," Gretchen said.

An 11:00 wedding would have to do.

"At least, she wants to be married in a church," Solome told Stephen.

Solome called the St. Paul Club again. Could a wedding brunch be arranged at noon on June 28th? No, the club was booked. They were sorry. There was nothing they could do.

"We could remove our membership," Solome said.

They made no further apology.

"A canopy on the lawn of the church?" Solome asked Gretchen.

"No."

She called the St. Paul Club again. "We've been members for 15 years. We need a place for a reception."

June was a busy month. There was nothing they could do.

Solome called the University Club and booked it before they could turn her down.

Gretchen came home the following weekend with Dennis.

"We'll stay in my room, mother. We're nearly married," Gretchen said. "We live together in New York."

"But I send your mail to the same address," Solome said. "I didn't know you'd moved."

"I just moved down the hall. My old roommate saves my mail."

Solome had lunch at the University Club with Gretchen and Dennis. They gave instructions on the arrangement of the ballroom. Solome continued to talk with the manager while Gretchen and Dennis continued their errands.

In the afternoon, Gretchen and Dennis registered at various stores. They came home that evening for supper, tired and cranky.

Gretchen came to St. Paul over her spring break later in March. Dennis stayed in New York.

On Monday, Solome and Gretchen looked for Gretchen's dress. Gretchen wasn't happy with any of them. She would keep looking, even though they were running out of time.

On Wednesday, when Solome worked at the Historical Society, Soos and the baby accompanied Gretchen to look for bridesmaid dresses at Daynard's. But Soos soon ran out of patience with the baby, and Gretchen continued by herself.

"You could do something different," Solome told her that evening after dinner. "Look for dresses the girls can wear again."

While Gretchen was on the phone to her bridesmaids and Dennis, Solome sat in the family room looking through the modern art book she kept for perspective.

She studied the work of Salvador Dali. His markings were like so many boats on the water. Where was a word for the sea? Maybe Salvadore knew a structured life cut into. Maybe he knew an erasure of form and structure.

What if the sun moved backward and gave her life back to her? What if Gretchen had stayed at school over spring break and Solome had her days to herself? What if Solome told Gretchen about Stephen? She had said she was worried about Stephen, but she hadn't told Gretchen why. When would they tell the children? Weren't they a family that shared things? No, Solome was there to help her daughter. She would endure the disruption of Gretchen's rudeness when she was stressed, and not burden her further. At least, Stephen was himself. There were times she thought his forgetfulness would go away.

Gretchen had decided on a black and white wedding. Her bridesmaids would wear tailored, black dresses. The four girls liked Gretchen's idea. That would make it simple and practical.

"Is this a funeral or a wedding?" Stephen asked.

Stephen, who was slipping, sometimes could get to the point. But often, it seemed his judgment was impaired. He said what he thought without weighing its effect.

They took Gretchen to the airport on Sunday. She felt everything was up in the air. Out of her control.

"Sometimes things are that way," Solome said. "It will turn out all right," she assured her. "You can look in New York for a dress. I'll fly there if you want."

Stephen Savard

I lived in a world of shifting objects. What was on my desk was not there any longer. Things disappeared. Things I didn't know appeared. What was the use of this? What that? It jumbled until I threw my briefcase in fury. That would take care of it.

Plans for the wedding was all I heard. In the middle of it all, the president of Cobson invited Solome and me to dinner.

"You're not the same, Stephen," he said. "Do you need a sabbatical?"

"No no."

Solome sat politely frozen at her place. She was up against the wedding— now this— the accusations that I was not the same.

There was a time I lectured without notes. There was a time the students didn't mind staying beyond the hour. When I talked, fact moved to fact, departed into anecdote, came back to the point, moved in another direction again. The students listened, took notes, sometimes forgot to take notes because they were intent on listening. Sometimes my lectures had been *electrifying*. That was what one student course-evaluation said.

As chair, I held the large history department together despite backbitings and feudings. No, by Christ. It was not going to be that way. I held

meetings in which we talked our way through the arguments and griev-
ances until they reached *departmental understandings*. We came through
that disruptive period as a solid department that remained solid. As division dean, I held other departments together through discussions and decisions regarding curriculum and allocation. As provost, I maneuvered the
college through the challenges it faced, with the president, of course. I was
instrumental in hiring the new treasurer who would guide Cobson through
a necessary *tightening of the belt*.

"I had a dream of you, dad," Soos called one morning. "You had wings.
They were small, but they were on your back."

"Maybe I'll fly through the wall ahead," I said. I don't think Soos heard
me because I heard Susan crying in the background and a hurried, "I have
to go, dad."

I also gave guest lectures, but found I couldn't talk as long as I had, and
then I couldn't talk without notes.

Now the wedding was taking everything. The reception would be
$20,000 minimum with all the guests. I heard Solome on the phone. What
menu? What wines? What band? Where would cake sit? Stephen what do
you think?

Solome Savard

Solome flew to New York to look at the dress Gretchen found. Stephen was
supposed to take her to the airport, but at the last minute, had a meeting he
couldn't get out of. There was a time when he could leave Cobson College,
get back the minute the meetings started and know exactly where he was.
Solome could have taken a cab, but she told Stephen she would call Jane
instead.

"Do we ever realize what we're getting into when we have children?"
Jane asked when they slowed in airport traffic.

Solome had hoped to visit the Metropolitan Museum and St. Patrick's
Cathedral, but didn't have time. Gretchen also was in the middle of exams
and did not want Solome to do anything but help her with the wedding.

What would Solome wear? She had a dress from Soos' wedding, but
it was frothy. Why did they make dresses for the mother of the bride like
that? A battle ship? Because she felt like she'd been in a siege by the time the
wedding arrived.

When Solome returned to St. Paul, she found a straight silk dress with sleeves at Daynard's. Was it too simple? No, it was better than looking like the wedding cake. She wanted to take Soos to look at it. She delayed the purchase, and it was gone when she returned with Soos and the baby.

The next week, Solome found another dress at Daynard's. It wasn't black, but a dark blue, almost purple. *Periwinkle*, the clerk said. What a name. It was a storm front on the horizon after an overly warm afternoon.

Solome wanted petunias that spring, but she didn't have time to hoe and weed. She told the yard man to plant them along the walk in front of the house. She only hoped he would get it done before the wedding. He usually told her when he would work, and what he would do. He also shoveled their snow in winter, letting it accumulate sometimes before he came with his snow-blower.

Late in April, when the yard man was working, Solome went to the post office and stood in line to purchase stamps, both for the invitations and the inner envelope with the R.S.V.P. card. Then she addressed the invitations to all the guests they decided on after long discussions. Stephen stamped the envelopes. They drove to the post office and put them in the mail with a feeling of accomplishment.

Stephen Savard

I had another appointment with the doctor. Again, we returned home silently in the car.

We had been safe all our lives. Or was safe just a condition that seemed like it was safe, yet was not, for any of us? The doctor's appointment had steered me into clarity. Safe was a mirage. It was tenuous. It was there by a thread. The physical world was not stable. Was not sure. Could not be counted upon. It only seemed that way.

Solome and I had spent our lives together. We had been blessed with opportunity, which we had taken. Now I sat in the chair in our living room and knew one day I wouldn't know Solome. She must have seen it in my face because she looked away.

Where would my mind go? My being? My soul?— if that was the word. What was the soul, other than the term in the long history of inquiry? The soul did not have a map. It dwelled among lions. The soul was arid. The soul was contradiction. It went south when it should go north and north when it should go south.

Solome Savard

Where was Stephen going? Solome wanted him back. She didn't want him to go. Or she wanted him to go quickly, before there was time to suffer. Solome knelt on the floor in front of Stephen in his chair and cried with her head on his knee. He put his hand on her head. When she looked up, she saw the distance in his eyes. It was as though she were on one promontory and he on the next, and there was no way between them.

Solome cried at her Monday night Bible study group. She had not attended regularly because of the preparations for Gretchen's wedding. She also had given up her Thursday discussion group and cut back on her hours at the Minnesota Historical Society. She began sifting through her friends, calling those she could be honest with, discarding the others, for the time being anyway. Jane Mead was the only constant. The Faculty Wives Club was out. She had caught their glances toward Stephen at a Christmas party.

Stephen was going to a place he didn't want to go. He was facing nothing. But nothing did not stay nothing. It had a ghost. At times, she thought she could hear Stephen in the house. She thought she heard him rush in the door the way he did as a young man when they were first married. Maybe because she wanted him to. Maybe because she longed for him to return to himself and say he was going golfing, or maybe they could go somewhere and eat and she didn't need to bother with dinner. The phone rang and she wanted it to be Stephen, but it was her daughter, Soos, who wanted her to watch the baby, Susan. She had some errands to do, and by the time she got the stroller from the car and the diaper bag and bottle, she might as well stay home. Solome agreed to watch Susan and felt anger that she agreed. What else was she doing? She had some errands to do herself.

What about candles for the windows and altar? Gretchen called with more concerns for the wedding. Would they show up in morning sun?

Dennis had a nephew who would be ring bearer. What about the ring bearer's pillow? Gretchen liked simplicity. The pillows she looked at were all full of bows. Could Solome sew one? Did Solome want a corsage? No. What would they do with baby Susan? Gretchen didn't want a baby's cry interrupting the ceremony. What music would they choose? Gretchen wanted a trio or quartet. Maybe Bach's *Jesu*. Handel's *Hornpipe* and *The Rejoicing*. Pachelbel's *Canon in D*. What order would the family be seated? What about the seating arrangements at the rehearsal dinner? How many Kamrar's were coming? What about the logistics of changes and maneuvers between church and the club? A limousine? A friend's vintage car?

Then there was the buying and wrapping of gifts for bridesmaids and groomsmen, the reader, the ushers, the friends who handed out the programs. What was the minister's fee? Did they want the woman at the church to oversee? She had a needle and thread and safety pin if needed at the last minute. She knew the timing, when the bridesmaids and maid of honor started down the aisle. The ring bearer. What order and when. Anything to make it easier.

Stephen Savard

We met Dennis' parents a month before the wedding. They were pleasant. They stayed at the St. Paul hotel. We picked them up for dinner before Gretchen and Dennis arrived from school in New York City.

The children were late because of Friday evening air traffic into the Minneapolis / St Paul. We had to wait twenty minutes at Hudson's Restaurant. We all felt awkward and tense. We tried to compensate with too much agreeable conversation. Solome had made reservations so Mrs. Kamrar could see if Hudson's was acceptable for the rehearsal dinner. I talked with Mr. Kamrar while the manager showed the women the banquet room.

Solome Savard

Solome didn't think the Kamrar's noticed Stephen's forgetfulness. If he forgot what he was doing, or who the Kamrar's were, he didn't ask. Solome had coached him before the evening. "You might forget their names, but don't ask. We're having dinner with these people we don't know, but we'll act like we know them." Stephen seemed to understand.

But Stephen remembered their names. He knew what to say. Solome felt the edge of her worry lift like a lid that had been pushed down too tight.

Gretchen had arrived tense and stressed. This would not be a pleasant weekend. She had a folder of final papers to grade. She carried another folder of wedding plans.

Solome felt like she had when a storm came up on Crane Lake and the wind blew in off the water— she remembered she felt the lake was a veneer that would lift. Did Gretchen realize how much work the wedding was for Solome?

On Saturday, they met with the photographer who wrote down the names for the groups in the photographs Gretchen wanted. There was Solome and Stephen. Soos, the baby Susan and Brian Stiple. Mark. Her mother. Mrs. Kamrar wanted more time to think about her list. It seemed official— like a list of who got into heaven. There was something sacred about the family. She felt it then. She knew there were tears in her eyes. She knew she couldn't let Gretchen see them. Her father had died just before Soos' marriage. Maybe Solome was remembering him.

Solome knew so little about Dennis' family. His parents. Brothers and sisters. Who would be coming? Their spouses? Children? Grandparents? It seemed unfair to Solome— she had raised Gretchen as her own and now had to give her up to a family she didn't know—

Mrs. Kamrar would fax her list the following week. She still wasn't sure who was coming. Solome wasn't either. How about Stephen's sister and a cousin who would bring the sister?

"How many pictures with the bride's and groom's attendants?" The photographer continued his questions. They would look at her wedding pictures the rest of her life. It was an investment they decided to make. They were in it. They would carry through and not stop short.

Family. That's what she had. But Mark, her son, didn't understand how precarious his father was. He didn't want to know. Neither did the girls. Mark's life was bound up with his friends at college. Stephen's and her pre-dicament simply wasn't in the range of Mark's interests. She wanted to sit him down and talk to him. She wanted to say how much she needed him, but he was in his life that did not include worry about a father who was losing his memory, his mind, his language, himself.

At times Solome wanted to be immersed in the details of the wedding forever. It took her mind off Stephen.

Stephen Savard

One day shuffled into another. There were more problems with the new student center on campus. Construction would have to be delayed. There were new problems with students. They protested this or that. I couldn't always sort through what they were disgruntled about.

Gretchen flew to St. Paul for several showers given by friends and families for whom Solome had attended showers and sent gifts and attended ceremonies. It was fair play. You gave. You got. It was part of our lives to help set the course for our children's lives also.

One evening, Gretchen called in a panic, saying her dress didn't fit. Solome flew to New York and met her for a fitting. There wasn't time to have it altered in there. Solome brought the dress back to St. Paul and took it to a seamstress she knew.

When Solome was in New York, she called the night before she returned.

"Have you fed Brown?"

There was silence.

"Go out and do it now."

I hung up without thinking to say, good-bye.

Solome Savard

Solome and Stephen had new material from the Alzheimer's Association. *Someone to stand by you.* The heading read. She looked up from the chair angrily. Where was the someone? Not in her living room. She looked at the sofa. The arm chairs. The small tables. She looked at the lamps. The recessed lighting she'd put in the ceiling to light the corners of the room. She looked at the pictures. The room was her. All her. She was happy with her house. But who was the someone standing by her? She looked at the pamphlets. No, there was no one in her house.

Great strides had been made, the summer issue began. Two new drugs had been approved by the FDA for treatment of the disease. Tracine and donepezil hydrochloride. She couldn't even pronounce them. Several other drugs were currently in development to help improve memory and alleviate or postpone symptoms of Alzheimer's disease. More pharmacological treatment options were expected with the next eighteen months.

What were these words saying? They were sunflowers with heads too heavy to hold up. Had she seen a picture of sunflowers? In the travel section of the Sunday paper? Not that she remembered.

She returned to the pamphlet. One of the communication systems in the brain, the cholinergic system, is defective in individuals with Alzheimer's.

In the brain, acetylcholine, one type of neurotransmitter involved in nerve cell communication, delivers messages from one nerve cell to another. An enzyme called, acetylcholi-nesterase, breaks down acetylcholine after it is used. Otherwise it accumulates between nerve cells.

These words are monkeys, she thought. Chattering to no one. Solome felt her throat close momentarily as the lump brought up the tears.

Research has shown that there is not enough acetylcholine in the brains of individuals with Alzheimer's. By inhibiting the enzyme that breaks down acetylcholine, scientists hope to keep higher concentrations of acetylcholine intact.

Tracine and donepezil hydrochloride function as acetylcholinesterase inhibitors, and decrease the breakdown of acetylcholine.

Solome turned to the first of the article. Were Tracine and donepezil hydrochloride the two drugs mentioned at the beginning? She'd forgotten, but found that they were.

Could she hand out Alzheimer's pamphlets with the wedding programs? The beginning and the end.

Late in May, Gretchen faxed the program for the wedding. Solome had to find the printer and then fax Gretchen the choice of fonts. She sat in the print shop proof reading while she waited for Gretchen's response.

Prelude
Seating of the Parents
Processional
"*Canon in D*," Pachelbel
"*Trumpet Voluntary*," Clarke
Call to Worship
Scripture Reading
I Corinthians 13:1–8
Prayer
Appreciation
Questions of Intent
Meditation
The Prophet, "On Marriage," Kahlil Gibran
Vows of Marriage
Exchange of Rings
Lighting of the Unity Candle

"*Concerto for 2 Violins & Orchestra in D Minor*," Bach

Scripture Reading

Ecclesiastes 1:9–12

Prayer

"*The Lord's Prayer*," Malotte

Pronouncement

Benediction

Introduction

Recessional

"*Hornpipe*," Handel

"*The Rejoicing*," Handel

Solome proof-read the names of the Maid of Honor, Bridesmaids, Best Man, Groomsmen, Ring Bearer, Reader, Parents, Minister, Greeters and Ushers.

Solome tried to pick up the programs from the printers on Wednesday after work, but the store was closed by the time she got there in traffic. On Thursday, she called the Minnesota Historical Society and told them she couldn't come to work on Friday. She might have to miss more days because of the wedding. She didn't even have time to read the newspaper. Why was her voice shaky? Why did she nearly cry?

How inconvenient it was to have Gretchen out of town. How many phone calls? How many questions would Solome have to answer by herself? She decided to clear a place in Soos' room. She couldn't return with the baby before the wedding. The yard man moved a picnic table upstairs for the wedding gifts.

Mark couldn't return to his room because Dennis was there. He was angry that he was moved out of his own room. But he suggested they help him pay for an apartment he found near the college, which he was going to ask them for anyway, which they already had anticipated.

"Dennis is only here for the weekend," Solome told Mark. "You can stay with a friend for a day or two."

"They're all moving. No one has a place. They want to stay with me."

"Stay in the new apartment then."

"There's no bed."

"Use your sleeping bag."

"On a hardwood floor?"

"Go buy a bed this afternoon."

43

"I want my own bed."

"You can have it after the wedding."

"I just finished my finals. You didn't even ask."

"Mark, I have more on my mind than I can handle at the moment," Solome said. "Why can't you see that? I'm sorry I didn't ask about your finals. How were they?"

"Nothing you would care to ask."

Stephen Savard

How had we become disrespectful to one another? Had it always been there under the surface? Where had the nastiness come from? How many of my own outbursts did I have to quiet? How long would I know to quiet them?

I heard the vacuum cleaner running upstairs. I felt like I was listening to the buzz inside my head. I felt I was at Crane Lake with my children in water wings that were slowly losing air.

I knew I would last a while longer. Maybe even through the wedding. I could live many years. The medicine I was taking seemed to help. I was physically healthy, but inside my head, I was full of holes. No, it wasn't holes. It was clutter. Little filings that stuck to open circuits, clogging them. My face was as it always was. It was my brain that would deteriorate, no, was deteriorating. There would be lesions, open spaces. I thought of the doctor's words. How long would Solome have to live with my body after my mind had gone? No, it was going to be harder than that.

The day would come I would call out for death, and it would not come.

What was this disease? Where did it come from? How did I get it? How fast would it come? What was ahead? How could a man forget how to sit down? Would I eventually stand at my chair and not know to bend my legs and sit? Would Solome push me behind the knees to let me know to bend my legs? It hadn't happened yet. Why was I rushing ahead? No, it was not here yet. But it would come. I would lose words, the basis of our relationship.

Maybe it was a joke. A hollowness that filled a man. I was active. I still ran a small college. At least, Solome said I ran it. I handled problems for which there were difficult answers. I managed students, prepared taxes, planned for retirement. I could work with numbers, but someday, I wouldn't even know what numbers were. Four. Three. Two. One. They would be hollow— A gray fuzz of matter cleared away.

Where would my words go that Solome had listened to all our married life?

The stress of the wedding wore on Solome. She called me at the college as she had in the past when she was under stress. I had to tell her I couldn't help at the moment. She said she called her mother to talk, but was soon in tears.

Her mother came to our house and sat with her. What if her mother outlived me? Would she live with her mother again? What happened when her mother died? She would be left by herself.

Mark returned home one evening, asking what furniture he could take for his apartment.

"You know you can't take your bed until after the wedding," Solome said.

"Where do you expect me to sleep?"

"The couch— I don't know, Mark— " Solome said. "Your grades came— You didn't even ask."

"I've got a lot on my mind— " Mark looked at his grades.

"You can rent a bed," Solome told him, "or buy a Coleman air mattress."

"You rent a bed for those people," he told her.

When Mark left, Solome was angry. She complained to me that night.

"Mark's still a boy," I said.

"No, he's not." Solome told me.

But I didn't want to talk about Mark. I wanted to remember my own boyhood. For some reason, I thought of the cinder drive where I skidded and fell from my bicycle. Solome had asked once about the dark place on my knee, and I had told her about my fall into the cinders.

I remembered one of my friends had a father who did taxes. I said I thought that would be a good way to make money. Solome listened to me while I talked. She seemed patient as I was drawn to my own history.

I remembered the times I traveled with my father, who had worked for the Federal Land Bank during and after the Depression. Or maybe it was my grandfather. When I was young, I could not see over the windows of the car, and my father placed a typewriter under me in the front seat.

"Did you ever hear such a dark voice?" I asked.

"What voice, Stephen?" Solome asked.

"They wouldn't let me sing in grade school."

"I like to hear you sing," she held me.

Diane Glancy

Solome Savard

Solome could buy the cemetery plots and get them out of the way. That would take her mind off the wedding for JUST ONE MOMENT! It would be easy. To lie down and not get up. To fall asleep and dream of light.

Presents for Gretchen and Dennis began arriving each day.

One afternoon, after the delivery man left more boxes on her step, she couldn't stay awake. She lay on the bed and slept instantly. She dreamed of sunflowers. A field of them. Why sunflowers? Their enormous stalks. Their round faces. Their heavy yellow heads looking down at their toes. The leaves like wings. She dreamed of them with many wings. But the wings had been trimmed. Had her yard man cut them back? Solome heard the dog bark and woke from her nap. What was happening? She looked from the window. No one was there. Solome told Brown to be quiet, but he barked again and again.

Why did he bark? Maybe it was Stephen's disease. That was the intruder, the prowler. She could advertise to get rid of the dog, but she felt safer with him in the backyard. She wanted to hear him bark if someone came.

Maybe Alzheimer's was striking her too. Maybe they could share the disease. Maybe when they slept, Stephen's disease crawled across the pillows to her. What would it be like to forget her husband? Where was Stephen in his empty sunflower head? Bees eating his face.

Alzheimer's was crueler than death. At least then he'd be gone. But no, he was still in her house. Would eventually have to be cared for someplace else. When she could no longer handle him. He was sprawling across her life with heavy heads of sunflowers.

Stephen Savard

I had a speech to give at a history conference. It was a conference I had attended for years. Sometimes Solome came with me, but this year she had the wedding.

History was a force of remembering [I began before the group]. Or was it a focus of remembering? History was a forward direction. It was not motionless. History was a similitude. A game of chance charged [changed] by the forces writing the events. Interpreting them in their own way. History de-solidified the unknown. It was known to those in it, but not to us.

History was a game trying to get to something that no longer was. [It was trying to shuffle a teakettle along a floor.] It was reconstruction. It was the cause of likeness. A fight against forgetting.

[I stood before the group hoping they understood what I was saying. My words somehow did not connect with my thoughts. But I trusted what I read on the paper.] History was a transparency through which some vagueness passed. At most, it was the portions of a guessed-at whole. It made a structure for pedagogy. Or indirect thought. [Had I read the talk to Solome before I left? Had she made comments? Did I pick up fidgeting in the audience?] History was a signpost that could not convey what was there. In a point of place, where something happened that affected something else [for instance, I could know I had Alzheimer's because I saw its effect. That was what I was thinking,   and not saying.] which was   more conductive of history— [I continued] [somehow.] As always, history was a difference of opinion. History was a whole being given over to someone [who has Alzheimer's] to write. History was a skewed portion, a likeness of something. History was reason and imagination. There was a new creative historicity. A movement toward the interpretive act of history. How can history be more about the historian   than the history? [Could there be a historical Alzheimer's?] Otherwise, history was a flock of migrating birds. That somehow knew by instinct its pedagogy. [Was my historical theory flying? If so where to?] History was lost   in history a relation of relationships—   going toward the hoped-for end. History and critical theory. Theory and critical history. A philosophy at most [in the name of clarity, which is a   point-of-view.]

I sat down to applause.

"How was the conference?" Solome asked when I returned.

"Before I retire, I want one last semester teaching history."

Solome reasoned with me. I knew she was right. I would get upset, she argued.

Though my illness. I know doing.

Solome Savard

Mid-June, Solome picked up Gretchen's wedding dress from the seamstress. She hung it up, hoping the weight would pull out the wrinkles. Otherwise she'd take it to the cleaners. She called the church. They had a steam press.

The woman who helped the brides would press the dress. The veil? Solome asked. That too.

Solome wrote a notice for the *St. Paul Pioneer Press* to appear in the wedding section the Sunday after the ceremony.

Gretchen and Dennis arrived three days before the wedding. Mark picked them up from the airport. They opened gifts, numbered them. They made a card file with name, gift and a place for the date when a thank-you note was written.

The florist called to make sure someone would be there when they arrived at the church at 10:00 with the two vases of flowers.

The Kamrar's arrived with other family members and a few close friends.

There were thirty people at the rehearsal dinner at Hudson's.

There was a men's party afterwards.

Around midnight, Solome heard Mark, Dennis, Brian and one of the groomsmen. They were helping Stephen up the stairs. He had fallen at the bar. He had a bruise on his face. He had been drinking. They all had.

The young men helped Stephen into bed.

"Are you all right?" Solome asked him.

"Yes," he said.

"I don't think you are," Solome told him, but he insisted that he was.

Why had they let him drink? Why had he drank? What was the point of all that drinking?

Solome suggested that the young men sleep downstairs because she didn't want them driving again. Brian wouldn't stay, but the others agreed. Solome took bedding down to them. They could sleep on the couches in the living room and Stephen's study.

Solome returned to the bedroom and talked to Stephen a while. He seemed all right after all. She let him fall asleep.

For a while, she listened to him sleep.

Stephen Savard

The bar was   loose flooring uneven   kept lifting the bar was there the boys talking I was saying to them? I didn't know grew disinterested what's going on? I wanted to go back. Leave. Here's   another drink, dad. They didn't want to go yet. Didn't want   to take me I was leaning too far over the floor suddenly rising there was a sink hole   I let myself fall into then carried home   someone upstairs in bed their voices underwater   just lay down stay in bed the welcome dark   fall into.

Solome Savard

On June 28th, the day of the wedding, Solome woke at six. Gretchen was already in the bathroom. Dennis and his groomsmen were asleep downstairs on the couches. Mark was in Stephen's study.

Solome called Mark to wake the men and take them to the hotel so they could dress. Mark was groggy also.

The Kamrar's called, concerned that Dennis had not returned to the hotel. Solome explained that Stephen had fallen and hit his head. Dennis and his friend had stayed at the house. Mark would bring them to the hotel to get dressed for the wedding.

But they had rented a car, Mr. Kamrar said. They could come and get them.

Stephen was mumbling. He didn't know where he was. Solome tried to wake him when she hung up, but he wouldn't wake fully. Maybe she should let him sleep a little longer. He had a large bruise on his face.

She called the doctor.

He would send an ambulance. Solome would follow in her car.

Brown barked without stopping.

Gretchen was in panic.

"He's all right, Gretchen. They're taking him for observation."

"On my wedding day?" She cried. "Who will walk me down the aisle?"

"Mark will."

"I don't want Mark. I want my father."

"I will go with your father. The Kamrar's will be here shortly for Dennis and his friend." Solome explained how they had spent the night. "I'll call you from the hospital. You shower and eat something and get to your hair appointment by 8:00. Be at the church by 9:00 if I'm not back."

"Drive myself to the church on my wedding day?" Gretchen sounded hysterical.

"The Kamrar's rented three cars," Solome tried to calm Gretchen, but Gretchen was in tears.

"Their own family can barely crowd into them."

"One of them will have to make two trips." Solome was exasperated. "Gretchen, I'm sorry I don't have time to be with you. I have your father to worry about."

Solome called a woman from the church who helped the brides and told her she would be at the hospital. One of Gretchen's bridesmaids would come to the house to help her with her wedding dress, shoes, bag, hose, and make-up kit.

"Get my dress and shoes also," Solome told Gretchen. "It's hanging on my closet door. And you're going to have to take your father's tuxedo and shoes to the church. We won't have time to come back here."

Solome started to leave. The ambulance was on its way to the hospital.

"Why didn't I think?" Solome said to Gretchen. "Drive Stephen's car. I'll leave his keys on the kitchen table. Call Soos and tell her to pick up Grandma. Don't forget the bag of candles and guest book and pens. Don't forget— "

"I'll remember everything, mother," Gretchen interrupted. "I'm only working on a Ph.D. I'll walk myself down the aisle."

If Gretchen made one more comment, Solome was going to tell her what was behind Stephen's problem. Then she would have something to be concerned about— But no, no, this was about Gretchen shaping her own world— hers and Dennis'.

At the hospital Stephen was awake. They took x-rays while Solome waited in the emergency room where she made a list of the medicines he was taking.

Could he go to the church and walk his daughter down the aisle? Solome asked.

"No," the nurse guessed.

Solome waited impatiently for the doctor. "We have a wedding this morning." She felt flushed. Her heart pounded. She had worked for this day. Stephen's face looked terrible. Solome thought of the storm on Crane Lake again. She saw herself flying through the sky with their cabin, the fishing boat, the bait store down the road. A wedding was windy. There were fish in it.

Finally the doctor came in. He examined Stephen, who was quiet.

"My daughter wants him at her wedding."

The doctor pulled Stephen to a sitting position on the table. He helped him stand. Stephen looked at Solome with what she thought was embarrassment. At least he wasn't combative.

The doctor shined a light into Stephen's eyes. He gave him an aspirin. "Since it's his daughter's wedding." The doctor said. "I think it's mostly a hangover at this point. Keep my number with you."

Solome drove Stephen to the church, praying they would make it in time, though she knew they wouldn't.

Gretchen was waiting in the bride's room, nearly hysterical with nervousness.

"The quartet is playing," Solome told her. "Your guests are listening to the music."

Solome helped Stephen dress quickly. She put make-up on Stephen's bruise. Then she got dressed herself.

The wedding started nearly half an hour late.

It was worth it all to be seated in church. To hear the quartet. To watch the bridesmaids come down the aisle in their black, tailored dresses. To see Soos smiling. To see the Kamrar nephew as ring-bearer carefully carrying the pillow. To watch Gretchen at the back of the church on Stephen's arm. But Solome could see the concern on Gretchen's face, even from the distance. As she started down the aisle with her father, she looked worried. Stephen, himself, looked dazed. The make-up did not cover his bruise. It was as if Stephen had gone into a closet somewhere inside himself. He knew something was happening. He looked at Gretchen as though she knew and would tell him, or could wipe away the confusion like sweat from his forehead.

Solome's mother leaned to her and whispered something.

"He's all right," Solome assured her as they stood for the bride.

Solome felt tears as she watched them coming toward her. *Stephen,* she said with her lips, but he didn't notice. Stephen had Alzheimer's. The thought hit her again. Something caused nerve cell communications to malfunction, eventually leading to nerve cell death. Was the soul and spirit and language of a man wrapped up in nerve cells? Were they reduced to synapses and the little patterns of nerve cells and electrical impulses along their trails? Why hadn't God explained that in his Bible? She would ask her Bible study group. Had Jesus died on the cross for nerve cells and electrical impulses? She would ask Reverend Croft, who waited at the altar. It wasn't just cells walking down the aisle in a lovely dress. It wasn't just cells in the black tuxedo beside the bride.

There was an investigation into insulin. Into strokes. Into other connections and causes and reliefs. Why was the wedding and the Alzheimer's information shuffled and dealt to her like cards? She felt faint for a moment, but she would not let herself faint. No. She was going to stand still.

Stephen, she wanted to call. She wanted him to know he was walking his daughter down the aisle to be married. It was a significant event in their lives. Surely he knew. For the moment, their wounds were covered under their new clothes.

Stephen Savard

We talked to colleagues at the University Club. I explained several times I had fallen at Dennis' bachelor party. Stupid accident. They laughed. No matter. Gretchen was smiling. Neighbors. Solome and I danced. It was still afternoon.

Solome Savard

Imagine Solome in the cabin at Crane Lake by herself, not afraid of being alone. Imagine the wedding no longer ahead of her. Solome had brought the dog, but he was restless, hearing the bark of another dog somewhere, wanting to go out. But Solome kept him locked in the cabin. Stephen was at a meeting at Cobson, where usually, he could still fit in his old groove. Before Solome went into the cabin for the night, she sat on the screened porch looking at a star through the trees. It was in a piece of sky the size of the dog's bowl. She knew the light of the star was from long ago. Its light traveled from a sun that had once burned. Solome thought about Stephen. He was going to go out too, but his light would keep traveling after him. It would reach others. He had provided for his family. He had given his children a course to follow. They could follow it, or not. They could choose to follow some combination of his course and their own, or others.

Where were the people in the next door cabin? Where was the retarded daughter? Had they lived there snowed-in in winter because they had no place else to go? Had they stayed there by choice?

Solome listened to the squeak of the dock in the waves as she sat on the screened porch the next day. The dock sounded something like the printer in Stephen's office in their house, an old dot matrix. He had a laser printer in his office at Cobson, but wanted to keep the old one. Solome had used Stephen's word processor for wedding guests and gifts that had been received. How would Gretchen write all those thank you notes?

The word, "buffalo," came to her that evening as she sat on the couch in the yellow pine room. It was a word outside her experience. The buffalo had been exterminated. They had roamed the Minnesota prairie. The Dakotas. Nebraska. Kansas. The word did not belong to the English language. It was one of America's words that had been added to English. What were others? Coyote? Ford assembly line? Interstate?

Solome felt fractured as she looked through Brown's fur for fleas and ticks. Was it because Stephen wasn't there? No, she had come to the lake by herself, though not often. She'd always been with her parents, then her mother. She'd been with Stephen, the children and their friends, or the friends of hers and Stephen's, or his colleagues, in various combinations. It was because of herself that she felt fractured. There was something she had not found in herself. Maybe it had nothing to do with Stephen. Or the children.

The cabin had a raised ceiling. Not an A-frame. They were too hard to heat in Minnesota. But a raised ceiling and a small, birch-bark canoe hanging there. Solome's mother had collected birch-bark baskets for a while. Now they sat on the yellow pine shelves in the cabin. Solome had made the checked curtains. Some of the kettles were from Solome's grandmother's house when they sold it. What had happened to the table with the drawers with metal bottoms? How could her mother let them get away?

Solome thought of Stephen as she sat by herself in the cabin. She missed the words that had been bridges between them. Words that had been a road out of isolation. Words that could solve problems between them. But Stephen's disease would scramble his words. She'd already heard it happen. They would not convey his thoughts. Maybe there wouldn't be any thoughts to convey. His words would be marbles rolling loose. The board tilted one way, then another, and he could not stop any of them from rolling away. He could still hold on. He was facing difficulties at the college. Multiculturalism was the next hurdle. She had asked him about it. He seemed to have less to say each day.

What were words? Dust from the fallout of comets. She saw one through the window of the cabin for a brief moment. A yellow light fell and was lost beyond the trees. She hadn't had time to make a wish. The wind brushed the trees. Winter was never far away in Minnesota with its mantel of snow. It was Minnesota. Summer felt like something was missing, like an animal without its fur.

She thought of her son and his friends. She wished he were still on the dock looking for birds. She remembered him at the lake with his bird book for boy scouts. He had to find ten different birds for a woodland merit badge. Solome sat with him while Stephen fished.

Eagle.

Bluejay.

Crow.

Sparrow.

Red bird.

Grackle.

Crane.

Mark had wanted to see an owl. But never did. Solome couldn't remember seeing one either, though she had heard them.

What were the others? Loon? Hawk?

Later, she had framed his badges. Not for Mark, but for her. She liked their round shapes, the boy-scout green, though Mark called it, army green.

Solome thought of her children. They too would have to find their way through the structure of language, making words do what they wanted, until they found the structure was making them do what it wanted— until they found that they were made for language, and not language for them. It was words that formed them and words in which they lived.

Mark called about money. Someone had made long distance calls at his apartment.

"How much?"

"$648.00"

"Mark!" Solome said. "How could you be so careless?"

"We had a party— someone went in the bedroom and called friends in Chicago— maybe overseas also. I don't know. It happens."

"You're going to have to be more careful."

"I need to pay the bill."

"Call the numbers on your bill. Ask them who called. Call them and tell them they have a bill to pay."

"It was more than several calls," Mark said. "It was more than several places." Mark sounded irritated. He was having to admit to Solome he'd been taken advantage of by friends. Friends who were working with him for a better world.

"Cancel the phone service in your apartment and use your cell phone," Solome told him.

"It's strange how memories come back," Solome told her mother when she stopped by her house. Solome would be doing something, and she would think of a table her grandmother had— the drawers with metal bottoms, large and concave to hold flour. Her grandmother scooped out flour when she baked bread or pie crusts, using the top of the table for a breadboard.

Solome still had the kerosene lamp on the mantle at the cabin at Crane Lake. She had some old kettles and birch bark baskets. Her grandfather's pipe. A few utensils hanging from the beam of the kitchen ceiling. Butter paddle. Ice pick. Some tall grasses from the Minnesota prairie. Pine cones, pine nettles. She liked the brownness of the cabin, of the earth without snow. It's what she named the dog when they found him as a puppy on the road— Brown.

Her father's old birch bark canoe was suspended from the ceiling of the cabin on Crane Lake too. He had bought it long ago and had it restored. It was a small canoe, probably a child's.

Solome's mother remembered what they had sold.

"Crocks. A divided, square wooden bowl with handle. Lanterns. Jars. A few trunks. You can't keep everything, Solome. You have to let some things go. Some of them must have sold in antique stores in Stillwater." Solome's mother said. "I wish I had my father's wooden tool box."

Solome remembered the table was on rollers. A lot of her grandmother's furniture was on rollers. They lived in a portable, movable world. Maybe her grandparents realized that more than Solome's generation. The purpose of Stephen's planning had been to make them secure. But they weren't. That's what she saw now. That's what she had to learn. She felt less fractured. She felt more secure when she held that in her mind. They were all on rollers. She thought again of her grandmother's furniture. She imagined what they had sold. She was disappointed in her mother that she had let it go.

As a child, Solome had lain on the floor under the table. She liked the metal curves above her head. Tin, she guessed they were. They sounded like rain in the gutters when she tapped them with her fingers. They were curved as the moon. Solome felt a determination within her as she remembered. In facing loss and brokenness, Solome could feel whole. She could face it. She would not turn away. It would make her stronger.

Wasn't the Depression a part of American language? Didn't it still show up in their lives?

What else could Stephen take? Calcium. Vitamin E. Ibuprofen. Estrogen had even been shown to help memory in women, but then again, maybe it had not.

When Solome returned from her mother's, Soos had called. When she called her daughter back, Soos wanted her to watch Susan the next day. Could she bring her by?

"I can come to your house," Solome said.

"My house is a mess. I'll bring her there."

Solome held Susan the next morning. Though she was 2 ½, she liked to be held. Susan was plump and blonde. She looked like the Stiples, Mrs. Stiple had said. And Solome agreed.

Soos was easy-going. She didn't always follow schedules and it was hard to get Susan to nap. Solome talked to Susan as she made their sandwiches. She held her on her lap as they ate. She held Susan at the window to see Brown. She walked through the room still crowded with Gretchen and Dennis' wedding gifts. Solome rocked Susan while she read to her, and finally got her to take a short nap.

Soos returned mid-afternoon. She took the baby and left in a hurry to start supper before Brian got home. Then Solome walked the dog in Hill Park. She put the dishes in the washer. She finished reading the newspaper. She talked on the phone. Her Thursday discussion group called. Could she return now that the wedding was over? They could send her the next book they were going to read. Her discussion group also was a book club. Often they digressed from the book and got into other issues. But that's what books were supposed to do. That's why they called themselves a discussion group. Did she want to join them again? A friend asked on the phone. She had called to talk about the wedding. Her own daughter was getting married. She might have to ask Solome advice from time to time.

Solome didn't know about the discussion group. She didn't know what to tell the volunteer office at the Historical Society when they called. She needed the quiet after the wedding. Yes, she was still interested in volunteering. Yes, she would attend the discussion group when it was possible.

They could send her the book. She would add it to the books beside her bed.

Stephen Savard

Solome and I went to a retirement dinner at the University Club for one of my colleagues. I told the group that Cobson would miss the man. I listened to the other speeches. Tom Marshall, one of history professors, went on too long. Someone joked that the next dinner would be for me. I joked back. I could feel my old self from time to time. I could feel the struggle to remain myself. I could feel the spots where I slipped. I had spent the afternoon in my office trying to read the faculty addendum to decide on merit raises. I had spent the morning with development and financial officers trying to work our way through various applications to foundations. I could hold passages in my mind, but not the whole of them as we changed language to fit the particular stipulations of each endowment and granting institution.

The man who was retiring would miss work. My thoughts wandered as the man talked. I fell into disordered thoughts. I pulled out of them. Solome would want to travel when I retired. We could spend more time at Crane Lake. She would watch me slip away. She would face the pain of our loss. She would cry during a discussion group. She would cry at her Bible study. She would cry by herself. But I knew she would not cry at the Faculty Wives Club.

Solome Savard

Gretchen and Dennis flew to St. Paul to open the rest of their wedding gifts. They returned some of them at Daynard's. They would take some of them with them. They would leave other gifts behind for Solome to store. They would pick them up later when they had a permanent place to live.

"You need to write thank you notes, Gretchen. My friends will be asking."

"I can't rearrange my life for your friends."

"I rearranged mine for you," Solome said.

"I'm working on a dissertation. I have a committee to please. I have to write letters for job applications," Gretchen argued. "I can't be worried about notes."

"You don't have to worry, Gretchen, you just have to write them. How can I answer my friends? Gretchen is too busy to thank you for all the trouble and expense you went to?"

"Stop it, mother."

"Gretchen is too busy to be decent?"

Gretchen stormed from the room. Solome was left facing Dennis.

Stephen Savard

I had to leave the table when Gretchen and Solome argued. Their voices sounded like gravel in my head. They weren't alarmed when I left. I heard their voices continue when I shut the door to my study. I wanted to stay there and never come out. The president of the college was at a conference for few days. A colleague from political science, Grant Harner, approached me in the faculty dining room about the need for another faculty member in their department. His direct approach wasn't the proper channel. We weren't adding faculty at the moment, but trying to eliminate. There was talk of an early retirement program. A forfeiture of tenure at half-pay with a four-year sabbatical to work on projects or teach part-time followed by full retirement. I told Harner his request would have to be brought up in allocations. I saw others looking at us. Was Harner planning a coup?

Later in the day, I met with the newly elected officers of the student body. There would be more trouble there. The whole world seemed volatile. I felt I was spinning my tires on a gravel driveway somewhere as I hovered in the corner of my study waiting to go to bed.

Solome Savard

After Gretchen and Dennis left, Stephen found they needed a new roof on their house. In the aftermath of the wedding, he found a hollow corner under the basement floor when he noticed a crack.

As he talked to workmen in the yard, Solome read another pamphlet she kept in a drawer under her towels in the kitchen. She didn't want Stephen to find them. She didn't want him to know she was concerned. In the later stages, he wouldn't be aware of the disease anyway.

This pamphlet was from the America's Pharmaceutical Companies.

The causes of Alzheimer's disease were not known, but were the subject of intensive, ongoing scientific investigation. There were several theories. Genetic predisposition played a role in some families.

Although there was no cure for Alzheimer's disease at this time, there was much that could be done to manage the disease and to treat its symptoms.

Solome liked the clear words of the pamphlet. It made Alzheimer's seem manageable. Endurable.

Behavioral symptoms were common in Alzheimer's disease, such as paranoia, delusions, depression, agitation, sleeplessness and anxiety that could benefit from a wide variety of psychiatric medicines.

But Stephen didn't have any of those yet. Was it what was coming? No wonder she kept the pamphlets hidden. No wonder she read them when Stephen was gone.

Solome and Stephen were in their bedroom. She sat on the edge of the bed while Stephen sat in the bedroom chair with Brown at his feet. Solome watched Stephen pet the dog. For some reason, Solome remembered when she had met Stephen at a dance. She and Jane Mead had gone together. She had the flash of a memory— a pink dress with a net skirt, a pink corsage. Maybe that was later. Stephen attended Seitman, a private boys' school, and sometimes girls from the nearby high school were invited. After high school, Solome had gone to Augustus College in Northfield while Stephen had gone to Cobson College in St. Paul. She returned to St. Paul nearly every weekend to see Stephen. He continued with graduate school at the University of Minnesota where Solome studied art history. They were married a week after he received his M.A. in History. Solome worked while Stephen finished his Ph.D. By then, she was pregnant with Gretchen.

What would Stephen do with those years? When he forgot, part of Solome would be forgotten too. She was being erased as well as Stephen.

"What have I meant to you, Stephen? Before you leave, tell me."

"You're my wife. We've been together most of my life. You're the mother of our children. We're partners. We're not alone because of the other. We're a couple. I go to work. I have my office at the college, but this is where I live. My home is with you. What else can I say?"

Solome had tears at the clarity of Stephen's words. "Do you love me?"

"Of course. I long for the day to be over— I want to feel you next to me. I like the evenings here with you. I can't imagine not knowing what I'm doing," Stephen said.

"When will we tell the children?" She asked. "You have to think about it," Solome said.

"Why?"

"Because it's significant. It's the new thing between us. It's our next child. Illness and loss and change and departure from what we've known— what we've been."

"What will happen to us?" Stephen asked.

"You'll continue to lose your memory. You'll be in a home when I can't take care of you anymore. You'll be content, I suppose. I will have to go on without you. Then you'll die. I'll be miserable without you until I die also."

"Then what?"

"I wish you'd come back to church with me," Solome said. "It seems clearer there. I wish you'd come to the Bible study. We talk about *what next*."

"I don't think it would help," Stephen said.

"You could listen, Stephen. What's your relationship to Jesus Christ?"

"I'm a Christian. I've been a Christian all my life."

"Yes, you've lived a Christian life. You've done your work. You've been a good husband and father. You haven't caused me grief the way Brian hurts Susanna through neglect. You are here. You helped me through it all. But do you know Jesus as your personal Savior?"

"Yes, I think I do."

"Do you confess Jesus as your Savior?"

"Yes."

"Do you realize he died for your sins?"

"Yes."

"All right, Stephen."

Stephen Savard

No, it was not Gretchen who was pregnant, but Soos. She called one morning crying. I was still at home, waiting to talk to the foremen of the work crews. I was still there when she arrived with Susan.

Soon, the roofers were pounding new shingles on the roof. A man with a jackhammer was digging a hole in the basement floor. Brown was barking wildly in the backyard. Solome took him to the garage, then put him in Soos' car for her to take to her house for the day.

Soos didn't stay long, but left with Susan in her car seat, and Brown barking from the rear window. Solome would pick him up that evening.

Solome Savard

There is language that is just language. There is language that is a crowbar that lifts a lid nailed down. To let in the air. There is a language that is a bridge over something that needs to be crossed. There is language that is a direct hit. An opening where there was none. To air out— to let in air in. To give bounty to even the most diminishing thing that happened.

Solome looked for that kind of language in the backyard with Stephen later that summer. The roofers had finished their work after several days of pounding. They had gone over the yard with a magnetic rake to collect nails. Solome picked up some roofing detritus she saw in the grass. She thought of the plaques and tangles that were cluttering Stephen's brain. She pulled a few weeds from the flowers. Then she sat beside Stephen again who was petting Brown.

"Tell me things will be all right," Solome said as dusk covered the yard. "What will I do when you don't come home of an evening? When you don't call during the day? What will I do without you?" Solome was crying. She was asking Stephen to help her through his disease, his absence, his death. He had to give her words now so she could follow them as if they were a road when he wasn't there to help her— when she wouldn't hear him speaking to her, saying, *here, this is the way.*

Stephen Savard

That fall at the opening convocation, the welcoming of new students, the return of others, under the canopy of trees on the lawn, I thought of the house, repaired, in place. A covering for Solome and me. I saw Mark in the group of students. I saw the progress on the new student center. Who would Solome invite for dinner? Who would Mark bring home? Would Soos stay with her husband? The president stood at the podium saying what he usually said. When would Gretchen come for the rest of her wedding gifts? What would I know at the end of the academic year that I didn't know

now? Look at the students watching me on the platform. Look at the rows of faculty. Their eyes like squirrels' eyes drilling into me.

Solome Savard

When Solome returned to her volunteer work at the Historical Society, she heard about another job opening. It was the job she had considered before: cataloging and researching historical information. Assisting the assistant. An old friend of the Savard's, Bill Richter, was on the Board of Directors, but Solome didn't want to call him. She wanted to apply on her own. The job was only two days a week, the same as her volunteer work, Wednesday and Friday. She would receive pay. She would share a small office space with another woman who did the same kind of part-time work. Solome went for an interview. The Historical Society called her the next week.

Solome would log incoming contributions. She would open boxes of old photographs and manuscripts sent to Acquisitions. Sometimes there were walk-ins. She would write a general description of what it was. Write an acknowledgment note.

"If something is old, people think the Historical Society wants it," her advisor said. "Coins, artifacts, diaries and journals."

The Historical Society was not interested in weather, though weather was often the topic of the journals. But weather was significant. What if the weather came first, and determined the people who could live in it?

"We ask, is this person significant? If not, does their story fill in a gap? If a farmer kept a journal, how is it different? How does it stand out? The Historical Society is not interested in single manuscripts, unless the person is famous. If there is an interesting story, the society wants the correspondence, the accounts books, the photos that go with it."

Solome looked up information on Red River oxcarts. She found an old photograph for an exhibit. She proof read the text for a forthcoming catalog.

Solome read the women's diaries, farm women who knew hardship and loss. She looked at loose photos without dates. The German and Swedish immigrants without names. That's what Stephen's disease was like. A series of faces and places with no names, no dates, no recognition, no meaning.

Once Solome's study of art history had been centered in Europe. But it was the significance of the American midlands she found in her work at the Historical Society. There were disasters, floods, tornados, the Hinkley fire. But it was the strength of the ordinary lives that now seemed *art* to her. Maybe her job would be the oxcart that pulled her through Stephen's illness. Or would it?

"Sometimes they forget how to swallow," Solome remembered a woman said in her discussion group, who had a distant relative with Alzheimer's.

Solome kept literature about Alzheimer's in her towel drawer in the kitchen. Sometimes she would look at it when she was cooking for family or friends. One pamphlet had a cheery picture of a husband and wife. He had just been diagnosed with Alzheimer's. He had been a workaholic, now they had time to play golf, enjoy one another. Solome put the material back in her towel drawer when she heard Susanna's car in the drive. She preferred the grim statistics over a heartening story of the glories of Alzheimer's.

Solome fixed lunch for Soos and Susan. She had called her mother to join them, but her mother was on her way to visit old friends. After lunch, Solome took Susan upstairs to the crib she had nearly outgrown in Susanna's old room, while Soos ran errands and got her hair cut.

In the afternoon, when Soos returned for Susan, and they had gone, Solome decided to go for a walk. She got the dog's leash and left by the backyard gate.

The word that stayed with her was *inappropriate. Putting things in inappropriate places. Dressing inappropriately.* Inappropriate in whose opinion? She felt rebellion against the material she read. She wanted an alternative. She would create options with her words. She could develop a language that would accommodate Alzheimer's.

It was a disease. No, erase disease as a word. It was a condition in which the sufferer— no, another word— in which the *recipient* was free to lose the details that had bound his ordinary life and travel elsewhere. Nepal. Bangladesh. Yes, that was Alzheimer's. Traveling third class through a third world country wiped out by tidal waves and hurricane.

Solome looked in her towel drawer again. Alzheimer's was a possibility of finding new areas of existence. Freedom— But freedom from what? Everything that any other ordinary human being considered vital and sacred? Thought. Language. Control. Life.

Diane Glancy

Stephen Savard

I wrote checks that evening. There were the usual bills that came every month. As I paid dues at the University Club and the St. Paul Club, I remembered the evening dinners and Sunday brunches with our three children. We had been confident— even arrogant— taking our place for granted. We had lived in a solid world. Now, for the first time, I was standing outside the family looking back at how we must have looked to others who had not been settled in themselves. How could we have been wrapped up in our own importance? How could I have been blind? I had been the recipient of benefits. What have I ever done to help? I tithed to the church and served on committees over the years. But I was suffocating in my shortcomings. I choked on my thoughts. I would become a thunderous weight on Solome. Something to be pitied as she helped me stumble into the clubs with my walker. She had been everything to herself, and it was going to be ripped away. I felt alone, destitute in myself as I sat at my desk in the study at my house.

Merciful God, where are you when the stars begin to fall?

Solome Savard

If insurrection ruled her country, the insurgents were her family. What troops could she send? Gretchen, her oldest daughter, married two months ago, had not written thank-you notes. Susanna, her youngest daughter, with a shaky marriage, found herself pregnant for the second time. Her son, Mark Stephen, the youngest, in college, was oblivious to every bone of common sense. Her mother, still pouty with widowhood, was often on the phone. Her husband, in the early stages of Alzheimer's, still held to his work, but retirement from the college loomed somewhere ahead.

In the meanwhile, late in August, Solome took another week away from her work at the Minnesota Historical Society and drove to Crane Lake, five hours north of St. Paul, with Brown, to close up the cabin, and to see what she could do by herself for a few days. She had asked Jane Mead to go with her, but Jane was seeing a new man, and didn't want to leave.

The dog rode in the backseat with his nose out the window. Solome tried to keep the window open for a few miles, but soon had to close it, catching the dog's snout as she closed the window from the front seat. She reversed the button quickly and freed the dog. She told Brown to lie down as she maneuvered through traffic on I-35 north. Then the dog slept as she continued north to Cloquet, where she took Highway 53 past Ely until she reached Buyck, Minnesota, where Solome stopped for milk and a few groceries.

She left the dog leashed to a post outside the store. As she stood in line, she heard the commotion of a dog scuffle, not a fight. Brown was barking at a large dog that a woman was trying to pull past him. Solome got Brown into the car, the woman got her dog away from the store, and Solome went back inside for groceries.

The first morning at the cabin, she woke with a dream. Her mother was hanging one end of a large bed sheet on the line. She was at the other end, hanging it up, but she saw the sheet had twisted and knotted in the middle. She had to unpin her half and untwist the sheet, then hang up her end again.

In the same dream, she threw a scarf to her daughter but missed, and the scarf fell to the ground picking up the leaf bits and dirt in its fringe. Which daughter was it? Susanna, probably, who needed it most. But Gretchen, also, was frantic. She had her dissertation to finish. Solome tried to remember which daughter she dreamed.

The dream itself was in two parts, hinged by a knot.

The morning was filled with dim gray light. Solome read a newspaper she had brought with her: *Troops in a third world country. A military coup.* But what could she do? Brown was napping at her feet, groaning sometimes with something he remembered, the encounter with the dog outside the Buyck grocery, or some previous confrontation.

After breakfast, she dressed. She had picked up her shoes from the shoe repair and they still didn't fit. She realized stretching would not adjust them to her feet. Why had she bought the shoes? They were just loafers. What was it about them that hurt, even after she had spent an afternoon not walking but driving? Why hadn't she noticed in the store? She had, but decided stretching would correct the misfit. She knew now she'd been wrong. It probably was too late to return them.

She stood at the window looking at the lake from the cabin. She remembered the old x-ray machine in the children's shoe store where her family had shopped when she was a girl. Inside the machine was a green luminescent light, something like the numbers on the clock in the night, or early light on the lake. The machine looked something like a small pulpit to which she stepped up, and moved her feet into the slot at the bottom.

Through the viewer of top, her parents, the salesman, and she, herself, could look into the dark, iridescent, greenish world that showed the bones of her feet inside the shoes, like a viewer she held underwater to see the fish.

She remembered the glowing skeleton of her feet in their new shoes, the jointed bones like sticks whittled to blunt points. Later the machines had been banned, but damage had not been done by the early x-rays. No one got shoes often in those days. A school pair, a dress pair, and ones for play.

She applied mosquito repellent and unloaded the gallon of antifreeze from her car, and the boxes she brought for packing. Then Solome pulled weeds and carried the heavy storm windows from the shed to the cabin. A man would come in the morning to install them and she wanted to wash the glass. Brown romped in the woods by the cabin, or lapped at the lake, or barked at the ducks, over and over, circling the outposts of his activity as she worked.

The next cabin had sold to a couple from Minneapolis, the cabin where the retarded daughter had lived with her parents. Solome heard one of the parents had died. The other was with the daughter in a home somewhere. The new owners didn't seem to come often, but their children, in their early 20's, if that old, were there with their loud music. How late would they play into the night? She listened to pounding of the bass guitar. She wanted to yell at them to turn it off. Solome wanted to sit on the porch with the dog and listen to the lake, even though Brown was restless. She usually didn't bring him to the cabin for fear he would wander off. Once, when he was young, he had gone off, and returned a few days later full, of fleas, ticks and scratches. Sometimes he had brought the ticks back to St. Paul. She had the house sprayed several times. There also were large dogs somewhere. She heard them barking from time to time. In the night, Brown would bark when he heard the dogs, until Solome told him to be quiet.

That evening, she went to a nearby resort for dinner, no longer crowded with summer tourists.

When she returned, she saw the dog lying on the steps of the cabin. She could see his sides heaving in the shadows. At first Solome, didn't realize he was hurt, but in the porch light, she saw the blood.

Something had attacked the dog. A small bear? She thought. She felt the sudden fear that an animal was waiting in the dark and would attack her also. She called out for Stephen, her husband, who, of course, wasn't there. She knew it as she tried to calm the dog, pet him, tell him he was all right. She would get help. But who would she get? She went into the cabin, looked in the phone book for the vet, called the emergency number from her cell phone.

"My dog's been attacked," she told the man who answered.

The vet would meet her at the clinic. He gave directions. State Road 24 past Buyck, then 116 toward Ely. It was probably ten miles.

How would she get the dog into the car to take him to the vet?

"Can't you come here?" Solome asked.

"My equipment is at the clinic."

She heard the music. She hurried through the dark to the cabin next door. She could see the lights as she hurried, panicked the bear would confront her.

She pounded on the door. Two boys opened it.

"My dog is hurt. I need help getting him in the car."

The boys followed her.

They looked in the shed with a flashlight for a board to lay the dog on. They couldn't find anything. Did she have a tarp? The blood would get on the upholstery. Was the dog hurt worse than she thought? The boys looked at him. Solome could hear the loud music still coming from their cabin.

One of them ran back to their cabin. He returned with a half-tarp. Solome remembered the storm windows. A man was coming in the morning to install them. It was the only thing she could think of. Would the glass break with the weight of the dog?

"Would you turn off that music?" Solome snapped at them. "How can you think?"

She got a window from where she'd leaned them against the house, while one of the boys ran back to the cabin again. He returned with a board that looked like an old shutter.

"You can't use that window," he said.

Solome held the board while the boys tried to pull the dog onto it. Brown yelped with pain. She ordered the dog to hold still. The boys put their hand under its belly and eased the tarp under the dog. With a shriek of both Solome and the dog, they pulled him onto the board. The boys lifted the board and carried it to the car, and pushed it into the backseat.

"We'll go with you."

Solome noticed for the first time that the woods was quiet.

The boys drove her car to the vet while she sat in back with her hand on Brown. She looked at the directions she had written in pencil, trying to read what she'd written under the dome light of the car, struggling with her handbag to find her glasses, trying to keep her eye on Brown and on the road. It was a long ride, but soon she saw the clinic, the vet, his dark figure was waiting in the bright door.

The doctor x-rayed Brown. There were internal injuries. The dog would need surgery. The jaw was broken. There would be a long period of rehabilitation. The dog was old. He needed to be *put down*. Solome turned away from Brown on the table as the doctor injected the needle into a vein.

What did she want to do with him? Cremate?

"No," Solome said, "I'll take him back to the cabin."

The boys said they'd dig a hole in the morning. She would bury Brown by the cabin.

"What bit him?" Solome asked.

"Another dog," the vet answered.

"I thought it was a bear."

"It would be timber wolves if anything," one of the boys said.

"The dogs up here resent other dogs that come from the city."

"I know he didn't like to come to the lake," Solome paused. "Well, he was a different dog at the lake."

The boys carried Brown's body to the car while Solome paid the vet. The boys wanted to put Brown in the trunk, but Solome wanted him in the backseat.

"He must not have stayed on his property," one of the boys said.

"Or else the other dogs came to your cabin," the other boy said as they drove back to the cabins. "I heard a large dog barking. Maybe more than one."

"You didn't hear a fight?" Solome asked.

"No," they answered.

"Your music is too loud," Solome told them.

"There's a lot of dogs around here," the boys said, ignoring her comment. "We run into them. They bark at the canoe if we get too close to the shore. Sometimes they swim after us."

The boys carried Brown's body to the car and drove Solome back to the cabin.

"What do you want to do with him?" The boys asked when they arrived at Solome's cabin. "We could leave him in the car for the night."

"Put him in the shed," she answered.

In the morning, Solome couldn't find any bloody place where the dog fought. Maybe Brown had gone off the property.

Why hadn't she left him locked in the cabin? If she had left him in St. Paul, he would still be alive. What would her children say? They would be sorry to hear about Brown, but they wouldn't grieve. What about Stephen? He also was in his own world. No one would blame her. No one would be upset she lost Brown through carelessness.

Where were the boys? She opened the door of the shed where Brown was, still wrapped in the tarp on the board. She got a shovel and looked for a place to bury him. She decided on a place on the south side of the cabin, toward St. Paul.

The boys dug the hole Solome had started, and laid Brown's stiff body into his grave. Solome thanked them, then stood alone at his grave. She wanted to tell Brown that he'd been a good dog. He'd been faithful, even when they had not paid attention to him. She thought of how often he had been ignored, or told to go away. He had annoyed her with his barking. Maybe she was relieved he was gone. She cried when she thought of him in the backyard waiting for attention, or even recognition that he was there. She shoveled dirt into the grave, and covered it with a brick she used for a door stop. A brick removed from a street in St. Paul by the city before it was paved, the bricks left for anyone who wanted them. Yes, Brown had been tolerated, but not loved, Solome thought as she buried him at the lake.

By afternoon, the handy man had still not come. Solome called Stephen on her cell phone and told him about Brown. He seemed unaffected. He was in the middle of meetings at the college. There was a new crisis over multiculturalism. Some students had a sit in.

"They chained themselves to the flag pole in the center of campus. It took several hours for the guards to cut them loose."

"You should have left them," Solome told Stephen. "They eventually would have freed themselves. Was Mark involved in the protest?"

"Yes, though multiculturalism isn't his main mission."

Solome called Susanna after she talked to Stephen to tell her about Brown's death. "Your father had no reaction. You might want to call later and make sure he's all right."

After getting through to Mark the first time she called, Solome went to the next cabin and asked the boys to come for supper the next evening.

"Why are you still here after the summer?" She asked them.

"We live here," they told her.

"All winter?" Solome asked, but then assumed the cabin must have been winterized by the older couple.

How could she tell the boys to be quiet with their music? They had been with her when her own family hadn't.

It was evening before the handy man came and got some of the storm-windows up, but soon it grew dark. He would return the next morning. He also would help her pull the canoe from the lake, turn it upside down, and chain it to a tree.

"Of course, they can always cut the tree down," the handy man said shaking his head. Each winter, there had been more break-ins. She also noticed a tree had been cut down on the edge of her property.

The next day, she rowed a short way from the shore in the canoe, then walked up the road. In the afternoon, Solome boxed her mother's collection of birch bark baskets and antique kettles. She looked for other belongings to take back, fearing their loss. She didn't think the boys in the next cabin would take anything, but she didn't know about their friends. She would have to leave the old birch bark canoe her father had suspended from the ceiling.

Stephen called her in the afternoon. He seemed to accept Brown's death.

That evening, Solome fixed supper for the boys for helping her with the dog. The boys said they were step brothers from a first and second marriage. Their father had married a third time, and they didn't like the new step mother. They didn't want to finish school. They didn't have jobs. Their father agreed to let them stay at the cabin all winter.

"It gets cold," Solome said, "30 and 40 below."

"We've camped out in the winter before. We cross-country ski. We've got our snowmobiles. We had a cabin before— on Superior."

Having someone next door all winter might keep her cabin safer. It was comforting as she thought of the lake edge eroding, as she thought of her husband eroding. Stephen, she thought with her hands to her face when she was alone. There was an enzyme snipping protein that protruded from his brain cells. The enzyme's name was beta-secretase. Alzheimer's was a disease that left the microscopic clutter called amyloid. It was like the clippings the handyman left after his snipping. Had Solome memorized the pamphlet? Would there be a drug in time to stop the snipping? Could she tell it to go home, the way she could tell the handy man he'd done enough and could go?

Stephen was in the first forgetful stage. It was evident he had Alzheimer's. Solome had to remind herself Stephen's disease was not going away. What body of water was lapping at the shore of his brain? What ducks flew south? The loons, wolves, bears, wild dogs? What storms would come and blow down telephone poles? Fill the lake with ice, push it onto the shore as the ice expanded in the cold.

Solome washed the dishes after the boys left. She remembered how Mark had brought friends to the cabin in winter. How she worried something would happen. One of them would freeze to death and they would be responsible. How often had they warned Mark of the cold? Solome remembered the x-ray, showing bones, skeletal as winter trees. She remembered the bones of her feet were like kindling. No, the bones of her thoughts were a fire of thorns.

Solome wanted to go to the door and call Brown. She wanted to tell him to come in from the night. She looked into the darkness. The moon and stars were the bones of the night, x-rayed in the sky. Solome sat on the porch wrapped in a quilt. She heard the small lap of the waves. The wind in the trees. She remembered the summers the family had spent at the lake. The evenings the family had watched the Northern lights. Now she sat alone in the darkness.

The boys next door must have gone somewhere after they left her cabin. Maybe they wouldn't come back until late, after she was asleep. Would their music wake her again? What was ahead? What would be uncovered by the days passing? Whatever happened, the insurrection would leave her by herself. That was certain. What had happened to the parent and retarded daughter? Why hadn't Solome shown more consideration? Why hadn't she been more charitable?

Someday she would sell her parents' cabin if the girls or Mark didn't want it. Gretchen would always live somewhere else. She had Dennis, her new husband, and her studies. Susanna would soon have two children. Brian, Susanna's husband, was not interested in coming to the cabin. Maybe someday Mark would have a family, though that was years off. For now, he would use the cabin for parties.

Solome listened to the little waves on the shore, one after another. She was glad the story was coming slowly. All of it at once would be too much for her to listen to now. That's why the lake took its time with each word.

Solome had the house in St. Paul to winterize too. Her yard man had checked the chimney for loose masonry and cleaned out the gutters. She had made a list in her yard-book of where her flowers had been planted. Her yard man could rotate them in the spring. There was something about the words she liked: caulk, putty, weather-strip, duct, vent, insulation, plumbing, soffits, sump pump. The hot water heater had been checked, the furnace had been cleaned last year, making sure the flame was blue and not orange or yellow from the lack of oxygen. There was something she liked about maintenance. Getting things into shape.

Solome tried to call Jane Mead, but she didn't answer.

The next morning, Solome got out of bed and put on her loafers. They were tight on her feet. She put on her old pair, and went to the shed for the shovel. She dug a hole and buried her new shoes on the north side of the cabin, toward the lake. She buried them like the two pieces of the sheet she had dreamed about the first night at the cabin, one end going one way, the other end, the other, the way the shoes came in the shoebox.

The next day, Solome turned off the water. Put antifreeze in the toilet. She finished packing the small boxes, light enough she could carry them to the car. She could hear the lake throwing its little buckets of waves against the shore. She started packing up the waves that were tossing her and tossing her.

Stephen Savard

We began by writing history on the wall— the Indian massacres, the slave ships, the internment camps. I didn't know where we were headed. Yes, I did. I thought about the car I had bought earlier that afternoon. The slave ships pushed across the ocean by wind in their sails.

I had to go through the racism training at Cobson. It was required because of my position and because the students demanded it. Solome had come with me. Not that it was a requirement for her, but it would look good if she did. Actually, she was glad to come. Solome usually liked the programs she attended with me. I think she felt she needed to be with me, to calm me, to keep me focused. But I hoped she liked being with me. She wanted to protect and help me.

Racism was more than minority and white. It was minority and minority. Mixed heritages too. It was being dismissed, not considered, left out.

Had I left out students? Overlooked them? Misunderstood their needs? Was I a racist? Yes, that's what I'd learn in the workshop. I knew it now.

Was I part of the wall of history? History according to what was written in books, taught in school, believed as the whole story when it was only part of the whole? I was drifting. I didn't want to be in the workshop. But I had to. I had the opportunity to be self-determined, which others did not have. The minority others.

Solome looked at me. I was listening to their words. She listened also. Knowledge was language. And what was language? The dominant language, they meant. A net in which they were trapped. The English language was a construct of racism and power against minorities. What an irony. America was a gathering place of diversities. Yet its language eliminated diversity because it was owned by the power structure. I always had spoken the top layer of the American language.

We were all in the boat. But who rowed and who rode? My job as provost at Cobson College was to hand out the oars. What were they saying? There were dynamics I might not be aware of. A student may not be studying because the father was shooting the mother and the brother was tripping out and the ex-boyfriend raping the sister with the kids screaming the dogs barking. Why couldn't he study?

It depended on who ran the show. Well, I did, to some extent. Who asked the questions? Who wrote the history? Who remembered the answers? Yes, I remembered— whoever spoke the language.

I began to realize I felt combative. I didn't want them telling me what to think. But I had to keep it to myself. I was here to learn. I had to remember not to speak out. I had to remember that I still had the power to edit my thoughts.

I thought I should make a contribution to the dialogue, but the students were there to take down what I said. To record it. Whatever I said, would be wrong in their opinion. Other than letting them run the college. Letting them make the decisions. They thought they knew best. Didn't my own son think so? How could they be so naive? To think they could determine what they needed to know. How limiting it would be to know only what you thought you should know. They wanted to determine their own education. To set their own limits. And where was Mark? Sitting out of sight with his radical friends? I felt my language ripping again.

Mark had not wanted to go to Seitman, the private high school I had attended. But after public high school, he had chosen Cobson College, where his father was provost. It seemed odd that Mark wanted to be at Cobson. The children of other faculty had chosen other colleges. But Mark liked to be at Cobson. Maybe his father's position gave him power he needed.

"Being white meant not having to think about it," the speaker said.

The afternoon felt crooked. It was hard to get it straight. Sometimes I felt blank.

When a break came, I went to my office to answer messages and take care of calls. Solome would talk to the others.

The European Americans say, I have no identity, no race, or racism. They suffer a cultural Alzheimer's. That was the reality of white power and privilege. No one white questioned or defined their whiteness as privilege. Power. Wealth. Ownership. I heard a string of words.

Solome Savard

When Stephen and Solome returned home after the two-day racism workshop at Cobson, the proofs of the photos of Gretchen's wedding were in a box by the front door.

"Why didn't they call me?" Solome asked. "I would have picked them up. What if it was raining?"

They opened the box and looked at the photo proofs for an hour. Solome would ship the proofs to Gretchen to choose the ones she wanted, then Gretchen would send them on to the Kamrar's. Then Soos would have her turn, and Solome's mother. Maybe even Mark would want several. They would all return their choices to the photographer, and maybe in another six months, they would have their wedding albums.

Stephen Savard

"I fear disappearing," I said that evening.

"You won't disappear as you drift into Alzheimer's," Solome told me. "Your memory will climb into the attic and shut itself off and seem to disappear, but it's packed to be returned like luggage when you reach your destination."

"After death?"

"Yes," Solome answered.

"It's not exactly like going to New York."

"It's more of a foreign country on which there's no information. It's an act of faith."

"You make it sound like a vacation," I said. "It's not a trip you take by choice."

"It's a flight you step into as a necessity, because you have Alzheimer's. It's a trip you're scheduled to take and nothing can be done to change it."

"I can hope it will be canceled," I told Solome as she made soup and we ate together in the kitchen.

"What made you feel like you're disappearing?"

"I couldn't hold onto everything they said today."

"I couldn't either," she said.

Solome Savard

Solome held Stephen that night. She felt him quiver as he did the time early in their marriage when they nearly collided with another car and he had pulled off the road, shaken. She remembered that first threat now as if it had been an omen. It was something that could have taken their lives. Was it the first time he had felt vulnerable, open to the possibility of an accident? Without power?

"I wish I wasn't taking you with me."

"There are support groups. There will be things that happen to make it bearable," Solome said. "You've got a long time yet, Stephen. It will be slow in coming."

"There are times now it hits," he said.

"I can't stand to think you will be sitting in the room and I won't know who you are."

How had he gone all those years without facing vulnerability again? Had he gone through his life without feeling it? Maybe he'd felt it and she hadn't been there to see it. Maybe he'd pulled off the road when she wasn't with him. Maybe he'd gone to his office and pulled himself together and gone on and she'd never known it. Is that what their marriage had been? How much of her husband had she not known? Had they tolerated one another the way they tolerated Brown? Had they arrived at the potential of knowing one another without going beyond? How long had Alzheimer's been in Stephen's head?

Before Thanksgiving, Solome called her repairman and painter, her *house man*, she called him, in contrast to her yard man. She had Gretchen's bedroom painted salmon. She had the man rebuild the bookcases on the wall, replacing the old, sagging shelves. She took the birch bark baskets and kettles from the boxes she had brought back from Crane Lake and arranged them on the new shelves.

She put a bathroom in the bedroom. There was a closet over the bathroom in her kitchen downstairs. It was not difficult for the man to connect the plumbing.

Why was she doing this? To sell the house. To get the most for it. She would have to, what was it called?— downsize. Scale back. Move to a smaller place. What would she have to live on? How much would the college pay? How long would Stephen be in an institution? How much of his care would be covered? When would she have to start looking for an apartment? A condominium? She didn't want a yard to care for. She didn't want to pay for snow removal. But there were maintenance fees at a condo. She'd heard Jane Mead complain. Would she have to begin to think of how little she could get along on? No. Stephen had planned for his retirement.

What else was it she remembered? Her discussion group had read Chaucer. What was in *The Canterbury Tales* that haunted her? She looked up the passage she remembered. There had been women along the road dressed in black, crying. Their husbands had not been buried because they were enemies of the new king. They had been left to be eaten by the dogs. Why had Solome remembered that? Had it been a premonition? Had she known from the beginning what would happen? Was it what had terrified and haunted her before she even knew it? Had it come from signals she picked up from Stephen, the ones she recognized, was receptive to, before she recognized them?

Solome didn't feel good. She was tired. She had a cough. Her skin hurt where her clothes touched her. How could she face Stephen's Alzheimer's? How could she face a place with no words? Was that why they hadn't told the children? That's why she hadn't told her mother. It would make the disease real. Once it had been named. Once it had language. There would be no turning back once everyone knew.

Solome remembered the resin that oozed from the yellow pine at their cabin at Crane Lake. It was Susanna who said the cabin was crying.

Solome and her mother had lunch at the Minneapolis Arts Institute though snow was forecast that afternoon. There was a new exhibit. *Impressionism of the 1870's.* She looked at Claude Monet's *View of Argenteuil* in the snow. 1874–75. It was the Boulevard St. Denis in Argenteuil, which disappeared in the distance. The pedestrians were bundled against the cold. There was a woman in a black coat walking— Solome felt she was in the painting.

There was meaning that accompanied words, but it stayed silent if the words were not spoken. All these words that were no words— that could not say anything. Yet when words were together, they joined in support groups. Like friends. But sometimes Stephen's words tumbled around on their own. One day his words would be gone because his mind had shut them out. Language needed the mind, or was it the other way?

Solome felt the loneliness, the isolation of the *View of Argenteuil.* She wanted to say that living with Stephen was like walking through the snow. With a slap, the words about Stephen's Alzheimer's burst from Solome's mouth, creating a new world, an unwelcome one. Her mother was stunned. "I'm sorry. I'm sorry," Solome said to her, holding her mother up, her voice louder than she realized, echoing against the walls in the empty room of the museum.

Did Cobson want a definition of *otherness* for its multicultural program? *The other* was Alzheimer's.

Stephen Savard

Thanksgiving that year was the Stiple's turn to have Soos, Brian, and Susan at their house. Solome told me she offered to buy plane tickets for Gretchen and Dennis, but they were going to the Kamrar's. Gretchen was making progress on thank-you notes, five months after the wedding, she told Solome as they talked on the phone.

Solome's mother would come for dinner. I would drive and pick her up because of the threat of another snow storm. The rest of the places at the table could be filled with students. I invited two international students, and Mark brought several friends home with him, friends who lived too far away to go home, or didn't want to go home. It would be the same at Christmas, only the Stiples and Kamrar's would be there too. In the past, I had dominated the conversation, not wanting the students to feel at a loss for words. Now I listened to the students talk.

I also heard Solome talking to her mother. Gretchen looked forward to her album wedding photos. They had looked through the proofs again and again, and finally the decisions were made. Two months later, the albums had not arrived.

"Was there a problem?" Solome said she asked the photographer.

"No," he said. "Often it was six months after the wedding before the albums were ready. The Kamrar's also had taken a long time to return the proofs with their family's orders."

Solome Savard

After Thanksgiving, Solome brought the Christmas decorations down from the attic. She had an open house for her neighbors on the cul-de-sac. She shopped for gifts. She had an open house for Stephen's colleagues. She and Stephen went to an open house at their neighbor's, the Grunswald's. The Christmas activities were a snow-wall around her.

In January, Gretchen called Solome to stay with her. Dennis had to be gone and she needed someone to be with her as she went through exams. Solome didn't want Gretchen to be alone with worry, but she lay awake at night thinking about Stephen. She hated leaving Stephen, but Gretchen needed her. Soos needed her also. At least she felt Mark did not. He was now in another apartment, this one in Minneapolis, with a new car to drive back and forth to the college.

"Can I tell her about you?" Solome asked before she left. "Without you there?" Stephen agreed.

Solome flew to New York to stay with Gretchen. They ate at ethnic restaurants. During the day, Solome shopped while Gretchen was at the university. She read the *New York Times*. She read Gretchen's work on her dissertation, *Medieval Women Mystics*. One evening, Solome and Gretchen saw a play at the Promenade Theatre on Broadway at 76th Street. Solome thought it would take Gretchen's mind off her exams. Solome didn't say a lot to Gretchen. Gretchen was stressed and snapped at her if she did. Solome was supposed to be there with Gretchen as a support, not as someone dispensing advise.

Columbia University was at 116th and Broadway on the Upper West Side. Gretchen and Dennis had an apartment on 105th between Broadway and Amsterdam. They paid $1700 a month rent. The Savard's and Kamrar's each paid $850 a month. Dennis and Gretchen were responsible for the rest of the rent and utilities. It was a walk-up in need of painting, with a kitchen that could hardly be used. Solome didn't like to stay there.

One morning, Solome took a taxi to Fifth Avenue and visited St. Patrick's Cathedral. She stood looking up at the high, vaulted ceiling, the round, blue stained-glass window at the back. She remembered being full of hope on other trips. Gretchen had been accepted at Columbia graduate school. Her son, Mark, was a student at Cobson College. Solome was the wife of the Provost. She had a grandchild, would soon have another. Solome's life had felt solid, but the solidness had been veneer. Her life was different now. Every time she came, she had less. She walked up Fifth Avenue and took a cab back to Gretchen's apartment. Later, Solome went to the National Arts Club for a lecture. That evening, they went to a reading by an author Gretchen wanted to hear at a bookstore. Solome spent another afternoon at the New York Historical Society at 77th and West Central Park. There was an exhibit on aging called, *Elder Grace.* "None of us know how we will fare, what loved ones will be with us, who will leave us behind." Solome also looked at another exhibit, the *Diaries and Letters from American Wars.* She could add one from the battle with Alzheimer's.

She sat in the reading room reading the *American Historical Review.* She looked at a review of Robert Larson's *Red Cloud: Warrior / Statesman of the Lakota Sioux.* ". . .Not enough documentation exits to permit the writing of a real biography." Solome knew the argument well. Yes, to go back in history, rely on what we have, Solome thought, but somehow fill in the missing pieces. This subject would have interested Stephen. They could have talked about the construct of history through language.

Solome felt disconnected from her life. Or from the life she wanted. What parts were missing? Stephen, certainly. But there was something else. What was it? Solome looked at her watch and closed the *American Historical Review.*

Outside on Central Park West, the taxis passed like swaths of margarine.

Solome wondered about her B.A. degree in art history as she sat in the cab on the long ride back to Gretchen's. Solome had been out of school 30 years. She had abandoned what she had learned. Could she retrieve any of it? What did she remember? A few painters. A few movements in art: Romanesque, Gothic, the Italian Renaissance, Baroque, Rococco, Neoclassic, Romanticism, Realism, Impressionism, Modern. Solome was surprised she remembered the movements so easily. But the details were gone. Her studies had suffered a form of Alzheimer's.

The last evening in New York when Gretchen's exams were over, Solome told Gretchen about Stephen after a promise that Gretchen would not tell Soos.

The next day, she returned to St. Paul.

The life Solome knew with Stephen would stop and she was angry. It was a thought that visited her frequently. At times, she wanted to abandon him. Walk off and never come back. The meaning of her life had been bound up in marriage. Now the marriage would be pulled out from under her. Not all at once, but slowly. Stephen was going someplace where she didn't matter. She had been defined by Stephen and his name, Savard. But it was her name too, had been over half her life. Now meaning would have to come from herself. Maybe it had been that way, and she was just finding it out. How would it be not to be defined by Stephen? To make decisions on her own again? To know? To be? The doctor already suggested that Solome join an Alzheimer's support group.

That evening, though they were tired, Solome and Stephen went to hear the St. Paul Chamber Orchestra. They had season tickets which they were often too busy to use, and gave away more often than not.

Stephen Savard

Finally, late in January, the wedding photos came, the ones Solome had chosen from the proofs. Finally, seven months after the wedding, after many calls from Solome, from the Kamrar's, from Gretchen, WHAT IS THE PROBLEM?— the photos arrived. There was an apology note. They were sent overnight mail to the Kamrar's. They were hand delivered to Solome. She called her mother and Soos. They would come for dinner.

Solome made a cake for dinner, then looked at the photos all afternoon. In several of the photos, I saw the distance on my face. I saw my awful bruise. We looked at the photos over and over. Gretchen and Dennis. Soos and Brian dancing, holding Susan between them. Mark and his friends. Solome's mother. The friends Solome and I had had for years. The Kamrar's. Gretchen's lovely dress. The cake.

At dinner, we all looked at the photo albums and talked of Gretchen's wedding. Even Mark came, this time without anyone. I noticed how tired, pregnant and depressed Soos looked. Solome got out her photos of Soos' wedding, but it didn't lift her spirits. Later, we called Gretchen and talked to her about the photos. Mark stayed on the phone in his room to one of his friends. Then everyone was gone.

For some reason, I called Mark into my office at Cobson College and told him that doctors suspected that I had Alzheimer's. He took it in stride.

Solome was incredulous when she heard it.

"Why did you tell him there?" She asked as she fixed supper. "Why couldn't we have told him together?"

I looked at her.

"Everyone will know," she continued. "I think they might suspect. This isn't a secret we can keep."

"Sometimes I feel like myself," I said. "I get through meetings without any trouble. Other times there's a clown costume in my thoughts unraveling the arena."

"Clowns don't do that."

"These clowns do," I said. "You told Gretchen when I wasn't there. You told your mother."

"That was different," Solome said.

"It's my disease," I said. "Now Mark knows."

"Is it really *your* disease?" Solome's voice raised. "You will be the one who doesn't know. But I will be the one who does. It's my disease more than yours."

"I'm still the one it's happening to," I snapped.

Solome Savard

Solome fought a war with waiting. A war with anger. A war with frustration. She had to act civil when she wanted to throw a grenade on the world. As Stephen's Alzheimer's advanced, she would have more of the war with giving and not getting, of being asked to do what she didn't want to do, of being a woman, wife, mother, but feeling something different inside that wasn't a part of any of those.

She was in America. The safe country. Possibly the leader of the free world. Though power seemed to be shifting. Was America in decline? Solome was the baker of Susan's third birthday cake. Yet Alzheimer's could walk into her house and nothing could stop it. Was America also suffering Alzheimer's?

"What's happening?" Solome asked her discussion group. "I can't stop questioning everything. That's one of Mark's mottos."

The book they read in the Thursday discussion group— What was it? A middle-aged woman had walked away from her family— her husband and three children— well, they were grown children, nearly grown. She just stuck up her thumb and hitchhiked!

Solome remembered they had talked in the group. If their husbands died, would they remarry? Jane said, yes, but most of them said, no. No? Was marriage that bad? No, it wasn't. Maybe some of them meant that their marriage was so good, they wouldn't be able to find another husband that could replace the one they had now. That was the trouble with language. It could be interpreted several ways. Opposite ways, actually. Would Solome remarry? It wasn't time to think about that yet.

Stephen Savard

Late in the winter, Solome and I stood in our kitchen. It would be hardest to tell Soos about my sickness.

"She has a lot on her mind," Solome said.

"We've always protected her," I said.

"Isn't that what parents are supposed to do?" Solome asked.

Solome had asked Brian and Soos for dinner, possibly to tell them about my Alzheimer's, if the opportunity presented itself.

"We have to tell her before Mark or Gretchen does. I asked Gretchen to wait. It was up to us to tell her. We can't wait much longer."

Gretchen had cried when Solome told her, but there was a stoicism in Gretchen, or was it that she was preoccupied with her own life of new beginnings? Nothing destructive could possibly affect her. Nothing like the slaughter of brain cells.

I watched Solome fix dinner before Soos, Brian and Susan arrived. Was it in boy scouts? School? A field trip? I talked about a trip to the old stockyards in St. Paul I remembered.

"What a place to take children," Solome said.

"What a place to take our children," I said.

There is was— I heard myself as the old Stephen speaking. I was still there. The leader, the one Solome could count on. She came to me, held me as if I were leaving for someplace and she couldn't go.

At dinner, I could see Soos' discomfort. It wouldn't be long until the new baby was born. No, this was mid-March. The baby was not due until the last of April. Soos had almost six weeks to go. The turquoise flowers on the yellow wallpaper in the dining room were as intrusive as the information about my illness I had to tell Soos.

Solome served dinner. After the meal, she cut the pie she had baked. Then Solome looked at me as the signal for me to speak. The house surrounded us as we ate. The furniture, rugs, windows— all of it—

"I don't know how to tell you," I said, as Soos looked at me with alarm. But I began by speaking of my forgetfulness, my confusion at times, my difficulty following the conversation in meetings, my pockets of unrest that came up now and then. Soos was already crying. Did she know? Was she so miserable she picked up on misery wherever she found it?

Brian had his arm around his wife. Susan, in her booster chair, looked at them. Solome was crying also, hiding her face in her dinner napkin. I was at the head of the table, telling my daughter and her husband that doctors thought I had Alzheimer's.

"Everyone knows," I said. "Gretchen and Mark. Everyone is resigned. It will be all right. It is not the end of the world."

The clichés were disappointing to me. They were making Soos angry. But no other thoughts came to mollify.

"Why am I the last to know?" She demanded.

What could I say? Soos had enough trouble with her husband. She had a child. She soon would have the burden of another baby. We didn't think she could handle it? We were protecting her because she was the one we thought was weakest?

"I told Gretchen when I was in New York." Solome told her. "Your father told Mark at Cobson."

"We waited until it was time, Susanna," I explained.

Brian held Soos as she sobbed. Solome took the dinner napkin from her face. She watched Brian comfort Soos. He didn't say anything. He just held her.

I knew there were many reasons Susanna cried so helplessly. Mainly it was the disappointment of her own marriage. The comfort Brian gave to her at the moment only reminded her that she was often without it. She cried about the eventual loss of my support that Alzheimer's would cause. She cried over her own predicament, I thought, more than mine or Solome's. Soos cried because her life, so carefree only a short time ago, had picked up so many burdens it turned serious with no relief in sight.

Solome Savard

Solome continued with the Bible study through the winter.

John 11:25— *He will live even though he dies*. It was about Lazarus. But Solome thought about Stephen. Eventually, he would be dead to himself, to herself, though he would live somewhere, somehow. For a while, maybe years, Stephen would continue with his work. But he grew depressed more often.

Sometimes he said he heard his own voice. It sounded flat. Distant. *Alzheimerish*. He was going to loose his mind. Not by going crazy. Stephen was not going that far. His disease would be cleaner. He would be erased. Not the messiness of lunacy that pushed the mind into a thorny wilderness. No, he was going to become desert, though Alzheimer's could cause bizarre behavior, the pamphlets warned them.

"Stephen has Alzheimer's," Solome told Jane Mead after a brief phone conversation about their discussion group. They had been talking about how to keep the group on ideas and not just conversation when Solome told her.

Jane was silent.

"I've known it for some time. We've told the children. You should know too. I don't know what will happen." There wasn't much else to say. Jane was sorry. She'd noticed Stephen's distance. Were they sure? Yes, they were. The conversation ended as abruptly as it had begun.

She had women friends. She had gone out with them often over the years. She needed to be with women. Jane, especially, was like a sister to Solome. She could be who she was with Jane. But Solome could go home to Stephen after she'd been with Jane.

Solome sat at dinner one evening with Jane and three other women friends while Stephen was at a dinner meeting of his own.

Solome knew the women knew about Stephen. She was sure Jane had told them.

"I know I won't always have Stephen," Solome said.

"None of us have anyone forever," one of the women said.

"You've had Stephen so long, you don't know what it's like to be alone," another agreed.

Solome got up from the table and left the restaurant.

What kind of help were they? Her friends. Her discussion group.

Jane called the next day. "What happened last night? You owe me for dinner."

Solome had not thought to pay for her dinner. She apologized to Jane. "You can take me out."

"Not with the others," Solome said. "I'm not ready for them yet. You told them about Stephen?"

"Yes, I told them," Jane said, "but they don't know what to do— what to say."

Solome could tell by the way people looked at her— the faculty wives she'd known for years— she had been side-railed. The news of Stephen's disease was out. They were sorry to pass her by, but the train had to keep going.

Would Jane be able to stick by their friendship through Stephen's disease? So often she had retreated when Solome needed her, having her own needs that took her strength.

Stephen Savard

The student center was a concern. There were problems with construction. I had counted on completion. I spoke of it at faculty meetings. I had given a date, but progress was not made. One problem followed another.

In the middle of a difficult morning, Brian called from the hospital. It was April 27th. Solome said she looked at the calendar to make sure. She met them in the birthing room. I came as soon as I talked to the construction foreman. Brian's mother stayed with the baby Susan. Solome called me and told me it would be evening before the baby came. Jane Mead would stop by and they would eat in the hospital cafeteria. By afternoon Soos was in labor.

I wanted to be at the hospital, even if it was only to sit in the waiting room. I had a long-range planning committee meeting early in the afternoon. Jan, my secretary, reminded me of a meeting with a faculty member up for tenure after that.

I stayed in contact by phone. Solome told me that Soos had asked for medication for her pains. A monitor by the bed recorded her contractions with a yellow line across the screen. By late afternoon, I arrived at the hospital. A girl was born that night. Susanna and Brian named her Sarah.

The next afternoon, the doctor said that the baby's tongue was held down by a fold of skin called the frenum.

Several days later, when they were out of the hospital, Brian and Soos took Sarah to the doctor to have the frenum clipped.

Solome stayed with Susan.

I went to their house when I left the college that afternoon.

Soos was shaken when she returned home, but the baby slept.

"She screamed when he did it," Soos said, "then she was quiet."

"She got over it before Susanna did."

Solome Savard

There was a new book on WW II. Solome saw it when she shopped for books for her granddaughter, Susan. She wanted to buy the book for Stephen, but realized it would be frustrating for him if he couldn't follow it. How would Stephen face the loss of his own field?

"Don't tell anyone," he kept telling her.

Solome stood at the bookshelf holding herself up until a clerk asked if she was all right.

"Yes," she said and moved on.

Stephen would return to the revolutions, the invasions of conquerors and merchants, then the wheel— the fire. He would speak an ancient, unknown, nomadic language, where there was no word for the sea they would know.

All summer Solome helped Soos with the girls. She stopped by their house everyday. Sometimes she stayed all afternoon. When Brian was out of town, Solome paid her yard man to mow their lawn. Solome ran errands, or stayed with the girls while they napped and let Soos run the errands, getting her out of the house for a while. Sometimes Solome and her mother took them out for lunch.

Sometimes Solome asked Stephen what he wanted to do for a vacation that summer.

"Where would we go?" Stephen said. "I can't think right now."

"We could go up to Crane Lake for a week."

"I don't know if I can be gone a week."

"I don't either," Solome said. "Soos still needs help everyday. We could take them," Solome suggested.

But when she asked Soos is she wanted to go, she did not. It was too much trouble to pack up.

Susanna and the babies, Susan and Sarah, were dear. They didn't seem to know it. If only Brian could see the worth of his family. If only he could revere them and not make Soos come up with her own value on her own. If only he knew the difficulty of taking care of babies. It was just something he wanted to get away from.

When they had Sarah baptized at the church later in the summer, Solome had a brunch afterwards. She invited Mark, but he didn't come.

The rest of the summer passed with Stephen involved in his work, and Solome busy with Soos and the girls.

Stephen Savard

The student center was a nightmare. There were continuing problems with construction. The lower end of the student theater in the basement filled with water. A permanent pump had to be installed. There was an underground spring that filled with melted snow. Or the rain. Something they hadn't foreseen. There was talk of starting over. But finally the center seemed completed. There was an opening ceremony.

Later in the fall, after church one Sunday, I thought about God. Now saying something about him. Jesus and the Holy Spirit had to get God under control, send him away. Straighten him out. God had gotten out of hand—

Why was Solome looking at me?

My presence in the house was more of an empty room without the furniture, paintings, rugs that had once been there. They had been stolen by Alzheimer's and could not be caught. I could feel the spaces between my words. Maybe Alzheimer's was more like a Chagall painting.

Solome Savard

Solome stayed with the girls while Soos went to the doctor. It was easier than taking them with her. Solome wanted to call Stephen at work and hear his voice. He wanted him to tell her he'd be home in several hours. She should rock the baby and think what she would fix for supper. Soon the day would be over.

Solome rocked Sarah and fed her. The mouth sucked even when the bottle wasn't in it. The eyes closed. What was Susan doing in the other room?

"Susan?" Solome called and Sarah woke with a start. She started to cry, but Solome put the bottle back in her mouth. Susan came in the room with a book. Solome said she'd read it as soon as the baby finished eating. Then the phone was ringing and Solome let it ring. Then Susan was gone from the room again and Solome worried where she was. She put the baby in her crib. By the time Solome found Susan, Sarah was crying. How could she rock both? Besides, Susan didn't want to share Solome's lap with the baby.

"You read the book to me," Solome said as she rocked the crib. But Sarah continued to cry until Solome picked her up.

Solome took the baby downstairs. How did Soos manage the steep stairs? How did Soos manage anything?

"Here, sit beside me on the couch," Solome said to Susan.

Solome read the story of a runaway bunny to Susan. No matter where the little bunny went, her mother would find her. If she became a fish, she would put a net in the water. If she became a bird, she would be the wind that blew her back.

"What's the matter, Soos?"

"Brian and I don't want to be together anymore. He wants to be somewhere else."

"Does he have anyone?"

"I don't know for sure," Soos answered. "We just don't feel the way we used to."

"Marriage isn't about feeling."

"Yes, it is." Soos disagreed.

"You've got two children. They need both parents."

"Brian is always angry."

Solome had seen his impatience.

"Didn't you ever not want to be with dad?"

The question was unfair. Stephen wasn't himself anymore.

"Yes," Solome said. "I want to leave the way Stephen is now. I want to be with Stephen the way he used to be."

Solome ran the dishwasher and the washing machine. She saw Soos needed to go to the grocery store. The baby was crying. The dog next door was barking. Poor Brown, she remembered. The house was dusty. Solome remembered the disorder. Everything felt like it was slipping away. She couldn't stay on top of anything. But she made it through those years. Soos would too. If Solome wasn't careful, she would help Soos raise her daughters more than she should. But Solome had raised her own children with the help of Stephen and her mother.

Solome could work full time at the Historical Society. There were some retirements coming up. But no, Solome had Stephen. She wouldn't be able to handle a full-time job, or even a job more than two days a week, until Stephen was finished with his illness. That meant death.

She held the word in her mouth.

There was a marriage enrichment class at the church. Brian agreed to go with Soos. Could Solome watch the children one night a week for six weeks?

Solome read the same book to Susan every week. The runaway bunny ran away to the river to become a fish. Her mother went fishing for her with a carrot on the end of her hook.

The bunny had wings [she had become a bird].

The bunny had sails [she had runaway to the sea]. Her mother became the wind and was blowing her back.

When the girls were asleep, Solome folded laundry. She took the clean dishes, bowls and glasses from the dish washer and put them back into their places on the shelves. She washed bottles. She picked up toys. She dusted. Maybe Soos and Brian stopped somewhere for coffee after the meeting.

Soos and Brian had a two-story English Tudor house. It felt narrow and high. There was a living room, dining room and kitchen downstairs. Upstairs were three bedrooms. The washer and dryer were in the basement where frequent trips were made. With Solome's help, Soos had decorated the house in blue and yellow.

Stephen Savard

Mark's grades had fallen. He was on probation and decided to take the semester off and work at a coffee house in Minneapolis.

Solome worried how it would affect me.

She began to notice the silence in the house. She bought a Bose Radio. She held me at night while we listened to the new radio, buried like Brown in a place we didn't want to be, someplace other than where we'd lived our lives.

Later in the fall, Gretchen called us one evening, miserable. Dennis had to take a teaching job in another part of the country. Gretchen had to stay at Columbia in New York. She and Dennis were in separate parts of the country. They had two rents to pay, two sets of utility bills.

"We'll help you travel on the weekends," I assured her.

"So far it's been the phone calls."

"Use e-mail," Solome told Gretchen.

"Sometimes I need to hear his voice. It's more than the course work— being in class. It's the teaching assistant job. The grading. I can't always get away. Sometimes I travel with a load of papers."

"Can't Dennis come to you?"

"We've argued about that— It isn't fair for me always to be going to him. It should work both ways."

"Do the Kamrar's help?"

"Not yet. How are you, dad?"

"The same," I told her. "I've cut back on a few meetings. I have less to say about policy. It's probably a relief to some. There are times I'm not sure what I'm doing."

"That's the way I usually feel," she said.

Solome Savard

Solome saw others cry in the Alzheimer's support group at a local community center. She talked politely when it was her turn, saying little. She wasn't interested in hearing people talk. She had questions she wanted answered— how long would it take Stephen to die? What was she supposed to do? How hard would it be to love him? Why wasn't love more ameliorating?

She wouldn't go back to the support group.

When Gretchen called several times about missing Dennis, Solome decided to visit her again in New York.

While Gretchen was in class, Solome spent the day in museums. The crowded streets seemed like rivers at the bottom of canyons and the taxis were yellow kayaks riding the currents.

Solome stood against the gray short wall around Central Park. She knew the granite buildings were built on granite. She thought of the money it cost to keep Gretchen in school, the money it took to visit her. She thought of the money it had taken to marry Gretchen. Solome wanted to feel the granite of financial security.

"You have to get out of the city once in a while," Gretchen told her as they ate dinner at Louie's Restaurant on Amsterdam Avenue that evening. "There's always something in your way. You get angry from the frustration. I have to run ten different places if I need ten different things. We go up the east coast. The Berkshires in Massachusetts. Some of my friends' parents have seaside places. We go to Connecticut. None of them are easy to get to. All of them take time." Solome knew the Kamrar's lived inland from the coast in Wilton, Connecticut. Mr. Kamrar was a marketing executive. Dennis had gone to Storrs and the University of Bridgeport.

A group of men sat at the next table. Solome heard them talking. Imagine having an expanding portfolio and a sense of power.

"I could teach at a private boarding school. I would like to teach at Hunter or Fordham, but so would everyone." Gretchen said as they decided on dessert. "I could apply to Marymount Manhattan."

Afterward Louie's Restaurant, they stopped in front of a Korean market with fresh fruits, vegetables, pastries and flowers on the sidewalk. Then they shopped in Zabars.

The next day, Solome went to St. John the Divine Church for a lecture on architecture. She didn't like to stay at Gretchen's apartment when Gretchen was gone. That evening, they ate a cornbread pudding souffle at Spoonbread 2, a restaurant on 110th and Amsterdam.

Her last night in New York, Solome had a vivid dream. Crane Lake was yellow as the sky at dusk, as yellow as the sun going down in it, spilling into the lake to cool. What was the sun made of? In the evening, it was taxi yellow.

Back in St. Paul, Solome was on the phone with Jane Mead when she looked from her window. The squirrels were eating her marigolds! She had seen the marigold heads in the yard like pieces of a spilled sun. Like taxis passing in New York. She thought the neighbor children had picked them. But it was the squirrels!

"I'll be right back," Solome told her friend, and ran to the door. "Get out!" She opened the front door clattering at them.

What was wrong? Her yard man was going to pull the marigolds up anyway. Why were they still there? He'd nearly finished raking the yard. Why was Solome attacking the squirrels? Leave them alone.

"What am I going to do?" Solome asked, returning to the phone.

"We'll talk about how we are now," Jane said. "How we're going to be without Stephen."

"When Stephen goes, I go also, " Solome said. "It's already happened— the part of me that Stephen doesn't remember is gone."

"Maybe you'll have time to return to school," Jane sounded like she wanted to change the direction of their conversation.

In the early years of their marriage, before children, Solome had begun her M.A. in art history.

"I don't want to be the oldest living student," Solome said. "I wouldn't want to start over."

Solome continued with church and the Monday evening Bible study group. Marriage had been a decision she would stick with. Christianity would be the same. She was in for the long haul. She would make her bed in darkness, if that's what was required. One afternoon, as she waited for Stephen to come home from Cobson, she re-read the book of Hebrews in the New Testament. Another afternoon, she read some of the stories in the Old Testament— the lives of the men Paul listed in Hebrews as men of faith. Where else was there to go? But Barak came to her attention more than the others. It was Deborah who told Barak to go into battle. It was Jael, another woman, who killed Sisera, the leader of the army Barak fought against. Why hadn't Paul mentioned the women?

After Christmas, the sub zero weather set in, but Solome decided to attend the Faculty Wives Club luncheon at the University Club in January. She still had to fight for Stephen's place. She could not withdraw. She drove down Summit Avenue with the defrost and heater blowing full blast. The street was so cold and hard it rattled the car. There was something lonely about the cold. She didn't remember it that way, but she felt it now.

The University Club was paneled in dark oak. The plates of Mandarin salad were set before the women. There were lovely winter centerpieces of white poinsettias and the large glass windows were frosted as if the Faculty Wives Club met in an ice palace. There was a lovely speaker. It was all— lovely and— white. Solome felt the old order and dignity of the place. She needed a reminder that this would endure while she and Stephen set out across the cold sea of his disease.

Stephen Savard

Solome brought work home from the Historical Society. She had the books spread on the dining room table. Dakota history. I looked at them as Solome fixed supper. I held my head in my hands. when Solome called me into the kitchen to eat.

"What's the matter, Stephen?" She asked when I remained in the dining room, but I couldn't speak.

The Dakota removal after the 1862   from Minnesota to parched reservation   dead bodies thrown in Missouri River from the train to South Dakota. The history I forgot   the wars to look at   what I forgot was history a sharp something   sticking me what I didn't want to think to consider what had not been looked at.

From time to time, with new medication, I had moments of clarity. Other times, I bogged down. I could climb out of the morass. I realized I had forgotten the firewall that had covered the history I had known and taught. I had forgotten the official version, and now saw what seemed an actual version. My agitation came upon me in spells.

Solome held me. She saw how something— something about history— found the cloudy parts of my brain where it caught in the snag of my growing lapses.

Solome saw the Dakota uprising in the book. I had been reading. Indians had attacked settlers after they had been attacked, cheated out of their land by treaties, starvation, and whatever else— Solome closed the book, comforted me, coaxed me into the kitchen and to the table.

"Deportation," I said as we ate.

"It's part of our history," she said. "It is upsetting."

"What if it happened at Cobson? What if I became upset over something?"

"I think you should think about retiring." Solome said before she realized what she said.

I said nothing.

"We'll have the president for dinner to tell him," she said later that evening as we prepared for bed.

"I'll go to his office," I answered.

Solome Savard

Solome's mother wanted to visit her husband's grave. They didn't get out of the car because of the snow. They just parked a moment on the narrow drive through the cemetery.

"I think dad has Brown now," Solome said. "Maybe dad will— " Solome didn't finish her sentence. "I remember Stephen and dad working together on the cabin at Crane Lake."

Solome's mother liked to visit the cemetery, even when she couldn't get out of the car. Only the trees and the tallest stones were visible over the mounds of the snow that lined the road.

Stephen Savard

"I've been noticing a change in the way I think for a long time. I'm having difficulties. Episodes of forgetfulness. I think it would be better if I stepped down as provost next year. I don't know how long I can keep running through them without stopping— permanently."

The president looked at me. Did I expect him to protest? To throw himself against the door and not let me leave his office until I changed my mind?

I heard Solome. Have you closed the garage door? Was the car in the garage when it closed? Are the doors locked? Did you find the frozen dinner? Had I heated it in the microwave? Had I showered?

Was the president going to ask these questions? No, it was still Solome I heard.

The president looked thoughtful. He regretted my decision, but he agreed.

Late in January, there was a Board of Trustees meeting at Cobson. My retirement at the end of next year would be announced. Solome attended some of the meetings that included wives. She was tense. What embarrassment would she and I have to face? What forgetfulness of mine would she have to cover? Just let them get through it without incident.

Solome listened as I read my talk on the history of Cobson College. It was a small liberal arts college in St. Paul, Minnesota. Henry Cobson had been a lumber baron who looked for something to do with his money. When a minister named Edward Duffield Neill approached him to establish a college, Cobson agreed. The college was established in 1878. Originally it was for men, but the first woman had been admitted in 1902.

Neill's philosophy for Cobson was "an alternate to state schools that should educate children morally and intellectually but not religiously." There had to be separation of church and state. But the private college could choose to use religion in the curriculum. In fact, maybe it was the job of the private school.

I could remember when faculty meetings opened with prayer. I could remember when chapel was mandatory for students, but they sat on the front row reading their newspapers and showing their displeasure.

Cobson's history was filled with struggle for financial security and an endowment, which had been achieved, then wavered somewhat. Nonetheless, the college was on solid ground, even with its slight downturn. Now where would the college go? We listened to another talk on new directions. Wherever it was going, it would go without me.

Solome Savard

There were near blizzard conditions, yet Solome drove to an early 4th birthday supper for Susan, and then she went to her Bible study group. Only one other couple was at the Forman sisters' house for the meeting, and yes, the man without his wife, John Everett.

"You should come to church more often," he told Solome as they had coffee after the discussion.

When had he noticed she was not always in church? Solome was in disbelief over his comment. "I have family. Sometimes we're out of town. I have responsibilities," Solome answered. "But I'm here this evening." Why did she have to make excuses to him?

Her yard man had cleared the drive. The snow-removal trucks already had been out, and Solome had had no trouble getting to the meeting. Where were the others? Why didn't he comment on her Bible study group attendance? Solome always had driven in the snow. In Minnesota if she stayed in, she would be in all winter.

In Mark 6:3, Jesus' brothers were named: James, Joseph, Judas and Simon, but the sisters were left unnamed. In Matthew 13:55, the brothers were mentioned, but the sisters were not. Solome sat in the Bible study, angry. If women didn't count, why did they have to face what they did? How could Solome go on on her own? How could she drive through the snow?

"I wonder why Paul didn't mention Deborah and Jael when he listed Barak in Hebrews?" Solome asked John Everett. "Deborah led his army. Jael killed the captain of the opposing army. It seems they should have been mentioned for that."

"I've wondered that myself," he said.

Jane Mead returned to the discussion group on the last Thursday in February after her trip to the Philippines. The women took off their coats and boots, stomping off the cold. They visited with each other, shared photos of grandchildren. They talked about movies they had seen and new restaurants where they'd been.

"America is a colonizer," Solome heard Jane said. "It doesn't stick its name on other countries, or send its citizens to live there, but its economy, its products, are everywhere." Jane belonged to a travel club which she said Solome would like. "America has put a cigarette in every mouth I saw. *Golden America* was the name of the cigarette," Jane told the group. "America the tobacco peddler."

But America also had been colonized, not by one country, but many. It was a group of countries within one larger country. Little Italy. Other European communities. Chinatown. African American communities. Asian. They all had come. The world in its different parts had put its stamp on America. That's what America was: a colony of many countries and languages.

It was 1 below. Solome didn't have the dog to walk, but the habit stayed with her. She had to make her way through the unconnected line of days ahead of her. She bundled up, layering was the principle— lined boots, thermal socks, wool trousers, t.shirt, turtle neck, vest, sweater, muffler, wool scarf, earmuffs, headband, coat with large pockets, hood and a flap that snapped over her mouth, thermal gloves with inner lining. She was ready. The usual story—Minnesota below zero. She had known it all her life. Snow covered the yards like folded blankets she left on the beds at the cabin on Crane Lake. She wanted to lay down and not get up. The white blankets on the sidewalk had been shoved aside; the sidewalk had been cleaned, except for patches of snow and ice on the sidewalks of homeowners who did not do a competent job. She had heard her yard man shoveling all morning. Keeping the sidewalk clear in front of the houses was a law in Minnesota.

Solome started down Upper St. John toward Hill Park. The mile walk around the lake would be shoveled and cleared of snow. The lagoon was frozen. The below-freezing air stiffened inside her nose. She pulled the wool scarf up over her mouth and nose. The only place she felt the cold was around her eyes and forehead. She pulled the headband down further on her forehead. Her eyes watered. She kept them as closed as she could while still watching the sidewalk. She didn't want to slip on ice. Already, she was afraid of falling. It was a worry of her mother's also. The engines of several cars were running along the curbs. Their sound was muffled by Solome's earmuffs. The exhaust from the cars was a white stream of air, much like her breath in the cold if she lowered her wool scarf. Everything was stiff, the air was hazy with frost or ice crystals. The birds' chirps sounded shrill, but at a distance. There was steam rising from chimneys on the houses. There was smoke from others. She could smell wood burning in fireplaces. Children came along the walk in snowsuits headed to the corner to wait at the school bus stop. Parents went with them, making sure mittens and hats stayed in place. Solome felt insulated inside her winter layering. She put her gloved hands into the big pockets of her coat. Otherwise her fingers were the first to get cold, after her face. The cleat-like soles of her boots helped her over the snow ridges as she crossed the streets. In the summer, she could walk a mile from her house and back, but in the winter, she had to turn around after several blocks from the frustration of the slowness and the difficulty in walking. Her eyes were stinging and watering anyway in the frigid weather. Her eyelashes felt heavy and her eyes blurred by the time she got back to the house. She dried the moisture from her breath that accumulated under her wool scarf and blew her nose.

She poured coffee and read the St. Paul *Pioneer Press*.

Later Solome would go to Kowalski's and shop. She would take groceries to Soos so she didn't have to get out with the girls in the weather. Soon she would calls Soos and get her long grocery list.

Solome was Mrs. Savard. Would she take back her name, Holfgren, as Jane Mead Harrison Hopper had? No, she was Solome Savard.

What was she thinking? She was still married to Stephen. Would be married to Stephen a long time. Would always be married. It was what she had to do. But where would Stephen be? Who would help her? Where was that verse? Christ would come with a shout and she would be ripped from earth. She felt ready somehow. The long, gray days of February and March helped her long for release as she sat in a chair by the window and read pamphlets of faculty tours.

She was the bearer of family burdens now. She sat alone while Stephen got to go on, as usual, and left her behind. Stephen always had traveled. He always was on his way to a meeting or conference somewhere. Now the trip he was on was more of a return trip. They both knew it. Despair, depression was chemical. An imbalance was killing off part of the brain. He was a different person, a stranger.

Stephen Savard

Mark had not returned to Cobson, but was winter camping at the cabin at Crane Lake. Solome wondered if the two boys were there in the other cabin. There was no phone in the cabin, but Mark had his cell phone.

She asked about the boys when she called, but Mark had not seen them. Solome knew Mark was not alone at the cabin, but she didn't ask who was with him.

I thought the snow would never end. When I was a boy, I had liked the messiness of cars passing in the street, the slush and wetness. I liked the clear sound of my voice when I called to a friend in the cold. When I was older, I liked the sledding and skating of winter parties with the girls. I remembered the winter days when my mother had been to the store and groceries were in the pantry. There were candles in the drawer in case the electricity went off. There was a cord of firewood at the backdoor. I liked the silence of the winter storms, and above them, the roar of wind high in the clouds, beating them, making them to let go of their weight of snow. Later, I remembered pushing cars out of the snow in the high school parking lot. Alzheimer's was nothing more than a blizzard. There was a strange comfort in withdrawing from the world.

Solome Savard

In late March, Solome met Jane in a renovated warehouse restaurant in lowertown St. Paul. She knew she had to get out of the house. The rattle of the large window in the old building sounded like the ripple of sheet metal. It sounded like a thunderstorm in the distance. Or the rattle of her own heart. The thunder was a stomach growling. What hunger was gnawing at the world?

Snow continued into April. They were heavy snows full of moisture from across the upper Great Plains. One dark evening when Solome left the Historical Society, it was snowing again. She had taken the ice scraper from the car during a brief warm spell. She wiped some of the snow from the windows of her car and let the windshield wipers do the rest. The wipers made a groan as they crossed the packed ledge of snow at the bottom of the windshield. She stopped at Kowalski's for groceries. First on the list was a white cake mix for Sarah's first birthday. When Solome started the car, the wipers did not work. She drove a block and stopped the car to wipe the windshield with her hand. She rolled down the window and tried to see ahead. Little by little she made her way home. It was not far, but she traveled hardly able to see where she was going.

"You should have called me," Stephen said, but Solome knew she had to rely less and less on him.

The next day, she drove by Novick's, the neighborhood garage, where they replaced a fuse to the windshield wipers.

On Easter Sunday, Susanna said she would go to church with them. The snow had melted except the piles shoveled to the corners of parking lots and along the north side of buildings. The morning was damp and cold. Brian had decided to go to church also.

It was the church the Savard's had gone to most of their lives. Solome remembered sitting beside Stephen, the children small, in the nursery, or children's church, or later, sitting with their friends.

Susanna held the baby. The nursery would be crowded and she didn't want to leave the girls there. Solome had Susan on her lap.

Solome read the program. Easter: the Resurrection of Our Lord. *Concerto No. 1 in G: Allegro*, J.S.Bach. The hymn, *Jesus Christ is risen today, Alleluia*. The affirmation and prayer. Gloria patri. Time with children. Susan watched them go forward. Do you want to go? Susan kept her fingers in her mouth. Solome got up and carried Susan to the front row where they watched the children on the floor as they sat before the assistant minister. They listened to the story about Jesus and his sheep. The children returned to the pews. Then there were the tithes and offerings. The sermon: *How to Believe the Easter News*. It was delivered with poise and assurance. Solome thought of the years she sat beside Stephen, numb and unaware of the meaning of Easter. It was a ritual of Easter baskets and ham dinners, without recognition of meaning. Now it was over for her. She had experienced the living Christ, a few times anyway, in her Bible study group, and in prayer. Solome wanted to say to the congregation, *don't you see?* Solome thought of Christ carrying her sins to the cross, her sorrows. She thought of him alone in the tomb. She thought of him descending into hell preaching to the lost. She thought of him ascending into heaven to sit at the right hand of the Father. She gripped one hand with the other. She had to hold on. She would not let the tears come. She would not break down, which was the response she felt.

Yes, the minister kept a veil on the glory and majesty of the risen Christ. Otherwise the congregation would be like Paul on the road to Damascus when he was struck blind by the presence of the Lord. The congregation would break down and weep. They would rush forth praising God. They would see into the halls of heaven. Thousands upon thousands. They would realize the poverty of their spirit. They would fall down and worship. There was another hymn: *Crown him with many crowns*. Then the benediction.

The minister had done his job. He had held the fort. Kept them blind, therefore calm. All rowdiness was at bay. All recognition of the meaning of the risen Christ. The minister had kept them in line, Solome thought as he passed her on the aisle. Yes, he had done his job.

Brian was late again. Susanna was sick and Solome put the girls to bed. She waited in the living room while Susanna slept, in case one of the girls cried. Solome watched the evening news. She sat by herself in Susanna's house. Soon, she heard Brian's car in the drive. She waited while he came in the house. He didn't see her on the couch. He put his keys on the table, started upstairs.

"Brian," she said.

He was startled she was there.

"Susanna's sick tonight. I helped her with the girls. It seems to me that's your job. What's the matter with you?" What was the matter with Solome? The anger she felt at Brian for years broke loose. "Why can't you see your family? Why do you have to make them miserable?" Solome was trying to whisper as she let Brian have it. "What kind of husband and father are you?" Solome knew she should stop, but she kept talking. "You're like one of the children Soos has to care for."

Now it was Brian's turn.

"You're the one causing trouble. Always over here. Sympathizing with my wife. Making her feel the way she does."

Susanna was there then too. "What's going on?" She asked. "Mother, what are you doing?"

"Your husband can't come home after work." Solome couldn't stop herself. She knew she was forcing the issue, hurting Soos. "Where have you been?" Solome asked Brian. "What've you been doing? In all my years of marriage, Stephen never treated me this way."

"Maybe you never knew what he was doing."

Solome flew into a fury again.

"If you think I'm going to put up with this," Brian said to Soos, "you're crazy as your mother."

"Brian— " Susanna pleaded, but Brian left.

"WHAT HAVE YOU DONE?" Susanna screamed at her mother. "Don't I have enough PROBLEMS without you making them worse?" Susanna was screaming at Solome. "What are you doing here?"

"I was waiting in case one of the girls woke up while you slept."

They heard Susan crying out for her mother.

What have I done? Solome thought. Susanna was nearly hysterical with grief and anger at Solome. The husband Soos had waited for had left again. Her mother had chased him away. Where had he gone? Back to some woman? Her father had never done this.

"Why aren't you at your own house?" Soos shouted at Solome.

When did Solome want to be in Susanna's house instead of her own? Didn't she dread coming because of the problems Soos faced? Didn't it depress her? Wasn't she denying herself to help Susanna. All right, she wouldn't come again.

In the meantime, Susan was crying harder.

Solome started up the stairs.

"I'll get her," Soos commanded. "This is my house. I want you out of here."

"You need help— "

"Haven't you already helped?" Susanna asked her.

Diane Glancy

"Susanna, you're not being fair."

"What's fair?"

"Brian is working this to his advantage," Solome pleaded.

"Doesn't he always? When I have been able to do anything to keep him here?"

Solome tried to hold Susanna, but she broke away.

"If your father was here— "

"My father was not *here*, if you remember. When didn't he have a meeting, a crisis at the college, another excuse for absence?" Susanna yelled. "He's been slipping since I can remember."

Solome felt her anger again at Soos' words. "I have a lot on my mind and you're always in the way of it. I think more about you than I do Stephen."

Susanna went up the stairs to see about the girls. Both were crying now, and so was Soos. "Brian would be here if it wasn't for you."

Solome wanted to follow Susanna up the stairs, help her quiet the girls. Come back down, fix a bottle for Sarah, help Soos with the relentless attention the girls demanded. But Solome had been asked to leave. What did Soos mean, Stephen wasn't there? He had been there. But where was Stephen now? It was true. He had *gotten out of it* once more. He always was involved with his job at Cobson College. Even if he didn't have Alzheimer's, wouldn't she still be alone?

Stephen had been a help in their marriage. But Soos was right. Had some of Stephen's help been manufactured by Solome? Had Stephen been more than Stephen because Solome believed he was? No, he had been a definite help. What was wrong with Soos? Solome hit the steering wheel as she drove home crying. Was there a limit to her anger? She couldn't call her mother. It was too late. Would Jane be at home? Or was she staying with some man she was seeing? Solome didn't have Brown to comfort her either, though what comfort had a dog been? Would anyone in her Bible study group be awake? Who was left? Jesus?

"I yelled at my son-in-law. He'd been out late when Susanna was sick and his family needed him."

This was the confession Solome made to her Bible study group. They didn't answer for a while.

"I'm not sure what to say," Ralph Stewart said. The meeting was at the Forman sisters' house that evening.

"Don't say anything," Else Renke said.

"He's been insufferable," Solome said. "A terrible husband and father."

"You can't judge him."

"Should I just tolerate him?" Solome asked. "Watch him run over Soos and the girls without saying anything."

"Brian is the head of his family. Not you."

"He's not doing his job. My daughter is miserable most of the time because of him."

"Mercy triumphs over strife —James 2:13"

Solome told her discussion group about her argument with Brian.

"I wish I hadn't let Soos go back to him."

"You can't stop her. She's a grown woman."

"But now she has another baby. Her problems with him keep getting worse."

Later, when she and Jane had dinner at the 128 Restaurant, Solome tried to change the tone of her conversation. "I believe in Jesus. Not religion," she said.

"You've become a Christian?" Jane repeated. "That will eliminate a lot of men you could have gone out with. I mean, who would want to go to church on a date?"

"It's not about dating. I don't want to date."

"Wait until Stephen lingers. You'll be ready."

"Christianity is a decision you have to make."

"*You* have to make, not me," Jane said. "You're just under stress, Solome. I don't know what you're talking about. The church we've always gone to is Christian. We've been Christians all our lives."

Stephen Savard

Solome's mother, Margret Holfgren, had a desire for independence and dependence at the same time. She fretted over her house, often calling me at work. It was large and unmanageable. My mother's-in-law thoughts were fragmented into rooms. This was happening here. That was happening there. Could I stop by and look at it? My wavering thoughts should be filled with ideas and theories. What had occupied my mind all my life. But she had not been given the opportunity. Had I had a stroke? She asked. Not that I knew of. Didn't she remember? I think it's Alzhiemer's. Oh that, she remarked. Solome had to think of her children. She had Soos on her hands.

I noticed an impatience when her mother called. What next? Her mother's ideas were in objects. What intellectual life could she have among the cups and dishes? The architecture of the house? Was it interpretive history? No, she remembered it differently. Memory was a fabric. Memory was clothed with what she saw, and what she saw, she saw through memory. It was a construction I could no longer trust.

"I wish Solome wouldn't go to that church group," Solome's mother said as we ate lunch at her house. She had called me again to look at something.

"You know the problems Solome faces."

"We're all Christians."

"So I've heard," I said, "but is Jesus your Savior?"

"Yes, he is," my mother-in-law said as she ate the mixed greens, dropping a piece in her lap, putting it back on the salad plate. "You sound like Solome."

"This salad is hard to eat," I said when I saw her embarrassment.

"You don't like my salad?"

"Yes, I do. Very much."

Solome's mother was still able to take care of herself, but the day would come when she too would have to be cared for. Solome should begin visiting nursing homes and senior citizen centers. Should she find one for both of us so she only would have one trip to visit us?

"I never hear from Mark Stephen. I send him money and he doesn't call."

"He's busy. You know how boys are."

"No, I don't think. He could have the decency to thank me."

"I agree."

"Is he ever returning to school?"

"Yes, he's back," I said. "We do what we can do, and then let go. They're on their own."

"There was time I worried about Solome. I wanted to tell her to forget Jane Mead, and here they have been friends their whole lives."

"What didn't you like about her?" I asked.

"She was a big talker. She was going off here or there, and she ended up in St. Paul all her life."

"You think we should have gone someplace else?"

"By then, Solome was with you. I knew you weren't going anywhere."

"Not beyond provost of Cobson College," I said.

Solome Savard

Gretchen finished her Ph.D. course work at Columbia, but she still had her orals and then her dissertation to defend.

Solome flew to New York to fill the week before Dennis returned. He was giving exams and grading papers at his own college across the country. Gretchen would wait for him in New York.

In the city, Solome saw the couples sitting along the sidewalk with their dogs and newspapers. They had nothing more to do than spend the day with each other. She noticed one couple— a man with gray hair, a blonde woman, at least 20 years younger, a white dog. They were sipping coffee, talking to one another. They'd make love in the afternoon. She hated them. What did they know about responsibilities?

The taxis passed like yellow pencils spilled from a box. She wanted to get in one and find someplace that didn't exist as yet.

When Solome returned from New York, she called Soos because she wanted to see the girls. She had bought them some dresses and a few toys when she and Gretchen shopped. It was late in the afternoon, but Solome wanted to drop by.

"I have to work at the Historical Society tomorrow, or I would come then."

Solome drove to Soos' house. Susan was waiting eagerly at the door, her little face pressed to the glass.

"I would stay with the girls if you and Brian wanted to go somewhere," Solome told Soos.

"We'd just fight. I don't know what we'd do."

"Go up to Crane Lake for the weekend."

"Brian needs to mow the lawn. It's his day to do errands. He doesn't like to go to Crane Lake. It's your place, not his. He's struggling with his job. It doesn't do any good to criticize him, mother."

"I'm sorry. I know it doesn't help. I've got one daughter crying because she can't be with her husband, and one crying because she can."

"They haven't been married long enough."

"That's not true, Susanna. Your father and I took time to be together. We argued, but we worked our way through our disagreements."

"It doesn't help to hear about your marriage, mother."

"What does help?"

"Nothing." Soos was crying.

Solome tried to comfort her, but Soos backed away. "I'm married now. I can take care of myself."

Solome wanted to tell Susanna that she wasn't taking care of herself. That she couldn't take care of herself with a husband who didn't treat her as he should. What was wrong with Brian? Why was he centered on himself? Why couldn't he see his wife needed him? Why didn't he know how to be a husband? How had Stephen known? What was the difference?

"Brian has to prove himself," Soos said. "He thinks the way to do it is to get ahead. To profit. It takes all his energy. His father-in-law is a provost. His mother-in-law lets him know that he is not— That he can't take care of his family," Soos looked at Solome. "It's frustrating for Brian to be around you."

"Yes, because he knows he's not fair to my daughter."

"What's fair? Nothing's fair. Go up to Crane Lake and watch the mallards with their babies in the evening. Each morning there's one less baby because a snake got them or the raccoons— Think of the deer maimed in hunting season in the north woods— "

"Soos— "

"Think about the mother duck as the snake gets in her nest. Nothing she can do will make any difference— "

"Soos— When did you get so morose?"

"When I figured out how things were— "

Suddenly Brian was at the door. Soos had forgotten he would be home early to get ready for a business trip the next day. They hardly spoke. He went upstairs and Soos went to the kitchen. Soon he called down asking where his clean shirts were. Soos didn't hear his voice, and Solome didn't call for her.

Solome was sitting with the girls in the living room when Brian came downstairs. She saw his impatience. "I remember when Susanna had confidence. I remember when she was happy. What have you done to her?"

"What have you?"

Solome would get nowhere yelling at Brian. She knew it. Just leave. Just walk away. Solome left the girls crying and went to her car. At least she had remembered to park by the curb, and not block the drive. She sat in the car a moment. Susan was watching her from the door. How could Solome handle everything? She faced the impending loss of Stephen as a support, three children who would continue to need her help, an aging mother, two granddaughters who watched their parents argue, and a friend, Jane Mead, who was still thinking in terms of what man she could go out with. Had nothing changed for her?

Solome hit the steering wheel with her hands as she started the car. She didn't want to leave, but she knew she had to. She remembered her Bible study group. She wanted to go back into the house for Soos and the girls. She wanted to see Brian gone. What world was this Solome was in? Who was the God of this world? If he was all powerful and all knowing, why had he left her desperate? No, she wasn't desperate. She had a house and savings. What if she had nothing and had to live with Brian and Soos? At least she had money, she thought. But with Stephen and her mother's care, with three children to help, who knew how long it would last. She would have her old age also. The debt of Brian and Susanna. The girls who needed relief from the tension between their parents. Maybe if Solome had to live with them, she could protect the girls. No, she would only interfere. She would make things worse. No, she couldn't live in the house with Brian. Solome remembered the security she had once felt. How could she live all her life, careful of her family, of herself, and come to this?

Stephen Savard

I was in the middle of departments struggling for positions and space. I was accused of inconsistencies in my decisions. I favored a woman whom others did not like. It seemed I could satisfy no one. My politics tended to be conservative. The faculty was more liberal. I felt myself slipping. The turmoil often depressed me as I sat in my office at Cobson. I knew eventually I would have to retire. There were times when my thinking was clear. I wanted to stop some of the faculty's propositions. I didn't think they were the way the college should go.

"Stephen. You can't hold us back. Cobson needs to move in a new direction. You're close to retirement." I felt a hand on my shoulder.

Retirement? Is that what they'd been talking about behind my back? I stood for another moment in the faculty meeting. Had I mentioned retirement?

I saw their faces looking at me. There was an awkward silence. I sat down. I realized they didn't want to hear my opinion, especially when it differed from the way they wanted the vote to go. But I had a responsibility to direct the college in the way it should go. The way I thought it should go. I started to stand again. I felt another hand on my shoulder. It was a colleague next to me, letting me know I should not interrupt again.

I returned to my office after the meeting and tried to think what happened.

It was out. Everyone knew I was incapacitated. They probably were standing around in groups talking about it. If my incapacitation was on their minds, their incapacitation to understand what I was experiencing was on mine.

If my weather was in line with what they wanted, it was all right. I could vote. Had voted. But if it was against what they wanted, then I couldn't vote.

Some days, the weather was clear. Other days, it was foggy. There often were strong winds. I could post a weather report each day. Whatever was happening, I was becoming aware of weather. Interior weather. Not what was there outside my window. Though weather was often there too. And a growing fog coming in from some coast I hadn't realized was there. The thought of Minnesota as sea-coast amused me for a moment. But when the fog cleared to see nothing is there. That was the fright of it. The shame of it.

Solome Savard

Brian called late one afternoon. He was taking Soos to the hospital. She couldn't stop crying. His mother was there to take care of the girls. He didn't want Solome to do anything. He just wanted her to know.

Solome paced the floor. Stephen was out of town for a series of alumni meetings for the purpose of fundraising. He was with a colleague who would help if Stephen grew confused. It might be his last trip and Solome didn't want to interrupt him. Who could she call? The Bible study group? She didn't want to bother them. Her mother? No. Jane? Solome remembered she hadn't returned Jane's call.

Solome could call Stephen back to St. Paul because of a family emergency, but she decided against it for the moment. Soos would stop crying before Stephen could return.

"Brian has taken Soos to the hospital," Solome told Jane.

"Which one?"

"Memorial."

"Why?"

"Depression. She's having a break down."

"I'll come over, Solome," Jane said. "She'll be all right. They have shock treatments now. Cathy has a friend who went through a breakdown— "

"Shock treatment?" Solome asked when Jane arrived.

"Yes, it's not what it used to be. It helps many people over depression."

"I know," Solome remembered. "I've read."

When they arrived at the hospital, they found that Soos was in the mental ward, not the regular hospital.

"What's she doing here?" Solome asked in disbelief.

"She had a breakdown. This is the area where you come for that," the nurse said. She buzzed the door and Solome and Jane walked in. Jane waited while Solome went down the hall to Susanna's room. Brian sat beside the bed as Solome entered. Susanna was awake, though medicated. She looked at her mother dreamily.

She tried to say something, but tears came to her eyes again. Solome stood by the bed, then sat in a chair beside Soos without saying anything.

"I'm sorry."

"It will be all right," Brian said to his wife.

Soos seemed to sleep for a moment. Solome looked at her puffy face. She avoided looking at Brian, and he did not look at her. They could have been in two separate rooms.

Susanna was in the hospital ten days.

When Stephen returned from his trip with a colleague and found Soos in the hospital, he was angry Solome hadn't called him.

Susanna had shock therapy and a combination of drugs until she was *regulated*. Solome and Brian's mother took turns caring for the girls. Mrs. Stiple took Wednesday and Friday, of course, while Solome worked at the Historical Society. One day, Solome took the girls to the church nursery for the afternoon when she had errands. Other mornings and afternoons, Solome played with the girls. She watched Susan draw a tree. The trunk was flat at the top with thin branches rising from it as though stems from a vase. Solome remembered thinking how to divide a tree trunk into branches. She drew a tree trunk, then divided it into two large V-shaped branches from which the smaller branches grew. Susan watched Solome draw leaves.

"It's hard to draw," Solome told her.

Susan agreed.

Sarah drew a lopsided mark she said was a head. She hardly was old enough to hold the crayon. She soon grew frustrated because she was too young to draw like her sister. Sarah spilled the crayons out of the box and

Susan fussed at her. Solome took Sarah into the other room where they sat watching television.

When Susan finished drawing, Solome played dollhouse with the girls. They ate lunch. Sarah took a nap. Solome read to Susan. She thought about what to fix for supper. After Sarah's nap, Solome put on their jackets and they went for a short walk. Then the girls watched television while Solome started an early supper. When Brian came home, Solome went to the hospital.

Solome wished Gretchen was there to help. Solome's mother came once, but made more work. And, of course, Stephen was there.

Mark came to the hospital once. Solome wasn't there, but Soos told her he had been there.

She was feeling better. She was ready to go home. She didn't know what happened. She couldn't sleep. She was overwhelmed with sadness. But she had medication now to help her.

"Did you tell the doctor about your father?"

"Yes," Soos started crying again.

"It's all right to cry. I do it too. I still cry over my father. You've lost your grandfather, and soon it will be your father. You've got two babies without much help."

"Brian said he'd help."

"I'll take Susan to her swimming lessons," Solome said. "I'll help too."

"Just so you don't help at the same time," Soos returned.

Jane Mead called Solome when she walked in the door. Stephen was there, but he didn't answer the phone.

"I can't have dinner with you," Solome was frank. "I can't bear to talk to you. My life is a crisis. All you do is talk about men."

"I don't talk only of men."

"I have to be quiet— so quiet nothing else will find me."

"Solome, that can't be you talking."

"I'll call you when I feel better. When I can listen to you again."

"Just let me come over. I won't say a word."

"No," Solome said and hung up.

"I've never understood how you could be friends with Jane all these years," Stephen said.

"I've never understood how you could deal with all your colleagues," Solome answered.

Stephen Savard

Susan was going to a swimming lesson at an indoor pool. Solome and I would take her.

I watched the instructor help Susan across the pool. Swim, swim, I thought. That's what we have to do. Don't stop. There's water underneath that will drown you. Those lovely waterwings   will not hold   you up by themselves. Paddle   paddle darling that's   all we can   do.

Solome Savard

After a husband and family for most of a lifetime, would Solome end up with her high school friend? They were on their way to go shopping. It was Jane's idea. Solome needed to take a break. They stopped at a neighborhood restaurant for lunch on the way. The restaurant with the tables too close.

"Remember the dances at Seitman's?" Jane asked. "Remember that's all we used to talk about. Let's start over again." Jane said. "Jane Mead and Solome Holfgren. What would you do differently?"

"Nothing. I just want it all back." Solome answered. "What would you do differently?"

"Marry Stephen Savard."

"He's my husband."

"Well, I remember wanting to date him."

"But you didn't?" Solome said.

"No, but I would try if we could start over again."

"I wouldn't let you."

"What if you didn't have anything to say about it? My life would have been easier if I had married Stephen. Or someone like him. Look at the difference between you and me."

"You could have married someone different the first time. Someone more suited to marriage."

"Who?" Jane asked.

"Do you remember the boy who wanted to sit with us at lunch?"

"Chet?"

"Yes," Solome answered.

"I've been thinking about him lately."

"He liked you," Solome said, "but you wouldn't have anything to do with him. You wanted more flash."

"Yes, and I got flash," Jane laughed. "He flashed out of my life before I knew who he was."

"How can you laugh about something that hurt you? Can you imagine Soos laughing about her trip to the hospital."

"She's with Brian, isn't she? That's what she wanted."

"But not in that way," Solome said. "I wonder what Brian thinks. He's worried about what his company will think when he turns in the insurance claim. He's worried about his image more than he worries about Soos. Sometimes I wished we hadn't insisted on Soos working in that office that summer," Solome sighed, "Brian had just started as an intern."

"Let's go to the movies after we shop." Jane changed the subject.

"Stephen will be home tonight. I need to get supper for him."

"Your fridge must have some leftovers in it."

"I'm not sure he could fix supper for himself."

"What do you do, Solome, that isn't attached to duty?"

"Stephen's been depressed," she said. "I also work. I'm thinking about working one more day a week. Maybe there will be problems at the historical society worse than the ones I have."

"The place would have to burn down," Jane told her. "Let's go to a movie. What do you say? When was the last time we couldn't laugh?"

"Your last divorce."

"When, other than that?" Jane asked.

"Your first."

Stephen Savard

Solome told me someone would be there for me. But someone was not there.

I had flown to Atlanta for another meeting. I was there by myself. When I woke in the morning, I couldn't remember where I was. Travel could do that. I sat up in bed. I saw the desk in my room. I opened the drawer and found the phone book. I couldn't remember why I was there. Yes, I did. After thinking. After looking through my briefcase I saw my talk. I remember the conference I'd come to. I dressed and went down to the main desk and asked for a cab. I told the cab driver I wanted to go to the airport. At the airport I couldn't find my ticket. I had left it at the hotel. I couldn't remember the name of the hotel where I had stayed. I felt panic as the crowds pushed around me. I was alone and couldn't think of what to do. Did I have a receipt for the bill at the hotel? I didn't know. I showed them my papers.

The authorities called Solome. She told them the name of my hotel. Could someone retrieve my bag and ticket? I'd just been there one night, though it seemed longer to me. They told me my wife called the hotel and explained the situation. Yes, the hotel could gather up my things. They would fax the bill to the college for my secretary to sign. Solome called the airport. When my bag and ticket arrived, they could put me on the plane for Minneapolis / St. Paul. At least I had arrived at the airport several hours early. Did I have another day at the conference that I'd overlooked?

"Don't lose sight of him," I heard Solome say as they handed the phone to me.

Solome told me to stay at the airline counter until my bag arrived. "Just sit still, Stephen. It will be all right," Solome told me.

I heard the worry in her voice, and the the exasperation. There was a place where the ground came to an end. Everything stopped. There was nothing ahead. I had to wait for the plane to lift   to what was   there. "Just hold on, Stephen. You'll know where you are again."

Solome Savard

"Mark, you've got to go see your sister. Why don't you take your latest girl-friend and go over there? Susan and Sarah love to see you," Solome told him.

"I've got a late paper to finish on an incomplete grade."

"And a few parties and the world to change while your sister grieves over her life."

"You're always a load of cheer, mom."

"You have a responsibility to your family, Mark. I've got your father to worry about." Solome didn't tell Mark about Stephen's last trip, though she wanted to.

"I'll take one of my girlfriends who wants to get married. I'll show her what she's missing."

Solome hung up furious with Mark.

Stephen Savard

It took me a while to recover from my experience in Atlanta. I seemed to be having aftershocks. I wondered how far the story would travel. Who would be talking about it when I entered the faculty dining room in the fall? I grew more depressed through the summer.

"They're going to get rid of me," I said one evening in the dining room. "They're going to sideline me before I retire. A new provost will be appointed."

"You've already told the president you're retiring. It was announced at the faculty meeting."

"I still have my office. I think the president will name Grant Harner interim provost."

"From mathematics?" Solome asked. "I thought they would get someone from the outside."

"They may in time." I sat at the table with Solome. "There's another group at Cobson now. Our politics, our policies are different."

I didn't say anything for a while. Solome let me think by myself. Then she got up, moved her chair to mine, and put her arms around me.

It was the beginning of another school year. My last. Mark was in school again. Soos seemed to feel better about her marriage. Gretchen and Dennis would have a commuter marriage again. One would be at one college on the east coast. The other was in the Midwest.

Gretchen called crying one morning when she couldn't get ahold of her mother. Was there a position at Cobson for them? She asked me. No, I said. We weren't hiring anyone in their areas. There were several colleges in St. Paul. There was the University of Minnesota in Minneapolis, she insisted. Could I talk to them?

"At least you both have jobs," I told her on the phone. "That's difficult in academia."

Solome had decided to attend the opening convocation after stopping by Soos' house for lunch. At the convocation, Solome sat beside the wife of the president of Cobson. On her other side, was Mrs. Harner. I sat on the stage with the trustees and other college officials. I was more of an honoree this last year. Another provost was in place.

"I want Cobson to offer an education that enables students to face the fragmentation and inconsistencies of this world," the president was speaking. "I want them to find self-determination, to be an active member of the community who will make ongoing contributions to a sometimes fractured world."

I was thinking allocate to downsize to less frequent departments by students. Not that students could judge what was best for them, but through course offerings and the guidance and interaction of professors they would be able to carry on in an independent way.

Yes, the president had to mollify the self-educated students. He didn't want sit-ins and uprising and rebellion.

Mark had returned to school, to the relief of Solome and me. He was somewhere in the audience with his friends.

Solome Savard

Solome shuffled through her days. Her Monday night Bible study. Wednesdays and Fridays at the Historical Society. Lunch with her mother.

"We're getting away from ideas," Solome complained at the next meeting of her Thursday discussion group. "We're talking about our lives. We decided long ago that wouldn't be part of our discussions. Let's get back on track."

"I've always liked off track better," Jane said. "Ideas can only go so far."

"I read *The Girl with the Pearl Earring*— historical fiction in the voice of a girl Vermeer painted. I don't know what to think of it. Blundering into someone else's life," Solome said. "There's a lot of it lately. Speaking in the person of another. Someone even wrote about what Judas Iscariot was thinking. There's also a book about Pontius Pilate, and one about the Apostle Paul."

"We can make up what is real?" Jane asked.

"It got a good review in the *New York Times*."

"How can we know what someone else is thinking? You can't change history," Jane said. "You can't go back and rewrite it."

No, Solome agreed. You couldn't change what was happening.

"We could travel," Jane said. "We could travel as a group— The discussion group. We could join my travel club."

That's what Solome wanted to do. Only she wanted to travel with Stephen. For a moment she imagined being next to him on a plane on their way to Europe. Maybe they'd never come back. For a moment, Solome imaged they were looking up at the Sistine Chapel. They were trying to maneuver the narrow streets in Toledo. They were on another boat on the Rhine. Solome would have to get out their photo albums to remember all the places she and Stephen had been.

"When did life come to finding something to stay busy?" Solome asked. "It used to happen naturally."

No one in the discussion group answered.

When Solome returned to her house, the yellow wallpaper with the turquoise flowers in the dining room caught her eye. *Get rid of it*, she said to herself.

Life had always been upwardly mobile. Yes, that was the term. She'd always lived in an expanding universe. Now it was shriveling. Closing down. Decreasing. She would receive diminishing returns.

What was that ridiculous paper doing on her wall?

She called her repair man, her *house man*, and left a message that she wanted the dining room re-papered. She would leave the name of the new paper she wanted at Willard's.

Solome got in her car and went to the store to pick out new paper. Something more subdued. Mature. Defeated.

"I wondered when you'd get tired of that paper." The house man said at her house the next week.

Stephen Savard

I had a dream that night, or the next night. They all seemed to drift together. Solome had invited people for dinner, but the sink was full of dishes, and she couldn't find clean plates. She had to wash them first, but couldn't find the dishwasher. She couldn't find soap or a dishcloth. The people were waiting.

I thought about the dream as I looked at the family photos on the shelf in my study. I had to remind myself of our lives. Gretchen and Dennis. Brian and Soos. The baby Susan. The baby Sarah. Various birthdays. Mark and his college friends at Mark's apartment. Which one of them had gone into Mark's bedroom and phoned Europe, leaving us with the bill to pay? I looked at a recent photo of Solome's mother. Solome and Jane. I looked at a photo of the cabin on Crane Lake. Beside it was a photo of the ground which Solome had marked, Brown's grave.

Sometimes we looked through the wedding albums of Gretchen and Susanna.

Gretchen and Dennis were at universities 700 miles apart.

I listened to Solome comfort her. "Hang on," she said.

"It doesn't get easier," I wanted to say. "Wait until you can't find your keys."

Solome also visited Soos and the girls nearly every day.

I woke from a nap in a depression another afternoon. I had trouble rousing myself for dinner.

"I dreamed I was giving a talk I had written, but I couldn't read it," I told Solome. "The words were there, but I didn't know what they were. Afterwards I walked on a coral reef just under the surface of water. I could feel the holes under my feet in the shallow water." I knew I was experiencing another moment of confusion. Just hold on. It would clear.

"You're getting paranoid," Solome said.

Yes, I felt they were against me. They were trying to get me to leave Cobson, even my position with reduced responsibilities.

"You interpret everything in a negative way. You don't trust anyone. You think they talk behind your back."

"They do talk behind my back," I assured her. "There always have been factions in the faculty at Cobson. Uncivil liberties are a part of the contested territories of departments and college politics. I wanted to eliminate several courses, which would mean several positions. I thought Russian would be the place to start. You should have heard the uprising in faculty meeting."

"I'm glad you're retiring," Solome said. "We'll have time to travel while we still can."

"Maybe we could do something with the children," I said. "We could all meet someplace. We seem like strangers to one another. None of them has any idea of what the other is doing."

Solome Savard

Solome went to the doctor with Soos and the girls. She still called them babies, but Soos reminded her that at four and one, they were no longer babies.

Solome had missed several luncheons of the Faculty Wives Club. Soos needed her another afternoon, but she had to go.

"It's these long winter days when I can't get out."

Solome remembered dressing the children in their snow suits. She remembered the relief when spring finally came. Even when the weather was cold, it was easier to dress the children in coats and hats.

Soos had a dinner for her parents and Mark. It was Stephen's birthday. Mark was late. They had sat down to the table after Soos could no longer keep the food warm, and had started to eat, when Mark walked in. Soos was furious.

"When will you grow up and get married?"

"You don't make it look appealing," Mark answered.

Why had language broken? Mutated? Why wasn't there one common language? Why were there many languages? According to the Bible, the people could get together and do what they wanted if they shared a common language. That's why there were so many languages. Because of Babel. With only one language men would have the power of a common language. The power of words.

There had never been an American language anyway, but numerous indigenous languages, many unrelated to one another. But America had wiped out the Indians' languages. Cleaned the slate. Made room for the conglomerate of English language.

Imagine a people who killed the language of the land they came to. The words of the landscape— dead. The people mixed.

Stephen Savard

Language before it came a   word was thought. I had another thought in my head I couldn't get out. Was I   [talking] what   did it   matter?

Later that evening, Solome found me sitting in a chair in the dark.

"I'm afraid," I told her.

"Do you remember Atlanta— when you didn't know where you were and I was waiting for you?" Solome asked. "It will be that way. Someone will be there for you."

Solome Savard

Where was Jane Mead? Off with another man, leaving Solome alone. How many times had Solome helped Jane? Stood by her? Now Solome was alone without Jane. That wasn't fair, Solome thought. She was just angry. Jane was a friend with whom she shared her life. But even Jane let her down. No matter how hard Solome tried, despite civilization and retirement plans and savings accounts and family and friends, Solome was alone to face uncertainty.

The winter was piled with snow. Solome read manuscripts for Acquisitions at the Historical Society. People died and left letters and diaries, and their relatives sent them to the society. Often it was a drab diary kept by a farm wife forgotten by everyone. *Today the weather was severe. Today the weather was cold.* Often, it was a woman who had lived without recognition of her life or any accomplishment except having withstood the elements and the neglect. Or it was the journal of a husband who left notes of farm cycles but no word of *her*. How often the past suffered Alzheimer's. It was everywhere.

Solome also unwrapped boxes of artifacts. One particular box contained a Dakota cradleboard. Some of the slats were taped to the frame with duct tape by a new generation. The cradleboard had a loop at the top in case the mother had to pick it up during a raid and run. The loop was made from the small branch of a bent sapling. Solome thought of the children's life jackets they wore at Crane Lake. They also had a loop at the back so the child could be lifted out of the water in case it was necessary.

Solome knew she needed a loop on her collar. She needed to be picked from the waters she was in.

She would take the cradleboard to the restoration department in the basement. She got up from her chair and walked out of her office into the rotunda. To Solome, the massive building was something of a contemporary companion to Fort Snelling that had been established above the Mississippi River after the first explorer, Zebulon Pike, had cited the bluff for a fort in 1804. The Minnesota Historical Society, near downtown St. Paul, was a fortress of Minnesota granite. Solome walked down the large, open spiral stairs, the voices of school children and visitors echoing like a distant raid.

Stephen Savard

It was the time we dreaded—a time we had not prepared for fully. We dressed, drove to the University Club. Our friends and colleagues were there. Our children. Even Gretchen and Dennis were able to come, though they wanted to see one another, more than they wanted to attend their father's retirement dinner. After we ate, there were the speeches. The president of Cobson led the group. Then Grant Harner, the new provost, spoke. Tom Marshall from the history department followed. Then a line-up of my former students. Blessedly, I would not be able to remember any of it. It went by quickly. I saw that Solome concentrated on keeping control of herself. She concentrated on supporting me. I was doing better than she was. I knew there were words and words, but I couldn't hold them in my mind. Solome looked at me as people said something funny. It was an enjoyable time. A closing of what had been a privileged career. Did it matter that I would topple like the giant northern pines that had provided the money to build and maintain Cobson College? I had achieved something with my life. They gave me a clock for my desk with the Cobson seal to remind me that time was running out. They gave Solome a photograph frame with the Cobson seal. They knew she liked photos. They gave us a camera for our retirement years. Mercifully it was over and we drove home not saying much more than when we had come. Gretchen and Dennis had ridden with Soos and Brian.

"You've done your work, Stephen. You can be proud." Solome encouraged me once again.

"I knew something was wrong several years ago," I confided to Solome. "I forgot meetings. I couldn't remember names. The only way I could find the car was that I knew it was in the provost's parking space. Sometimes I would have to think to remember that. I had dreams of sitting in meetings, forgetting why I was there. I was there to say something, and I didn't know what the meeting was about. Sometimes I would say something and realize later how rude or angry it sounded. I would chide myself, sometimes realizing I was speaking out loud. I kept the door to the office closed. I was afraid they would hear my voice. I would tell myself to be quiet. I never knew who was listening." Solome listened to me, not knowing how stressful it had been. "They wanted me to leave. I knew it before I agreed to retire." I paused. "There's a relief it's over— that I got away without worse embarrassment."

"Yes, we've been blessed," Solome said, wiping the tears that fell down her face.

The summer after my retirement, we went to Crane Lake with the granddaughters, now ages five and two, while Soos and Brian took a vacation.

It reminded us of when we were young and had Gretchen and Susanna, before Mark was born.

Soos had not wanted them to go.

"Can you keep the girls out of the lake and watch dad too?" I overheard her ask. Had my family started talking behind my back also?

Solome took several books to read to Susan. I sat beside her holding Sarah while Solome read. We played games. We walked on the shoreline among the reeds. We waited while Solome prepared dinner, looking through weeds and finding bugs.

In the evening when the girls were asleep, Solome and I planned a trip to China.

In the first year after my retirement, Solome and I traveled as we had planned. We visited Gretchen while Dennis was gone. They were still at different schools, never closer than several hundred miles. I felt that Gretchen held me responsible for their hardship. Solome and I also took Soos and the girls on several short trips while Brian worked.

In late February, Solome and I went to China on a tour of retired university professors. With medication and Solome to help me, Solome and the doctor felt I could go. It was a long plane trip across the ocean. It took nearly a day with layovers in Los Angeles and Hong Kong. We were weary and groggy when we arrived at the Kunlun Hotel in Beijing. We had the afternoon to rest before they met that night in a restaurant.

Already Solome saw the differences in the couples. There were the quiet ones, the talkative ones, the ones who loved one another, the ones who had grown apart. There also were the forgetful ones. I enjoyed talking to the men. Often we stood in the hotel lobby talking while the wives gathered by the tour bus. We didn't have much to say, but talked together anyway.

The group spent ten days in Beijing and Xian. We walked on the Great Wall. We went through the Forbidden City and the Summer Palace. We saw Tiananmen Square and the People's Museum. We saw the terra cotta warriors. We visited theaters. Often, in afternoon and evening performances, I slept with my head against Solome's shoulder. She didn't understand the plays and operas herself. The only place I stayed awake was the Shaanxi Folk Art Theater for the shadow puppets. The program in English read, "Na Chi Scrambles the Sea." Afterwards, we saw how the Shaanxi shadow puppets were made. Solome bought two for our granddaughters.

We attended lectures on Chinese history. Solome brought *Wild Swans* by Jung Chang to read on the trip. She read passages to me about the brutality and torture of Chinese history, the famine and suffering, the communist campaigns.

The tour group spent an afternoon in the Tang Dynasty Art Museum. We visited other museums. Solome tried to keep them straight, but they began to blur. Was it in the People's Museum she saw the art of peasants and farms? The bronze hedgehog, the cow, rooster, hen, duck, pig, goat, rabbit, ox? She talked about function transferred when she saw a button in the shape of a snail. She also showed me a bowl with a roof for lid and a door for a spout. She thought of art as a tool to give form to ideas.

In restaurants, the tour group ate at large, round tables where the food was set in the center and circled. We visited with different couples, most of whom we didn't know, though I had read some of their articles, or thought I had, and they in turn, had read mine. We also visited as we rode our tour bus to the next site and the next where we were hounded by hawkers. I didn't always understand why they bothered us, but Solome told me not to let them bother me.

Solome looked at the Chinese people, bundled with socialism and bureaucracy. Most of them just wanted to sell their wares. How much could the Americans know of China? How much did we want to know? I listened to the conversation she had with others on the bus. It was as if the Americans had brought little containments of our own country and set them down in China to walk through. And further, there were little containers to open within the little containments we brought. There was a whole series of insulations between the Americans and the country we toured. If Solome closed her eyes, could she tell where she was? So many of her thoughts stayed in America. She worried about how Soos was managing with the girls. She thought of Gretchen. She worried about Mark's grades at Cobson.

At a Friendship Store, we bought a silk rug which we had shipped to St. Paul. In an open market, I got something for Mark, and Solome bought tea sets for Soos and Gretchen. From a hawker, we bought an ink drawing of a crane. In a museum, Solome bought a jade pin for herself and her mother.

Then it was the last evening. We ate Peking duck and exchanged addresses and e-mails.

At the airport the next morning, everyone got on the same plane to Hong Kong, and then to Los Angeles. After the long flight across the

Pacific, we arrived in Los Angeles and boarded our separate planes to their different cities.

When Solome and I returned to St. Paul several hours later, Soos, Brian and the girls, met us to help with our luggage. Solome was glad to see them. Even I was enthusiastic. We hugged and talked about the trip as we waited for the luggage.

When it arrived in the carousel, one of Solome's bags had a broken handle.

"Someone gave it a good kick," Brian said, picking it up from the baggage claim.

But nothing inside was broken. Even the tea sets made it across the Pacific.

Solome Savard

The next week, Solome took the bag to Ferdo's Luggage in downtown St. Paul for repair. It would cost $40. She was required to pay before they would fix the handle.

"Why is it so much?" She asked.

"We have to replace the handle," the repairman said. "It looks like it was hit with a hammer."

Yes, that's what they thought of Americans.

The silk rug arrived nearly a month after their return. Solome put it in the dining room.

There was an exhibit of photographs from China at the Minneapolis Art Institute: *Fifty Years Inside the People's Republic*. Solome met her mother for lunch and afterwards, they toured the exhibit. Solome saw a black-and-white photo of an open-air factory. The canals. The walks stained with duck-droppings. The surrender of Chiang Kai-shek's National Forces to the Communists in 1949. The establishment of the People's Republic of China. The tumult of tradition and modernization. The cultural revolution that destroyed the old Chinese culture.

"The overall poverty," Solome said to her mother, remembering the need for maintenance and sanitation. In one place in Beijing, Solome had seen an open gutter used as a urinal.

Solome always had liked the rooms of Chinese art at the Minneapolis Art Institute. She had walked through them as a girl. She had brought her own children to see them. Someday she would bring Susan and Sarah.

But the difference between the rooms of ancient Chinese art and the photographs from present China haunted Solome. It was the difference in her past and present life with Stephen. Alzheimer's was a Chinese revolution. It was a communist takeover of bourgeois decadence with a new plan for austerity and sameness.

In the spring, Mark Stephen graduated from Cobson College. Stephen sat on the platform with college offers and officials. He would hand Mark Stephen his diploma when his name was called.

Solome sat on the lawn under the large shade trees on the campus beside her mother. Soos and the girls were there too. Solome wanted them to see the graduates marching down the center aisle between the chairs on the lawn, then the entry of the president and trustees, and finally the faculty. It made Solome's eyes water to know it probably was Stephen's last procession. It also was their last child's graduation from college. She wanted her granddaughters to see their heritage. She wanted them to see their future.

Solome saw the new professors, some of whom were young women just out of graduate school, some of whom were minorities. What would it be like? Gretchen would know. What was Solome to them? A wife? A retired wife of a retired provost? Did they know she had thought? Did they notice her at all? They had made it to a world she had not, maybe didn't want. But she wanted to pull Soos out of her marriage and place her among the young women now in the processional. But that wasn't fair. Soos would make her own life. Did these young women know the rigors that were ahead for them? How would they come through their battle?

After the pomp of speeches and the ceremony of handing out diplomas, there was a reception in a large white tent in an adjacent field. She talked to many friends on the faculty. Would she continue in the Faculty Wives Club? No, she doubted it. She was always welcome. They would miss her.

Somehow Susan got lost. Solome heard her cry and went to look for her. Some students were with her, waiting for someone to find her.

That evening they had a buffet dinner at their house for Mark and his friends and their parents who had come from out of town. There was a large crowd, but Mark and his select friends came late and left early. They had other parties to attend. Parties without parents.

Mark had said that he wanted to take time off from school for a year or two, then go to graduate school. He continued to work at Morphew's Coffee and Book Shop in Minneapolis with his friends. He could pay some of the rent on his apartment, but Solome would have to help him.

Solome's mother asked if she was proud of Mark as they worked that evening in the kitchen after the guests left.

"Actually, I liked him better when he was earning merit badges."

Later in the summer Solome made a trip to Crane Lake with Soos and the girls. Brian was on a business trip and Solome thought the girls might enjoy the lake. She also took her mother.

Susan saw the canoe suspended from the ceiling and wanted Solome to take it down so she and Sarah could play in it, but Solome wouldn't. She told Susan it was too fragile.

The boys in the next cabin must have moved on because the cabin was vacant the week they were there. But that weekend, the man who owned the cabin arrived with his wife.

"Where are the boys?" Solome asked.

"One of them is working in Oregon, the other is in school."

As they talked, some men arrived in a truck, obviously locals.

"The old tree by the cabin has to be cut down," the man told her. "It's dead and nearly hollow inside. If it falls, it will fall across the cabin."

The men worked all day. The tree was the tallest on the point. Solome was saddened that it would come down, but she could smell the rotten core when they cut the first branches. The tree was at least 200 years old, the men said. It had probably been seen by the first French explorers.

Solome stood with the girls for a while and watched the men. She could see the small, wiry body of the one man who climbed up into the tree. He could be a descendent of one of the old voyagers. Solome saw her mother was crying. Solome felt tears also. Not because of the tree as much as the hollowness she knew was in Stephen.

Susan woke up early from her nap, held her ears. Sarah had trouble sleeping also because of the noise of the saw. When all that was left was the trunk, the man called Solome to watch it fall. The trunk and branches were notched so they would fall away from the cabin. Solome took a wedge cut from one of the branches. Inside, the tree was hollow.

The next day the men returned and continued to cut the branches into firewood. They stacked some of it in Solome's yard.

"They charged $400 to cut that tree down and cut the branches into firewood," the man told her later. "In the city it would cost $2000."

On the way back from Crane Lake to St. Paul, Solome drove behind a lumber truck for miles. It was loaded with the trunks of several huge trees.

"Can't you pass?" Soos asked impatiently.

"Not on these curved roads. I can't see far enough ahead. We've got the babies with us," Solome reminded Soos. "We'll be to the interstate soon."

Stephen Savard

I drove my car to have the oil changed. When I returned, I stood in the middle of the kitchen.

"Why don't you go sit in the living room?" Solome asked.

"They asked me what year the car was and I couldn't remember," I said. "The first year I thought of couldn't be right. It would have made the car twenty years old, and I know it's still new."

"What did you say?"

"I told them I couldn't remember."

"Where did I get these trousers?" I asked later in the day.

"We were shopping last spring," Solome told me. "We were passing through Daynard's and we stopped to look at men's clothes."

"I don't remember buying them."

Solome Savard

In the fall, Solome went to the Alzheimer's support group that met at Lockwood, a home where Alzheimer's patients were— what was the word— "kept?" She heard others talk about deciding to put their family member in a home. But what did that word mean? That kind of home was not a home. Sometimes language had Alzheimer's, forgetting what its words meant. Home was not Lockwood. Home in that sense lost its meaning. Sometimes Stephen talked about home. But Solome wasn't sure it was their home he meant. Where was Stephen's home? Was it back farther than Solome knew? The home he lived in with his parents? Was it before that?

Solome's attention was drawn back to the group. She would have to face that decision too. Stephen would wander away. He would hurt himself while she was gone. He would turn on the stove and forget to turn it off. Could she always stay with him? No. But didn't some people keep their family member at home? Yes. Was there someone else there? No. Could she afford to hire someone to stay with him? Did she know what that cost? Did she realize how tedious the care of an Alzheimer's patient was? Just wait until she got into it.

Solome did not like this support group either. She left as soon as it was dismissed without talking to anyone. The phone was ringing when she got home. Stephen must be asleep. Was the phone beside the bed turned off? He seemed to sleep more soundly now. Solome looked at the caller i.d. Caller unknown. Another salesman, she guessed. She didn't answer the phone. Was it Stephen calling from Alzheimer's? A place with no number. This man who was her husband. What was she supposed to say? How could she face a marriage without words? Without an American language that had known Manifest Destiny. Western expansion. Victory in most of its wars— until lately.

That night in bed next to Stephen, Solome dreamed she and Stephen were on a trip. Where were they going? Was it the old trip they had taken to Spain, or the newer one to China? They had not been able to sit together. Stephen was several aisles ahead. Now it was time to deplane. Where was her luggage? He had put it in an overhead bin. She couldn't find it. He would have to come back and help her. Meanwhile, there was a pillow on her seat. One of those small airplane pillows she liked. She saw it had an embroidered pillowcase. She took it— put it in the large shoulder bag she carried. She felt the bulge of it under her arm. Everyone was nearly off the plane— Stephen was on his way back to help her find her wheeled bag.

But they were not on a trip. Would never be on a trip again. Stephen was going nowhere and she was going with him. Solome couldn't tell Stephen her dream. He couldn't talk about something abstract. It would frustrate him. Thinking about something unclear as a dream was uncomfortable for him. The conversation wouldn't make sense. Now there was silence. Solome looked into Stephen's eyes. They were full of sparrows.

Solome didn't know what to do to pass the time. She read the newspaper to Stephen when they finished breakfast. A man had been murdered. A 54-year-old woman would have triplets. Why did she even read the paper?

That evening Solome went to the St. Paul Chamber Orchestra by herself. She heard Haydn's *Trumpet Concerto* and Poulenc's *Sinfonietta*. She saw that Beethoven's *Symphony No. 4* was scheduled for another concert,

Mozart's *Clarinet Concerto in A.*, and Gustav Mahler's *Symphony No. 3*. Yes, she would keep coming, even by herself. Solome spoke to a few friends and acquaintances at intermission and after the concert. They asked about Stephen. She gave an upbeat report, but she felt *boxed*. Husband, children, life had defrauded her. She was angry. America was not the land of the free. She had been bound since she could remember. But wasn't it what she once had called security?

Stephen's disease was as devastating and open as if it were an affair he was having with another woman. No, more unthinkable— as if an affair with a student. Stephen could hurt himself. He mentioned buying a gun. He dreamed someone was breaking into the house and would awake agitated, scaring Solome. She couldn't get him back to sleep. The doctor gave her medication for him, but it was difficult to get him to take it. He thought she was poisoning him.

Solome knew the time would come when she would have to put Stephen into a home. She decided on Lockwood, where there was a long waiting list. She consulted her lawyer, her financial adviser, her bank. When the time came, the money would be withdrawn monthly. In the fall, Solome filled out the papers, and Stephen was placed on the waiting list.

Solome remembered the large, old tree on the point at Crane Lake. The man who climbed the tree wore boots with spikes. Solome remembered he had jabbed his boots into the bark with each step. With one rope, he hooked himself to the tree; with another, he pulled the chain saw to the top. Another rope caught the branch that fell when cut, and lowered it slowly. He had to keep his lines separate. He couldn't let the fall-line cross the line that held him anchored in the top of the tree. But it was Stephen's lines that were tangled. Sometimes, when he would try to say something, his words got caught on one another. He spoke a shifting language. The meaning drifted from one word to another. It was all relative.

One evening, Solome sat in the chair in the bedroom with her feet on the ottoman. She had brought home some materials from the Historical Society. She paged through a history book for information the curator needed for an upcoming exhibit. Stephen had gone downstairs. She heard him turn on the television. After a while, she called his name. When he didn't answer, she went down to the family room. He wasn't there. Maybe in the kitchen— that familiar place she'd been in most of their marriage. He wasn't there either. She called his name. The door to the garage was closed. She opened it. Both cars were there. She went to the back door. It was ajar.

"Stephen?" She called.

Stephen Savard

I was sitting in the backyard.

"Come into the house," Solome said to me. "It's cold."

She helped me stand, and walked me back in the house.

"What were you doing out there?"

"I thought I heard Brown."

"Brown's dead, remember? He's buried at Crane Lake."

I looked at Solome. Brown's dead? Crane Lake? Why didn't I remember?

"Let's sit in the kitchen," Solome said. "I'll make some tea."

I heard the television and looked toward the other room.

"I'm tired of that noise," Solome said, and went to turn off the television.

She returned to the kitchen and turned on the Bose radio. I sat at the table. Had something happened?

"Do you want me to call the doctor?"

I did not.

Solome leaned over me and put her arm around my shoulder. I moved back from the table and she sat on my lap with her arm still around me. She held my hand with hers. I didn't know what to do. We sat together until the tea kettle whistled.

"You were all right in the backyard?" Solome asked as she poured the tea. "You're sure nothing happened?"

In the morning Solome called the doctor. "Stephen could have stumbled," I heard her say. "There's a bruise on his arm. He didn't know what he hit." The doctor wanted Solome to bring me in. They tested me for a stroke, but I had not had a stroke.

"Just be careful," the doctor said.

Did that mean she couldn't leave the room if I was watching a television program she didn't want to watch? She often thought I didn't watch it either, but stared at something moving to have something to watch.

Diane Glancy

Solome Savard

The next week, Solome found Stephen confused again. He was in the garage trying to take the aluminum ladder off its rack on the wall.

"What are you doing, Stephen?" She asked. Solome could picture him trying to climb to the roof. "Why do you need the ladder?"

"The tree's on the roof," he told her.

"You can't climb the ladder," she told him, but he didn't listen. He continued to work at lifting the ladder from the large hooks that held it. "Come on, Stephen," she said. "Let's go in the house."

She saw that he was not going to stop, and that if she stood in the way, he would grow angry. Finally, he lifted the end of the ladder high enough that it fell to the floor with a bang. Then he worked trying to lift the other end.

What could she do? He would carry the ladder from the garage, lean it against the house and climb. There was no tree limb on the roof. Maybe it was the sky he would climb into.

Solome was in her robe, but she went next door to the Grunswald's.

"Hetty!" She called to a light in the upstairs bedroom, but it was a light they also left on when they were gone.

The Grunswald's weren't at home, or they weren't answering their door. She looked to the next house, but she didn't know them. They had moved in when the Morgan's left. Solome looked to the other side of the cul-de-sac. There was a light on in the Bernard's house. She didn't know them well, even after many years. Why had she been unfriendly? She knocked on the door of the house that had been the Morgan's. The man answered.

"My husband has Alzheimer's. He's trying to get the ladder out of the garage. Would you help me get him back in the house?"

The man followed her. His wife came also.

As they neared the back door of the garage, they held a loud noise. Stephen had tried to carry the ladder, but it dropped on his car. He was on the floor with one end of the ladder across his leg. The man pushed him down when he tried to get up. "Just a minute. I'll get the ladder off you." The man lifted the ladder and Solome and the man's wife helped Stephen up. He stumbled. It took the man to hold Stephen upright.

"Let's get him in the kitchen."

Solome opened the door and the couple helped Stephen into the house. They sat him in the kitchen chair and looked at his face. It was scratched. He had a small lump on the side of his head, but the ladder must

130

have brushed him instead of hit directly. They checked his arms and legs. When they rolled up his trousers, they found a bloody scrape on his shin.

"That's where it hit him," the man said.

"If you help me upstairs with him, I can get him into bed, and put a bandage on his leg."

The man talked to Stephen as though he was visiting across the fence. It seemed to help. Stephen cooperated as the man helped him up the stairs.

"I can undress him," Solome told the couple. "You can let yourselves out the door."

"I'll be glad to help."

"No," Solome said, thanking them. "I have a son I can call," and the couple left.

Solome unbuttoned Stephen's shirt. She unbuckled his belt and unzipped his trousers.

"This will hurt, but I want you to help me take off your trousers."

She slid the trousers down to Stephen's ankles, past the scraped place on his shin. "You're bleeding, Stephen. Can you walk to the bathroom with me? I don't want you to get blood on the bedspread."

Stephen stepped out of his trousers and walked to the bathroom with her. She cleaned his wound with peroxide and covered it with gauze. She got his pajamas and he put them on.

She would have to watch him. She would have to close off their life together as she had known it, and not expect to get back.

If only it was simple as closing the cabin for the winter.

The next day, Solome and Stephen sat in the waiting room at the doctor's office.

Stephen thought he heard something— *in the backyard a meeting*— *to them*—

"No, Stephen, here, sit back down." Solome said.

Soon the nurse called Stephen's name. The doctor examined the bruise on Stephen's leg. The knot that had risen on his head had gone down. Solome felt guilty for letting something happen to Stephen as if he was a child she'd neglected.

"Name three states," one of the therapists asked Stephen during a visit to the doctor.

He looked blankly at her. She gave him time to respond, then named some states when he didn't.

"Kentucky," he said after a long interval.

"Any more?" The therapist asked.

Stephen couldn't think.

Solome did not like it when the therapist was in the room. Why didn't she leave him alone? Stephen was not going to respond.

The therapist continued looking at Stephen.

Minnesota, Solome thought. You've lived here all your life.

"What kind of car did you drive?" The therapist asked.

Stephen couldn't think.

Solome remembered China. A functional place which had destroyed much of its art history and permitted little contemporary art, unless it was propaganda. China was utilitarian. Institutional. Why had they gone?

Solome left the room and waited in the hall.

Stephen Savard

"Name three states," the woman said.

I did.

"Where did he get Kentucky?" I heard Solome ask the therapist. "You'd think he'd say Minnesota."

"But he didn't," the therapist answered. "I'm amazed he could answer as he did."

"Then why are you asking?"

The therapist didn't answer.

When the therapist left, Solome sat by herself beside me in the room.

Solome Savard

Several months followed without incident. Solome was hopeful. Maybe Stephen's Alzheimer's was in remission. He washed the cars with Mark. He and Solome took Susan and Sarah, now six and three, to children's reading hour at the library. But just as Solome was feeling confident again, Stephen had a car accident on the ice in a late spring storm. He wasn't hurt, nor the people he hit, but it was the last time he would be able to drive. He had taken his car while Solome was at the Historical Society. She had put his keys on a shelf in the kitchen cabinet.

"If he is competent enough to find the keys— " Solome said to the doctor, but she saw he was not going to agree.

"I'm going to have to put Stephen in a home," Solome told Soos on the phone that evening, "as soon as there's an opening."

There was silence on the other end of the phone.

"I won't always be able to take care of him."

"You can't do that, mother."

"You don't realize what it's like to take care of him. To worry about him every minute I'm away from the house."

"You're going to put him away?"

Solome could hear the flash of anger in Soos' voice. "Lockwood is able to take care of Stephen in a way I can't."

"Just because you don't want to be burdened with him?"

"It's more than that. He could hurt himself."

"Then bring him here. I'll take care of him."

"You're being unreasonable, Soos."

"I'm not having my father stuck in a home."

"You don't have the option of making that decision."

"Yes, I do." Soos hung up.

Soos was able to rally a hysterical call of protest from Gretchen, which Solome answered with reason and calm. Solome told Gretchen of Stephen's inability to understand nearly any task. She told her how he grew confused and frustrated and finally angry. How everything at Lockwood was safe for him.

"There are times of hope," Solome said. "I read in the newspaper or hear in the news— Japan has found a protein that keeps brain cells from shrinking— or a new drug is being developed— but the fact is, Stephen's capabilities are diminishing and the doctors can do nothing to stop it."

"It's that medical system in Minnesota," Gretchen said. "That administrative-run medicine."

"It's Alzheimer's, Gretchen." Solome answered. "There are days Stephen says something that makes sense. But those times are fewer and fewer. I've had to ask neighbors to help me get Stephen back into the house."

"Why didn't you tell me?"

"You're busy with your own life."

"Aren't my parents a part of my life?"

"Stephen is not safe in his own house," Solome said. "There— I've told you."

Soos was more persuasive with Mark who burst angrily into the house in front of Stephen and Solome the next day.

"I will stop you from doing this."

Stephen looked at Mark, not understanding his emotion.

"It isn't going to happen any time soon," Solome lead Mark by his arm from the room, "but Stephen will have to be moved from the house. You know that, Mark." Solome told him without wavering. "You're going to confuse your father even more if you don't settle down."

The next week, Solome wrote Stephen's sister and told her that Stephen had Alzheimer's and would be placed in Lockwood. Stephen and his sister had been distant for many years. She had had several marriages and Solome couldn't keep up with the episodes of her life. She was a wedding and funeral relative. After their parents' deaths, she and Stephen had not corresponded regularly. She lived in a different part of the country. Maybe Solome should have written more often.

Stephen Savard

That fall, after an uneventful summer, Solome decided we could attend the St. Paul Chamber Orchestra. It was Beethoven's *Symphony No. 4*, and the Mozart's *Clarinet Concerto in A*.

Solome drove us downtown and parked. We crossed Rice Park to the Ordway Concert Hall. Inside the glass doors, we greeted a few friends who also were season ticket-holders. They knew I had Alzheimer's. Was there anyone who didn't? They smiled at me and spoke to Solome. Upstairs, Solome stood talking to others. There was Grant Harner, the new provost, and Celia, his wife. Solome and I stopped and spoke to them. Then Solome led me into the redwood concert hall. After our trip to China, Solome said the walls around the stage looked oriental to her.

I sat through the first part of the concert, but began to grow agitated. I wanted to leave. When Solome looked at me, she saw I was crying. Solome took my hand. She put her arm around me. My sobs were heard above the music. There was something in Beethoven that I understood. It was as if I was on a sea. My ship could not sail back to shore. I felt utterly alone. I connected with my condition. I understood my loss. There was a moment of recognition. I was facing erasure, and it was overwhelming. Solome tried to quiet me. People were looking, she said. The Beethoven *Symphony No. 4* continued to play. I saw my place at Cobson, my family, children, grandchildren easing away from me. I saw myself receding into the symphony hall where I sat by myself in darkness.

An usher came to our row. The man next to Solome told her he would help the usher take me to the back of the hall.

"Let's leave, Stephen." Several men helped me stand and walk to the door of the hall, past the rows where our friends and the Garner's sat.

Solome Savard

The following winter, after more falls and spills, after more frustrations and near catastrophes, there was an opening at Lockwood. Solome took Stephen to the doctor, and from the doctor straight to Lockwood, so they didn't have to leave the house directly. She would bring the rest of his things that afternoon. Solome didn't want anyone going with her and Stephen. They had started out in their marriage by themselves. They would return from it in the same way. Solome wanted it to seem like a normal trip. But they were a bird caught in the grille of the car, each one of them had a wing. Nothing could give them flight again.

At Lockwood, Stephen was settled into a room with another man who suffered from Alzheimer's. They looked at one another but said nothing.

Solome unpacked the small bag of Stephen's belongings, arranging them in drawers, the way they had been at home. She didn't want Soos, Gretchen or Mark. She didn't want her mother. She wanted to do this herself. She had to do it herself. There was a mixture of shame, of self-pity, of anger, of awkwardness, of untruth. This shouldn't be happening. The Stephen she knew would hate it.

Solome remembered packing things for Mark when he went to Boy Scout camp the first time. Now she was sending Stephen into a room with someone he didn't know. She would return to their house by herself. That was it. Stephen would never be with her again. He might not even remember what he had lost. She kissed his head and walked out of his room and down the hall and out the main door into the parking lot. Solome was overcome with grief as she got in the car. She pulled to the edge of the parking lot and stopped. Another wad of grief caught in her throat. She cried until she felt like she was choking. She continued to cry on the edge of the lot, not caring if anyone saw her or heard. She poured out her grief in coughs. She cried until her crying became sobs. She was crying beyond grief now— into what was it? — Fury?

Brian, Soos and the girls came to Solome's house for supper for Susan's seventh birthday. It was the first time they ate without Stephen. Both Soos and Solome cried through the meal. Soos was still angry as though it were Solome's fault that Stephen was gone.

"You're in something you don't want to be in," Brian said to Solome. "I understand perfectly."

Imagine Brian helping. Imagine the something he didn't want to be in was marriage to Solome's daughter.

"Don't concentrate on your distractions; but on Jesus," John Everett, the man who was leading the Bible study group, said.

Is that what Alzheimer's was? A distraction? Is that what demons were? A situation she was in, but couldn't abide? Solome wanted to scream. She was angered at the Bible study group. What did they know? Their lives were still secure. They had problems, yes, everyone did. But not THE KIND OF PROBLEMS SHE HAD. Their lives were still intact. They had not faced the erasure of the mind of the one they had lived with over thirty-five years. Stephen was vacant! He was not there. Sometimes he could repeat what was said to him, if it were a few words. He echoed like an empty house. Solome wanted to hold onto Stephen. She wanted to rip him from Lockwood and bring him home. But the Stephen that had lived in their house was gone. How could she live with that? It was too painful. Her eyes filled with tears as soon as she woke in the morning. Sometimes she couldn't get out of bed. If Brown had been alive, he would have barked her out. She would have had to take him for a walk. That would have gotten her out of the house. Let God speak to her from the sky. Let him answer for what he had done. For putting his people on earth where there were diseases like Alzheimer's.

"You can't see the kingdom unless you're in it," Ralph Stewart said.

What was the man saying? Solome would have to pay attention again.

"You can't see inside the house unless you're in it."

"I've stepped into the house," she answered.

"But you haven't looked around. You don't know what's in it. The Bible is a house with many rooms. It fills your life. Anything you need is in that house."

"I'm only here because I don't have any place else to go."

"That's why we are here," Elaine Franklin said.

"Cast your cares upon the Lord— I Peter 5:7," Harold Franklin read. "When you give them to the Lord you no longer hold them."

"Don't fret," John Everett said.

"Don't fret?" Solome asked. "I've lost my husband. My married life. I have my mother to worry about. I will be facing the end of my own life down the road. I have a son-in-law who is hurting my daughter and grand-daughters." Solome saw everyone look at her, alarmed. "He isn't beating them, no. It's his hurtful attitude toward them. But I won't fret. WHAT HAVE I GOT TO FRET ABOUT?" Was it hysteria Solome was feeling? Why didn't Jesus restore Solome's husband? In the Bible, Jesus healed the sick, but had Alzheimer's ever been healed?

"I can't come to this Bible study group any longer," Solome said. "It's too painful. I have to go back to my old Fidelis class where the heart is sedated, where the pain is covered over by the mere shape of its being ignored, where pain and sorrow are not examined. I was safe there. The hurtful parts were ignored. I want church as I knew it in the past: a ritual without emotion. A place I went on Sunday where religion was kept. A historical research library that doesn't circulate outside the library. History that stays history. I want to be there in that fortress. You take church and spread it all over the place. It follows me home. It lives with me daily. What is this? I got along without it all my life."

"You're already come into the house, as you said. You've accepted Christ as your Savior. You can't undo your standing in Christ."

"I've always lived inland. I don't have words for the water. It's barren. Do you see anything on the sea? I know lakes, rivers, lagoons, ponds. But the sea? I don't have an oar. I don't have a boat. I don't have language for the sea."

No one in the Bible study group said anything. They sat in the circle in silence as Solome cried quietly in front of them. Else and Bill Renke. Elaine and Harold Franklin. Charlotte and Ralph Stewart. The Forman sisters. And, of course, John Everett without his wife. Solome could be herself in front of them, more than she could in front of her friends.

"Nonetheless," Solome said, "I feel a steady hand."

"Though the fig tree doesn't blossom, though grapes aren't on the vines, though there's nothing in the fields and olive orchards, though the herds and flocks are gone, I will rejoice in the Lord— Habakkuk 3:17–18." John Everett read from his Bible.

Solome looked at him. For the first time, she knew that John Everett had known defeat also.

Solome walked around Hill Park by herself. It was the first day of March and it was 20 degrees and the snow was piled high. She still missed Brown, but she didn't want another dog. She had enough to worry about without a pet to take care of too. She thought of the hollowness that followed death as she walked. But Stephen wasn't dead. His body was in the home at Lockwood.

Solome had a recurring dream of not being able to get where she used to go. Stephen must have dreamed too. "It's a lovely place," he told her when she visited him at Lockwood.

He must have found some place where he could accept himself. "What's it like?" She asked. But the way to tell it was gone.

Mark came to Lockwood to see his father while Solome was there. Mark obviously didn't want to be there. He didn't want to see his father with Alzheimer's. He didn't want to see his father incapacitated. Neither did Solome. Mark was never one to put others first. Was it something they had done as parents? After the two girls, they were delighted with a boy. Had they put too much emphasis on him?

Solome continued her Bible Study group. There were ways of trying to cope with Alzheimer's. Solome's would be faith. It was the only hope she found. At times, she had come up for air. The air she found was the reality of Christ in her life. If not for others, it seemed an inflatable raft, for the time, anyway. Maybe it would remain.

The next meeting was at her house. It was a small group. The Forman sisters were not there. A late spring snow was forecast, but only a dusting fell. Late snows were usually heavy, full of moisture, but they melted quickly into slush. The slush froze in the night, and turned back to slush the next afternoon. The doorbell rang soon after the meeting started. It was Reverend Croft and his wife. Solome was glad to see them. They asked about Stephen.

John Everett opened the meeting again with prayer. Bill Renke, the leader for the evening, began. "Proverbs 18:21— The tongue has the power of life and death— with the mouth we confess our salvation in Christ."

The discussion for the evening was the different Bible verses that had to do with the importance of what was said. The importance of speaking words of faith. Solome liked the thought. What she said could ease the tight place she was in. Look how the words of David in the Psalms led him through his troubles.

After the discussion, Solome served cake and coffee.

"Spiritual Alzheimer's is what happens when man forgets God," Reverend Croft said.

Soos and Brian came to Solome for help with a down payment on a house they had found. Solome thought of asking Stephen about it, but knew it wouldn't do any good. She would have to get used to making decisions by herself. She agreed to give them several thousand dollars, not as much as they asked.

On an early Saturday in May, Solome helped Soos get ready to move. She would take care of the girls while Soos put things in boxes.

"I'll take the girls to my house," Solome offered.

"No, they need to see the process. It's confusing to take them from their things in the old house, to their things in the new house. They'll be afraid it will happen every time they leave the house."

Solome supposed Soos was right. She saw that Soos was a long way from being ready for the movers. She was doing some of the packing to make the move cheaper. But the movers would be there before Soos was packed. She did not have her things ready to go. Solome found dishes in the dish washer. Laundry in the dryer. Small boxes on closet shelves that should be put in a larger boxes. Toys on the floor, under the bed. Pictures on the walls.

"Soos, let me help."

"Just feed the girls," she said. "I can handle it."

Solome heard impatience in Soos' voice. She took the girls to the kitchen and had to unwrap two dishes to fix peanut butter sandwiches for them.

Soos was unorganized. She was not handling it. Solome worried if they could afford the new house. It seemed that Brian and Soos were out driving one Sunday afternoon and saw the house and decided to buy it without much thought, other than it was in a school district they wanted for the girls. Maybe they were just running from the disappointment of their marriage. No, that wasn't true. Brian was a businessman. He knew what they could afford. But as usual, it was Soos trying to catch up with the work that followed in the wake of their decision. Solome had to take a back seat. She couldn't run Soos life, though she wanted to. She had to back off and do only what Soos asked her to. It hurt Solome to see Soos under stress. It made her angry to hear Soos insist that she could handle things while Solome, who could handle them better, had to sit back and watch Soos struggle. Fumble was the more appropriate word. The house looked like it had been turned upside down. For supper, Solome and the girls went to a drive-in and returned with hamburgers.

"Why don't you stay at my house tonight?" Solome suggested.

"No, I want to spend the last night at home," Soos answered.

"Bring the girls over tomorrow. Your door will be open for the movers. They'll be in the way," Solome said. "Be practical. They'll do better at my house."

Soos, in her tiredness, agreed.

Solome was relieved when the day was over. She drove to her house and welcomed the empty quiet. But as soon as she took off her coat, she began to cry. She wanted to talk to Stephen and she couldn't. She hit her hands on the bed until she grew tired of even that.

Solome took care of the girls the next day while the furniture was moved from one house to another. That evening, Brian and Soos came for dinner, exhausted.

"Stay here tonight," Solome asked again, and they agreed.

In the next week, Solome helped Soos unpack, hang curtains, arrange furniture. Slowly, they seemed to get settled again.

Solome cried again at the Monday night Bible study. It was a weeping that would not stop.

She drove home, dejected, but she had stopped crying. The attack of grief was over. But what if it came back? She didn't like to cry in public. It embarrassed her. It shamed her. Something was wrong that she couldn't handle. She had always been sufficient and self-possessed. Well, some years as a young mother had been difficult. But Stephen and her mother had been her supports. Now they couldn't help. Was her grief over the fact that she didn't have them anymore? No, it was more that she didn't have life anymore. She was in service to them now, not that they wanted it that way, but that's the way it was. What if Solome took her mother into her house? Solome wouldn't like it. Her mother would rearrange things, would upset things. Solome would be a prisoner to both her mother in her house and Stephen in the home. She couldn't leave her house without worrying what her mother was doing. No, she wasn't up to that. What if Solome took her mother to a counselor, or the minister, to help her let go? Solome would keep some of her mother's things, but most of them would have to go. She would keep the antiques for Soos and Gretchen. Her mother could have some of her own things in her room at the home. Or her mother could stay in her house until she was so incapacitated she would have to move her out and face going through her mother's house by herself. Soos would want some of the furniture for her new house. Maybe Gretchen would want more than Solome realized when she had a permanent position somewhere near Dennis. Would Mark want any of the furniture for his apartment? Solome doubted it.

Solome was nearly Stephen's age. What if something happened to her? What if they ran out of money? It could happen. They could share a ward with other indigents. Solome sat on the edge of her bed in the dark. She saw the shape of Stephen's chair and ottoman in the dark, his closet door. For a moment, the thought engulfed her. It was a cavern into which she fell. She wanted to call out. She did call out. "Jesus," she said.

Solome faced the unknown. Jesus died on the cross for this. Jesus was sufficient, he had said. She only had to believe. Jesus laid down a bridge, which was his cross. Solome only had to walk across it believing it was there. It was a form of walking on water. Would she find the courage to do it? Imagine wanting something, and wanting something, and not getting it, but, instead, getting something that she didn't want.

Solome met one of Stephen's colleagues, Tom Marshall, as she came from the cleaners. She had read the recent issue of the *Cobson Journal*. Tom had just published a book and Solome mentioned it. Tom was never a close associate, but he had become the department head on a rotating basis.

"How is Stephen?" Tom asked.

"These changes are hard to accept—" Solome began.

"Why are they hard to accept?" He asked Solome. "It's the history of the world. Something comes in and replaces another. One conqueror over another. In American history, the British over the French, the rebels over the British, the cavalry over the Indians, the immigrants over the open spaces. Alzheimer's over Stephen. Unbelief over the belief one had as a child."

"Or belief over unbelief."

"Yes, I heard you have become immersed in religion," Tom said.

"Where did you hear that?"

"My wife. She heard it from other wives. You know how women are."

"Yes I do," Solome said. "Thank you for the intellectualization of my situation. I'm glad to join in history's great march. I certainly feel like one of the defeated."

"I didn't mean to offend you," Tom said.

"I take no offense. You gave it to me like a man. I accept that."

Solome felt thoroughly dismissed. She took her clean clothes hanging in a plastic bag and left.

Some of the spouses of the Alzheimer's patients came to Lockwood every day. Solome was not able to because of Soos and the girls, her job, her mother. It took a long time for Soos to get unpacked and settled. Things didn't fit as she thought they would. She hated the wallpaper. She wanted new curtains.

"I'm not in the mood to paper a wall," Solome told her. "I can't take on anything that hard."

"You watch the girls, and I'll paper." Soos talked her into it. But Soos got into trouble; the pattern didn't match and she grew frustrated. Soon the paper was in a rumple on the floor, one fold sticking to another. Solome ended up calling her house man who did painting and papering for her. Solome bought more paper to replace what Soos had ruined, and the house man finished the job.

Solome's mother called that afternoon. She was having problems staying alone. For some reason, she was suddenly afraid at night.

"You're going to have to find someplace to stay eventually."

"I could stay with you."

"No, mother. I can't accept that. I want to work. My responsibility is to Soos and the girls."

"I suppose some of your responsibility is to me."

"Yes, mother, that's true. Have you realized I have Stephen to visit also?"

"Of course, I have."

"If you were in the same place Stephen was, I could visit you both."

"I'm not ready for a home. I can still take care of myself."

"That's true, but for how long? Have you turned on the stove and forgot to turn it off yet?" Solome asked. "I've seen the scorched place on your counter."

"Anyone can forget a pan."

"At least you didn't burn yourself," Solome muttered, "or burn the house down. I think you'd enjoy being with others. There are planned activities. You could play cards. You'd be surrounded with friends. How many more winters will you be able to drive? How are you going to keep up your house? I can't grocery shop for you all the time."

"I think I can and do shop for myself. I also think we do a good job of shopping together. It gives us time to talk. Besides," her mother said, "there isn't room in one of those homes for my things."

"Well, get rid of some of your things we need to get rid of. How many *Good Housekeeping* magazines have you got in your attic? How many clothes in your closet you never wear?"

"How many do you have?" Solome's mother asked.

"Why don't we clean out our houses together?" Solome suggested.

"Why don't we store some of my things at your house?"

"No, mother," Solome said, but it was the closest her mother had come to agreeing to downsize. "With your things at my house, it would be nothing for you to move in with me."

It was summer. Solome walked with a neighbor, Hetty Grunswald, in Hill Park. When she returned to her house, she sat in a chair at the window reading the *St Paul Pioneer Press*. There was a reprint of an article from the *New York Times*: Torture in China Getting More Press. Soon after arrest on trumped-up charges, Li Kuisheng was beaten to a bloody mess. He had been made to jog in the snow, he was shackled— one arm forced over his shoulder, the other arm forced up from behind— Solome read how the man, a lawyer, had defended an official the government didn't like. After 26 month in custody, Kuisheng was cleared of charges and released. Solome read of his torture, and the wide-spread ill-treatment of detainees. Imagine America in debt to the Chinese.

Solome felt the breeze and saw the curtain move. Why did she read the paper? Why was she safe in her house in America while people were being tortured, raped and murdered? Why had she been born in a country that prohibited such behavior? Why had she been spared? But had she? Alzheimer's ripped into her house, her heart.

Solome thought of the inhumanity in the world. How could people believe in the goodness of men without a savior? Didn't they know the human heart? There was a blackness— a blindness in it that only Christ could dislodge— and even with Christ, it was hard.

Several nights in a row, Solome woke around 3:00 a.m. Was Sarah crying? Was her mother awake also? If her mother was with her, they could get up and talk. Why did they all live in their separate houses? In primitive societies the entire family lived in the same hut. It happened also in poverty. There was something primitive in the middle of the night, and in the poverty of darkness.

Solome felt stretched between Stephen and her mother, between Soos and Gretchen, between Mark and Brian. How far could they all pull before she broke? She was the center post. The center hinge around which they all turned. She could not go back to sleep. She looked at the ceiling. She looked at the window. It would be dark for a long time. She could get up, but what would she do? She didn't want anyone outside to see the lights on in her house. Did she think they might knock? She listened to the house. What desolation she felt. Her heart pounded momentarily, but she spoke the fear away. She was not going to be afraid. The house was locked. The alarm was on. The Bernard's were next door. The Grunswald's. The phone was beside her bed if she needed to call 911 for emergency help. She lay in bed and asked the Lord to help them all.

Solome thought of Stephen in the home, in his narrow bed in the room shared by another man. It was as if she left him on the Wall of China. It was the same as if he had not come back. No, it was worse. Part of him came back. She couldn't move on because his body was still here. Solome made trips to Lockwood every other day. Sometimes there was a flicker of recognition in Stephen. Other times, most times, there was nothing. The time had come that he no longer knew her. She lay in her bed. Stephen was her husband. Yes, she still had a husband. He was somewhere, there inside his shell. And she was tied to him. It wasn't fair.

Mark and some of his friends spent a week at Crane Lake. They had taken a video camera, and one night, showed the cassette. Solome had fixed supper for them. Soos, Brian and the girls had come also.

Solome watched the boys' antics at the lake. But she also saw the lake through their eyes. She saw the lake in a way she hadn't. There was an intelligence in the video, a caring, which she hadn't recognized in Mark and his friends. They had even pulled weeds around the cabin. There was a shot of Brown's grave. They had a party with the boys in the next cabin, yes, and girls were there too.

Solome wanted to spend a few days at the lake also, and decided to drive up. The next day, she called Soos to ask if she could take Susan with her. Soos called back that evening and said that she and Brian had agreed. Sarah had been cranky, and it might help her to have some time alone with Soos. She would ask Susan in the morning if she wanted to go.

The man and his wife in the next cabin were leaving as Solome and Susan arrived. He told Solome he had called John's Tree Service to have another tree removed, but it was no longer in business. When he inquired in Buyck, he heard that John had been up in a tree, cutting a large branch, when the power saw slipped and cut off his arm. He bled to death before they could get him down. Oh God, there it was again. The Christian responsibility of witnessing she did not want. She had not asked if Jesus was his Savior. Did that mean he was in hell?

When Susan was in bed that night, Solome sat on the screened part of the deck and thought about the man in the tree. She felt the darkness around her. Had he not been able to hold the artery? Had he gone into shock and couldn't think? Had he chosen to let his blood run out because he could not face his life without an arm?

Solome wanted to put her hand in her oven mitt, reach into the sky, and pull the sun backward several years. It had happened in the Bible— II Kings 20:11. She remembered it from her Bible study. She had made a note of it. God had moved the shadow of the sun backward. She also wanted to be again where she had once been.

Stephen Savard

Late summer   Solome said   watched a political convention on television one morning. How programmed it seemed. How pat and buttoned down. Where was the substance? It was [veneer]. Is   that the word   she said? Alluvial. [Where did I get that ?] It seemed   distant. What *it* seemed distant? Life?   Something that would   never reach   again, no matter how far I held out   hand.

Solome Savard

Solome turned off the television, dressed, and drove to work at the Minnesota Historical Society.

145

She walked through an exhibit room where it was still quiet. The children from various summer camps had not yet arrived. She looked at the bark lodge. She looked at the old sled made of animal skin. She looked at the paintings on the walls and the writings beside the paintings.

"We made a treaty, and we were promised a great many things, but now it appears the wind blows it all away." Little Crow, or Taoynteduta, at Washington, D.C. treaty negotiations, 1851.

She read S. Holmes Andrews in *Harper's New Monthly Magazine*, July 1853, on the history of St. Paul. "Five years ago [there] were a few log huts now there is a large and rapidly growing village of almost 4000 white people with handsome public buildings, good hotels, stores, mills, mechanic shops, and every other element of prosperity."

Solome continued through the third floor and then walked down the stairs to her office on the second floor. She had to look through two catalogues from rare book dealers: *Rare Americana*, Catalogue Thirty-Four, A Selection of Rare Books, Pamphlets, Maps and Manuscripts, and the *William Reese Company* Catalogue 193 on Native Americans. The curator had marked several books he was interested in purchasing for the Society. Solome had to check to see if the Historical Society already owned the books the curator wanted to purchase, or if the Society owned the books, what condition they were in. If the Society's copy was 100 years old, and the book in the catalogue was in prime condition, Solome had to report on that too.

She made note of the books in the Indian catalogue first— *IU OTOSH-KIKI-KINDIUIN AU KITOGIMAMINAN GAIE BEMAJINUNG JESUS KRIST: The New Testament of Our Lord and Savior Jesus Christ*, Translated into the Language of the Ojibwa Indians, New York, Pr. by the American Bible Society, 1844. *Three Years among the Indians in Dakota*, Joseph Drips, 1894. *The Adventures of "Antelope Bill" in the Indian War of 1862*, Parker Pierce, 1862. *The Sioux Wars, What Shall We Do with Them*? James Taylor, 1862. *The Ojebway Language: A Manuel for Missionaries*, Edward Wilson, 1874.

Solome had work she had to do, but she sat at her desk a moment before she went into the research library. She was haunted by Little Crow's statement. "The wind blows it all away."

What was done unto others was received in return.

"It used to be called hardening of the arteries," the counselor of the Alzheimer's support group said. "It's a form of dementia. It begins with forgetting names and ends with forgetting to breathe. Pneumonia is a common cause of death. Not Alzheimer's itself, but something else. It can take from 3–20 years to die of Alzheimer's. Usually around 12. It depends upon a person's chemical makeup."

Solome wiped away a tear. Some of the women cried openly. She would cry later, in the car on the way away from this place— not like she had the first time when she had spit up her grief as if she was choking on a bone.

"I think sometimes he remembers," a woman said. "I walk into his room and he looks up like I have just returned from shopping. Something flickers, but it is gone as soon as it comes."

"Sometimes her attention span seems longer, and I have hope she will be there again, but I'm always disappointed," another woman said.

"He remembers how to do less and less. Now it's his bowels."

"At least our patients are manageable most of the time," the counselor said. "There are places beyond this where Alzheimer's patients go."

"Sometimes when I'm visiting him, I think, who is this person?"

"What do they do all day?"

"We had to take the mirror from my mother's room. She didn't know who she was in the mirror. She grew afraid. *There's an old woman watching me*, she would say. *Get her away*."

"The Alzheimer's patient retreats to the early 20's. They think they are young and it upsets them to see themselves in the mirror. They expect a young face in the mirror. They can't understand the reflection is them. The home has them on *adl* activities, the activities of daily living. Making the bed. Brushing the hair. We don't let them watch television. When there's been war on the news, they think it's something they lived through— a war from their era, and they go through it again. If there's an old movie on that is not threatening, we let them watch it as though it were a new movie that just came out."

"It's the inappropriate behavior that also is difficult. Sexual advances, for instance. Our ability to control our behavior deteriorates also."

Solome didn't want to hear any more. She wanted to bolt from the artless room and these depressing people. She wanted to get up and walk out of the institutional room decorated to look homey, but it was without life. She wanted to walk out of Lockwood, out of the world.

The leader of the group irritated Solome. She talked as though she were one of them. Did she have a relative with Alzheimer's? Solome wanted

Diane Glancy

to ask. Did she stand by watching while her husband's head was being eaten and there was NOTHING she could do about it but be CIVIL?

Maybe Solome should *witness* to them. Tell them about Jesus. Introduce them to *this awkwardness*.

Solome already saw the worsening of the disease. Sometimes Stephen would cry without apparent reason. Maybe he was remembering the Beethoven concert. Or the removal of the Dakota Indians from Minnesota. Or another part of the history he had known. The doctor had told her about his crying spells, then she saw it for herself. *No apparent reason,* she held the doctor's words. No apparent reason other than Stephen had Alzheimer's and was feeling all those EMPTY SPACES in his head where he used to have brains.

Solome walked to the car and drove home. In the kitchen, she laid her purse and keys on the counter. Her legs felt week. Her head buzzed. Maybe she was catching Stephen's disease. Maybe because she had kissed his forehead. She felt like she was coming apart. Maybe Solome should let her mother move in with her, in case she couldn't take care of herself, in case she was catching some disease. What made muscles feel week and uncoordinated? Polio or Muscular Dystrophy. Yes, MS. That was what she had. Her mother would pull her back together. No, her mother in her house would only cause more tension.

Solome lay in her bed. She swam in her thoughts. Just don't let Soos call with another problem. Don't let Gretchen call with another complaint. Don't let Mark call with his impatience. Don't let her mother call to meet her at the Mildred Pierce Restaurant on Randolph where they had begun meeting for dinner. Maybe Solome would die quickly and wouldn't have to go through the old age she saw at Lockwood. Solome imagined herself on a plane to visit Gretchen, the plane falling out of the sky into the trees. She saw the pines rising quickly to the plane. Suddenly she woke, realizing she had dozed.

Solome called Agnes Forman from the Bible study group when she had trouble walking down the stairs the next morning. Agnes came to the house. Agnes Forman with a name that could scare the demons. Solome felt she was falling apart. She called the Historical Society and said she couldn't work that day. Agnes sat with her at the table. She fixed coffee. She poured cereal into a bowl for Solome. She held Solome's hands until they stopped shaking enough that Solome could eat the bowl of cereal. She had no fruit to put in the cereal. Solome didn't want to go to the store. She didn't want to do anything but find a plane that was going down and get on it. She looked at the floor as though a stairway would open and she could step down into the darkness. Soos called while Agnes was there. In a trembling voice Solome told her she couldn't watch the girls. Soos asked why. Solome told her she had just received the first installment of the rest of Stephen's life, and she couldn't rise from it yet. Soos was concerned and wanted to help her mother, but Solome told her that Agnes Forman was with her, and Solome didn't want the girls upset. They were sensitive to sorrow. Solome had seen them pick it up from their mother.

"Who is Agnes Forman?" Soos asked.

"A woman from my Bible study group."

"Let me come over, mother. You need someone there from the family."

"No, I don't. And don't call Grandma," Solome told Soos.

Solome hung up with confidence that Soos was appeased.

"The girls won't have a grandfather." Solome continued to cry, or began crying then, she couldn't remember. She continued to cry until she felt sobs jerking her shoulders. The whole world seemed in the grip of something— What?— Alzheimer's?

Agnes stayed with Solome that morning. After they prayed, Solome went back to bed. Agnes would sit in the kitchen until she woke. She had brought her Bible to read. Agnes Forman, fortified with armor against the enemy.

"Turn off the phone in your room." Agnes said.

When Solome woke, Gretchen had called wondering if she should fly in. Soos had called her worried beyond belief. Soos also had stopped by the house, but Agnes refused to let her to up to Solome's room. Solome smiled, imagining that scene.

"I'm better," Solome told Gretchen when she returned her call. "I'm better by myself. You have too much to take care of where you are. The Alzheimer's support group was a momentary awakening. I'm losing life as I have known it. Give me a chance to grieve."

How could Solome understand her husband was not her husband? How could she tell her children their father was not their father? There was another person in his body. One not entirely unpleasant, but one who bore no resemblance to their father. He had vacated. She didn't know where he was. Oh yes, she did. He was in heaven, just waiting for his body to catch up. He would be restored to himself. God was the father of resurrection. It would just be a long vacant time with this substitute Stephen while the real one waited above. How could she believe that? How could she believe her father was at a summer cabin with Brown somewhere in the outer space called Heaven? Had anyone seen it? How could she tell Jane Mead what she believed when Jane questioned her about how she was handling the advancement of Stephen's disease? Certainly Jane could see into Solome and poke anything not genuine. Solome's mother was weepy. She was no help. She took her mother to Lockwood to show her where she should be on the waiting list. Solome could put her there without her knowledge. You didn't just walk into a place like that. There was a waiting period. Maybe Stephen didn't have to wait as long as others because he had been the provost of Cobson College.

Stephen Savard

Ask   She I couldn't   think go away go—

Solome Savard

Jesus suffered all our sins and diseases on the cross. Had he suffered Alzheimer's? Was there a blessed moment as Jesus suffered on the cross that Alzheimer's came up and he forgot where he was? Forgot his pain? Forgot who he was and was oblivious even unto the work of salvation?

Jesus was with her, the Bible study group said. She put her hand out for him. He felt like air.

Mark had traveled over the summer and into the fall. He and his friends had gone to Montana. They had gone to New Orleans. They had gone places she did not know. He was experiencing what there was to experience.

"I just want you to come back alive from your experiences," Solome told him.

Mark had come by the house to bring some boxes to store in his closet.

"I might sell the house sometime," Solome told him.

"Why?" He asked.

"It's too big for me. Your father isn't coming back."

"What will you do when Gretchen comes home?" Mark asked.

"She could stay with Soos. They have a bigger house now."

"You could keep Grandma here."

"That's what she says," Solome told him.

"This's the house where I grew up. I don't want you to sell it," Mark said.

"If I had my way, your father and I would be here forever," Solome said, "but it doesn't work that way."

Mark went to attic looking for something he wanted.

When he came back downstairs, Solome said, "You're going to have to get a job, Mark."

"I'm going to graduate school," he said, "I'm taking a year off."

"You need to work, Mark," Solome told him. "I'm not giving you more than your allowance."

"You will still pick up the car insurance?"

"Yes," Solome said, "— and you need to go see your father," she reminded him.

"I did," Mark answered. "It was like driving across Montana."

Soos and Gretchen both called Solome that evening about keeping the house. There were too many memories. They couldn't let it go.

Solome looked for a condominium with a real estate agent. She looked at smaller houses; one of them small enough it had only two bedrooms. Let everyone store their own belongings in their own closets. Even Soos had several boxes in Solome's attic and basement. Gretchen had even more. Jane Mead and several of her friends lived in condominiums. She liked them whenever she visited, despite the drawbacks. They had fireplaces and small, tidy kitchens. They were attached to others. Not as isolated as a house standing in a neighborhood by itself. Would there be enough room for her discussion group? She wanted a dining room also for family dinners and entertaining.

She walked through her house that evening. She didn't want to leave it yet. She wasn't ready to sell it. When the real estate broker called the next week, Solome said she didn't want to look at more condominiums or houses. Solome would let her know when she wanted to look again.

Sometimes Solome read the Bible. She made herself read the Bible. She struggled to make herself read the Bible. From the beginning, it was about the appositional forces in the world. Solome could feel them in herself. The word, *divided*, was there in the Bible from the first. Solome knew the two sides of who she was. Yet who could believe this foolishness? A death and resurrection on the cross. This absurd religion that Solome looked to for help.

Maybe this pull of forces was as it had to be.

Stephen Savard

Heavy snow a   tall on fence outside window   ready to topple a building it off the corner of something   lifted the ground   fall rubble dirt cloud down what nothing to   back not happen.   Yes   that was.

Solome Savard

Solome watched Stephen sitting by the window in his room at Lockwood. The snow was made of unique patterns of snowflakes. How many snow-flakes had she cut from white construction paper as a child? How many snowflakes had her children made? Was there ever a winter without snow-flakes hanging on a string in the windows? Solome thought of Stephen's brain scan. Each snowflake was different. Each storm of Alzheimer's changed the brain into different shapes. The man that shared a room with Stephen was different than Stephen. They each had Alzheimer's, but it was a different Alzheimer's.

Imagine a woman alone in her house with a silk rug in the dining room from China, and an ink print of a crane on the wall. Imagine that she could imagine. When the children had been young, she had imagined a time when they would be raised and not under foot all day. Now she had that time. How quickly it had come. How quickly it was over. It had seemed like it would last forever. But now she was free of all those duties she had wished would not last forever. Well, not entirely. Now she had granddaughters. Susan already was in the second grade. Sarah was four. Solome attended their church, school and pre-school programs. She had birthdays parties and dinners for her family. She still had the problems of how to deal with the intersections of their lives.

For Christmas, the children got Solome a dog. She heard it yip as Soos brought it in the house.

"I don't want it," Solome said. "I'm gone to much. I'm at the Historical Society or Lockwood. I can't leave a little dog like that alone."

"Just keep it for a while."

"No, I would grow attached to it. I have too much to do. A dog will not help. I appreciate the thought. I am alone, but a dog will not help me through my loneliness. I don't want to walk it. I do not want to clean up after it."

"It wasn't your fault Brown died," Soos said.

"What does that have to do with it?" Solome asked. "I don't want a dog. You are giving me an obligation and not a gift."

"We want to help you," Gretchen said.

"If I get a dog, I want it to be my decision," Solome told her children.

"It's a present," Soos protested. "How can you be so impolite?"

"How can you be impolite and buy me a gift which requires such responsibility without asking me if I wanted it? It seems you are imposing on me."

Gretchen was dumbfounded.

"You take the dog, Gretchen."

"I can't," she answered. "I put in whole days at the university. Dennis is gone. Soos has too many responsibilities with the girls. Besides, they've been feeding a cat, which probably thinks it's their pet already."

"Then you take her, Mark," Solome said. "She can stay in your apartment. There's always someone there to pet her."

Solome's mother was another possibility. Solome looked at her. No, she wanted her mother to go to Lockwood. A dog would give her permission to stay in her house, or to move in with Solome so she could take care of the dog while Solome was away.

The Christmas brunch was quiet, whether from Solome not accepting the dog, or the dread of visiting Lockwood, or both. No, there was more. It was the recognition of how different Christmas was without Stephen. The recognition that a season, which had once been a time of giving and receiving gifts, a time of wholeness for the family, a time of togetherness, had been turned inside out. Everyone felt it, but they could not say it. It was the secret knowledge they all shared.

After the Christmas meal, they got in two cars and drove to Lockwood. Stephen was in his shirt and trousers in a wheelchair in a row of chairs. They pulled him to his room. He looked at them without much recognition. They placed his gift on his lap. He didn't open it, but only looked at it. Solome began to unwrap it for him. It was a plaid robe with a long sash. He held the sash in his hand. They talked about Christmases in the past, remembering Mark shaking a box that set off the siren on his fire truck, remembering Brown nearly knocking over the Christmas tree with its ornaments. Gretchen and Soos sometimes wiped their eyes, or stepped from the room a moment, or into the bathroom. Sometimes they talked in artificial tones, as if everything was all right, when underneath, the sight of their father was too much to bear. Only Susan and Sarah were content in the room, oblivious of its meaning, exploring new objects— the sideposts on the bed, the crank underneath. If only they knew this was what they moved toward—this was the culmination of life. Stephen who had been Santa Claus, had been father Christmas himself, handing out the gifts, carving the turkey, making everything happen for them, now sat in his chair before these strangers. Strangers. Their star in the sky was gone. Their magi. Their coming of the promised child.

Stephen said something no one understood. Was Stephen remembering a Christmas long ago? Maybe a Christmas before Solome knew him. She couldn't recognize what he was saying. Then he said, *home*. He wanted to go home. There was that word again. But what home did he mean?

Alzheimer's was a form of dementia. Solome always thought of dementia as unrest, wildness, craziness. But dementia meant impaired memory and reasoning ability. Severely impaired, in the case of Alzheimer's. It was caused by a shriveling brain. Solome kissed Stephen on the forehead and wished him Merry Christmas. The family stumbled backward out of Stephen's room. Everything felt smaller in winter. Stephen's family hurried to their cars in the cold, the women drying their faces as they rushed away from the smallness of the world Stephen inhabited. They drove back to their houses where they could close their doors.

That evening, the dog went home with Mark.

Stephen Savard

It wasn't   people always in and   his room he look   at them not

Solome Savard

In January, Solome worked four days a week at the Historical Society. It was easy to get lost in work. To become involved in museum exhibits. To take on new responsibilities. Solome moved into Acquisitions. She was now an assistant, no longer an assistant to the assistant.

She also now was responsible for computer data. She had to go to classes to learn the computer. She had to create a list for the acquisitions committee meetings, a list of books they wanted to buy, a list of books they had been given. Solome sat in on the acquisitions committee meetings. Often the assistant knew more than the curator because of the research she had done. Often the committee relied on her opinion.

When Solome started out from the house for the Historical Society one morning, anxiety came over her. Was it a premonition? A warning she would have an accident? An irrational fear. Hadn't the accident already happened? Didn't her husband get hit with Alzheimer's. What was the next worst thing that could happen? Brian Stiple would leave Soos and the girls. Dennis Kamrar would turn out like Brian, but Dennis had the safety of distance. Would he grind down Gretchen's heart? Would he make her feel unworthy? Unloved? A wife he had chosen to marry, then regretted his decision. What did Solome have to lose? She started out for work. She was not going to be overcome by anxiety. She was not going to let the demons come. They were more than her, but over them was the One more than them.

One night Solome woke with a dream. She was climbing the stairs. Someone was with her— Stephen? He had something like a rocket ship tied on his back. A plane with two rocket boosters. He was panting. He fell over dead, turned into a dog that ran away.

Solome opened her eyes. It took her a minute to realize where she was. It was a dream. Only a dream. Was Stephen dying? She knew he was. But it could take years. He could outlive her. She felt hot. She pushed back the blanket and looked dazed at the room.

Stephen was at Lockwood in one of the *his and his beds,* she thought. She felt a wave of amusement? Was this a joke? Was she depressed and saw the distortion? No, depression meant seeing more clearly. She was depressed. Therefore, she saw things as they were. Unchangeable. Desolate. Moving toward an end.

Solome finally went back to sleep and woke groggy in the morning. What had she been dreaming before she woke? What was it this time? Something she had to remember. She turned her head into the pillow. No— she had dreamed of John Everett from the Bible study group in an unspeakable way. What was wrong with her? Where did these dreams come from? She thought of turning over and going back to sleep. Maybe another dream would wash that one from her head. But she had to get up. She had to write checks for utilities and her tithe to the church. She had to reconcile the check book. How much time it took. How tedious all the details of living. She had an appointment with their financial advisor to prepare taxes. Stephen always had paid bills and done the taxes. Now the sequence of numbers for him moved— four, seven, two, one. Nothing. But what did she know what moved in Stephen's head?

When Solome stepped outside for the newspaper, she fell on the ice in her drive. Her feet slipped out from beneath her and she slammed against the ground in a sitting position. Had anyone seen her? The Grunswald's? The Bernard's? The new neighbors? Would they help to pull her up? Was it because she had dreamed of another man? No, how ridiculous. It had been an accident.

"Hetty!" She called, but there was no answer. She remembered Hetty's voice calling her long ago. The Grunswald's oldest boy had fallen and broken his arm. Hetty had held him while Solome drove them to the hospital. She remembered how he'd cried in pain.

Solome sat a moment wondering if she could move. Why hadn't she been careful? Her back hurt, and her head. The sudden impact jarred her. She got up on her knees, and stood, slowly. Her foot slipped again, but she caught herself, jabbing her foot into the snow bank. She limped into the house with the paper.

The next morning, because she was in pain, she called the doctor and went into his office. He felt her tailbone and the bones across her hips. He wouldn't x-ray because he didn't think it was necessary. She would be sorer the next day, he said. He gave her a mild pain killer and she went home. She called the Historical Society and said she wouldn't be in for work.

It hurt to sneeze. Her head felt tight. She felt as if her hip was on fire.

Her mother came to the house and they had supper together.

Solome lay in bed on Saturday morning looking at the ceiling. The light fixture was the center around which the room orbited. Solome lay in bed without getting up. There was nothing she had to do. Usually breakfast pulled her out of bed, Stephen's breakfast. He had to get up and she got up with him. Now he was not there and she had nothing to get up for. Maybe Soos would call for help. Solome could turn on television and watch one of the morning shows as she had coffee. She could read. How could she continue to live in her empty world? That's why people visited Lockwood every day. The trips were a fortress against the waste. The ones who didn't visit Lockwood daily had something else to do, jobs or children to take care of. Solome's fortress was sleep. That's what it was. A place to escape. But she would have to get up soon. Start somewhere. The attic or the basement. The bedroom closets. The dresser drawers. Maybe it was easier to start thinking of what she needed to keep instead of dispose of. Maybe she should start with her mother's house. The dresses in the back of her closet were vintage. Where were the mounds of sequin earrings? But her mother wouldn't hear of it. Solome returned to thinking about her own house as she lay in bed. She wouldn't start with the kitchen. Not the kitchen, no, she wanted all her dishes and utensils, her pots and pans. She moved to Stephen's study. She thought of the boxes of personal belongings from his office at Cobson, his memorabilia and photos. At least, she hadn't had to clean out his office there. Most of his papers were disposed of, or kept in computer records. She thought of Stephen's large desk. His wooden file cabinets and lawyer's book cases. The rest of the bookcases were built in. She could get rid of some of the books and journals. That was where she could start. Then the bedrooms. The attic and basement were still full of the children's projects in school, their clothes, their costumes for various programs. Why was So-lome saving them?— because she couldn't get rid of them. She was losing too much already. She had to hold onto something. Otherwise, the weight-lessness of her life would let her fly off with the leaves from the backyard trees. She thought of the garage. The outdoor cooker, the lawn furniture, the old bicycles, Mark's hockey stick, the snow shovels and blower. She felt saddled with clutter. She rolled over in bed. She wanted to touch Stephen. She wanted to love him. She wanted to push off the awful emptiness that was in bed with her. That was her new companion. Solome and her own life. Maybe she would ask to work five days at the Historical Society. They had asked her to. Maybe she could get lost in her job. Maybe she could work six days, seven. Then there were the family photos on the shelf. She would keep all of them— The albums in the built-in drawers under the bookcases. What would she do with them if she moved? What if she was a widow in China? She should think of her blessings. Yes, her life was blessed. Then why did she feel the large empty ball of air above her as she lay in bed? Why couldn't she get up and go on with her day? She was a floating island. She was the recipient of life. She had never had to look within herself for the kind of strength she needed. Life had been given to her. How poor of spirit she was. How unlikable— she realized. A skater over the frozen lake that was thawing. Solome remembered the skating parties she had been to as a girl— the barrel fire where they warmed themselves— the winter air that crackled in her nose. She longed for the past before the downward slope of her life. Sometimes she thought about her thoughts. How they circled also. How they came back to the same place. She lay in bed and thought about her life and the freedom to just think of it. How many years she had wanted to stay in bed, but the children woke her? How long she had thought if she could just lie in bed?

Solome watched the ceiling fixture in her room. She watched the flat ceiling and the few irregularities here and there. She lay on her back, on her side, on her stomach. She drifted in and out of a dream state in which her thoughts traveled over the past and present without order. *The ceiling has a voice*, she thought. Where did she get that thought? She sat up. She had to think of something else to do. She had to set her life on an expanding course again. She had to get up. Take a shower. Get dressed. Eat. Listen to the weather. Back her car out of the garage to go where?

"Jane," Solome called from the phone beside her bed. "Let's go out for breakfast."

"I don't eat breakfast."

"Coffee?"

"I'm watching television. I have to write a letter to my mother. Otherwise she'll move back from Arizona. I'm having lunch with Carol. You want to join us?"

"No."

"It'll be all right," Jane said.

"No, I'll go out this morning by myself."

"Solome— "

"I'm looking for a reason to get up," Solome told her.

"Eat your cereal and come over for coffee. You can help me think of what to say to my mother."

"No, something else will turn up."

"Carol and I are having lunch at Zander's."

"I'll keep it in mind."

Solome hung up the phone and looked at the ceiling. She would get up. Put on her robe. Go downstairs. Fix coffee. Look at her calendar. Maybe something was on it that she had forgotten, other than going to Lockwood.

Where would she take a vacation? Would she join Jane's travel group? Who would she go with? Where would she go? She had heard women talking about traveling when she ate at a restaurant. They were saying how stressful it was to travel with someone. The one was saying how she and her companion had been two American women yelling at one another in the streets of Copenhagen, the people looking at them. It took years to learn to travel with someone. She would never have anyone like Stephen to travel with again.

Solome held her head in her hands. Her cleaning woman was coming. She had to get out of the house for the afternoon. She could go to her mother's. She could go to Soos' house. She could stay with the girls while Soos went to the store, or she could go with them. No, she wasn't going to be an add-on of their lives. She was going to take care of herself. She would go to Lockwood where Stephen would simply look at her. She could call John Everett and have an affair.

"Mother, do you want to go out to lunch?"

"I'm having left-overs from our dinner last night."

"Have them tonight."

"Come over and we'll have lunch together."

"I don't know what to do next," Solome was honest with her mother.

"I still haven't figured out what to do without your father."

Solome talked to her mother for half an hour.

"I'm going to stay here. I have to learn to get through this by myself." Solome hung up the phone. Hadn't Solo once been her nickname? Hadn't she made decisions by herself? But all the time, she had been surrounded and *clothed* with others. Now, here she was— a Solo act, a meaning that had turned inside-out on itself.

Well, look at it from Christian eyes. She was *clothed* with the blood of Christ, not just outside, but running throughout. That's what she needed to do: see the Bible in terms of art movements. See the Bible as art history.

Solome made an omelet for herself and read the paper while she ate, her silverware clinking against the plate like an old church bell in another neighborhood where they had lived nearly thirty years ago.

On Saturday, Solome took Sarah to *Half-notes*, a music class for children, which Susan also had attended. Sarah stood in a group with other children. They played percussion, drums. They shared. They interacted socially.

Susan had a cold and Soos had taken her to the doctor.

On the way back from *Half-notes*, Solome listened to Minnesota Public Radio. There was new research on Alzheimer's to stop amyloids from clumping in the brain. A molecule, SAP, stuck to amyloid fibers. There was a drug being developed to remove SAP from the blood and therefore from the brain, which would stop the clumping. Someday there would be a prevention for Alzheimer's.

Someday.

Jane talked Solome into going out one evening for dinner and a play with several women: Jane's divorced friend, Jane's daughter, Carol, and two other women. They saw a play called, "2" about the Nuremburg trial of Hermann Goering, the second man behind Hitler. "2" portrayed Goering as a human being, with complexity. He was caught in circumstances that got away from him. The play showed there were other sides to a story, even one as horrible as the Holocaust. Solome was moved by the wife and young daughter who came to the prison to say goodbye to Goering before his death. Was there another side to Alzheimer's? Was it something she could feel sympathy with? Could she see how the disease was caught in a slow stampede that moved toward its end? How could anything like Alzheimer's not take the rap?

Hitler Alzheimer's. Concentration Camp Alzheimer's. Hiroshima Alzheimer's. Atrocity Alzheimer's. Anti-Christ Alzheimer's. Solome kicked the bedroom door when she returned to her house. She kicked and kicked. It whammed the wall and whammed the wall. She bent the door stop, dented the wall with a sunken moon. She wanted her place back. Wife of the provost. The center of friends. Mrs. Stephen Savard. Owner of significance. Of source. Of envy. Of all the hollowness therein.

"Mother" Solome heard a cautious voice. "What's wrong?"

"Soos?" Solome asked, startled.

"You'll wake the girls."

"What are you doing here?" Solome asked, wiping her tears.

"Brian came home in the middle of the night last night. He was late this evening. I didn't want to wait for him again." Soos was crying, and Solome comforted her, her heart still pounding from her outburst.

"What were you doing?" Soos asked.

"I was kicking the door because of your father's Alzheimer's." Solome said, and they held each other in the dim room.

Soos didn't ask any more questions, but let her mother go back into her room.

Later, before she slept, Solome heard the phone, but let Soos answer it.

Agnes stood firm in her views at Bible study. Christ had come to upset Solome's world that Solome might see beyond it. Others did not agree. They had a long discussion on what events were caused by God, and what events came of themselves that could be used by God.

Look at the moon with its Alzheimer's, Solome thought as she left the meeting. There was a thin rope of a cloud, or a vapor trail in the sky, trailing it. Look at the moon wired to the earth so it wouldn't wander off.

In the summer, Solome went to New York for a short visit, and Gretchen and Dennis in turn came to St. Paul. Gretchen looked through Stephen's belongings and took a handkerchief and a belt buckle. Dennis wanted several of his books. He spent a morning going through the shelves. Solome saw he picked Gerhard Ritter's book on World War I and a book about Ritter's conflict with Fritz Fischer, another German historian. Solome tried to find a paper Stephen had given once, but couldn't locate it. Gretchen wanted the signed copy of Angie Debo's books on Native American history.

"Did dad know her?"

"I think someone gave him the book."

Dennis' pile of books continued to grow until he had to sort through them again. Solome would ship two dozen books to him, she said. The rest she would keep until Gretchen and Dennis were settled in one place.

"Do you want any of your father's things?" Solome asked Mark when he came by the house. "I'm going to get rid of a lot this summer."

"I'd sell most of them at the used bookstore," Mark said.

"There's at least a dozen boxes of his books the college sent from his office. If you help me get through them, the money is yours."

The next week, Mark and his friends came by the house and spent the morning in Stephen's study going through his books. They separated the ones they wanted from the ones they didn't. They also separated the signed books for Solome. She would keep a few of his important books. She would keep the history and educational journals in which Stephen's articles appeared. She would keep the book Stephen had written.

The boys loaded two cars with Stephen's books.

"How can you get rid of dad's books?" Mark asked.

"I had to face getting rid of your father." Solome answered. "Why don't you ask me about that?"

Mark's friends seemed embarrassed over Solome's bluntness with Mark. She decided to let it go as they ate the lunch she fixed for them. They talked about their own interests. Sometimes they asked her questions about the history of Cobson. Then they were gone with Stephen's books.

It wasn't as easy as she thought. In Stephen's study, she grieved over the vacant shelves. She took her dust cloth and wiped the dusty places behind the books, the thin dust lines between the places books had been. She wiped the shelves clean. She wiped her face that was damp with tears. She wiped the shelves again. Solome sat in Stephen's study. "Stephen," she said. The room seemed to echo, not the way a house echoes once the furniture is taken— before the furniture of the next family comes in. But the study echoed with a vacancy that couldn't be filled.

Solome looked through the books of historical essays Stephen had edited. She looked at the book he had written, *A Clear Distance: Post American Revolutionary War*, which he dedicated to her. Solome remembered when they sat at the table surrounded by children and decided on the title. *Cleared for Democracy* was another choice of Stephen's. Stephen had wanted to continue writing, but his teaching and administrative duties got in the way. There was some notes for another book, but Solome had forgotten what would have been the intent of that manuscript.

Later, Mark returned to the house.

"How could you get rid of dad?" He asked. "Wasn't that the question you told me to ask?"

"Because of love, I guess," Solome said after thinking.

"I don't know what you're talking about."

"You're going to miss these things, Mark, if you don't."

"You're always putting me on the defensive."

"I just expect more from you."

"What do you expect?" Mark was angry, and they hadn't even talked.

"Understanding. Help."

"What do you want me to do?"

"I want you not to have to ask those questions."

"I can't get dad back. I can't put your life together."

"My life is together."

"Then why are you bothering me?"

"Bothering?" Solome questioned. "What have I asked of you? It's always me giving to you."

"You have the resources. The house. The checking account."

"I don't expect you to support me. Your father took care of that." Solome said. "But I expect you to be a human being who understands what
I'm going through."

"I'm going through it too." Mark answered quickly. "Do you think I see
dad and don't know everything is gone."

"I want to feel love from you."

"I do love you." Mark said.

"What is love?" Solome asked. "I hear it at church. I hear it in my Bible
study. I just heard it from you."

"It's knowing you are my mother."

"It sounds like an obligation."

"It's different from loving my girlfriend."

"I can remember that kind of love. I remember when I only wanted
to be with your father." Mark looked away from her, but she continued.
"Love is feeling at first— a physical commitment. Then there's the idea of
marriage, or recognition of a contract made, of a decision that is kept. It's a
covenant between a man and woman that transcends the physical. Love is
something that keeps changing. It's the realization that you've become the
other. The two have become one. I think in terms of us. Not me. Or he. Love
is a transcendence that is more than the disappointments, the boredom,
the disinterestedness, the hurts that come from time to time over the years.
Love is the power of forgiveness. I don't always feel love, but I know it in my
head. I was given a gift— a marriage that worked because we made it work,
for one thing. We didn't give up. We were blessed with success. We had the
privilege of working for what we wanted and achieving it. Sometimes I look
at Stephen now and wonder if the next step is pity. I look at him in his next
state— his consciousness without ideas— maybe even without recognition
of that consciousness— and wonder how love will cover that."

Mark didn't answer.

"As his wife, I have been lost in Stephen's Alzheimer's. It has erased me
as a wife, which has been most of what I am."

Stephen Savard

I see   chair looked   people   my room   go   there

Diane Glancy

Solome Savard

The next winter, Solome was invited to the Faculty Wives Club Christmas luncheon, and a dinner at the college president's house, but had declined both. She wanted to slip into the holiday season without notice. She was even tired of sending Christmas cards, and cut her list in half. Later, she resisted the temptation to send out last-minute cards. Let them think she was losing her grip. Many of them had stopped calling her anyway. If she saw them at the grocery store, or music hall, there was a rushed greeting before they moved on.

The day before Christmas came on Sunday that year. Solome sat in the church with her family. Mark sat beside Solome. His girlfriend, Mary Case, was on the other side of Solome. She didn't mean to sit between them, but when Mark entered the pew she was behind him. Soos, the girls and Brian, were on the other side of Mary Case. Solome asked Mary Case if she wanted to exchange places, but Mary Case said she was fine where she was. Mary Case began talking to Soos, but Solome didn't know what to say to Mark. She wanted to tell him she missed Stephen. She wanted to tell him she would give anything to have him on the other side of Mark.

During children's time, Solome took Sarah and Susan to the front of the church. Sarah clung to Solome, but Susan wanted to be independent. Solome sat on the floor with the girls and the other children. Soon Sarah relaxed and moved away from Solome to sit with another girl she seemed to know.

When they were finished, Solome took the girls to their Sunday school classes, then returned to the pews. The only place to sit was by Brian. Where did Solome belong in the family? Didn't the Eskimos set the mother-in-law adrift on an ice floe? It wouldn't be that easy for her. She would live for a while. Even her mother was still alive. What would she do?

After church Solome took Mark and Mary Case, Soos and her family for brunch. Solome was still the head of the family. They wouldn't have gone out to eat without Solome there to pay the bill. Gretchen and Dennis arrived that afternoon. Soos wanted to go to the airport, but Sarah was crying and needed her nap. Mark and Mary Case had to go to her parents, so Solome drove to the airport by herself. She still worried about them flying, but she kept it to herself. She brought Dennis and Gretchen back to her house. Gretchen was glad to be home. She was tired and stressed. The semester was over. She had gotten her grades in at the last moment, staying up late to read her students' papers. Dennis also.

That evening was Christmas Eve. Solome had prepared most of the meal and had gifts under the tree. Soos and her family arrived about 6:00. Mark and Mary Case arrived shortly after. Gretchen and Dennis had fallen asleep while Solome set the table and finished preparing the meal. Mark went upstairs to wake them. When they came downstairs, the family toasted the season, ate, and opened a few gifts.

That evening, they returned to church for the children's program. Susan was one of the angels that announced Jesus' birth. There were several angels, as they had to use all the children. Soos had sewn the two sides of Susan's angel dress together. Solome had hemmed the dress that afternoon while Soos made a lamb costume for Sarah.

Christmas morning Solome opened a box she had wrapped for herself earlier in December. It was a long, wool *Geiger* coat she wanted. She also had a gift from Jane Mead she opened.

Gretchen gave Solome an art book from the New York Historical Society, and some note cards of different scenes in New York.

"Gretchen, how did you know I would want these?"

"I knew you always went to the Historical Society when you were in New York. I knew you'd like something from the museum shop."

Gretchen and Dennis had opened their gifts. They had given each other books.

Dennis fixed French toast for Gretchen and Solome. Later that morning, they drove to Lockwood.

"He won't know any of us, Gretchen," Solome said. "You haven't seen him for a while."

"I was here last summer."

"He has declined since then."

"Dad," Gretchen said.

Stephen looked at Gretchen without expression. He seemed to neither recognize nor reject her. He looked at Dennis as though he knew him. Dennis greeted Stephen. Stephen didn't know his son-in-law. This was the man he'd given his daughter to. Solome felt a tenderness toward Dennis. If only she could forgive Brian.

Solome looked at Stephen in his helplessness. They had dressed him in a bright necktie. He looked like the only ornament left on the tree.

Mark and Mary Case were late. Soos and Brian were ready to leave when they arrived at Lockwood. "I have to get dinner for us," Soos told him.

"Mom has to stop by her house and get the dishes she's bringing."

"Dennis and I made a salad," Gretchen told Soos. "We'll be right behind you."

"Want to ride with us?" Dennis asked Susan.

"She can't," Soos told him. "It's too hard to change the base of her car seat from car to car."

"I can remember you kids sat in the car without a seat belt."

"Now children have to be buckled in." Soos told her. "It's a law."

Mark and Mary Case were in Stephen's room. Solome looked down the hall for them. What could they be talking about?

"Who is Mary Case?"

"Someone Mark met."

"Where?"

"I don't know."

"Don't worry," Soos said, "he's never with anyone long."

"It might be another girl by evening," Brian said.

But Mary Case lasted past Christmas. Mark was with her in the spring. Solome planned a picnic at Hill Park where she and Stephen had taken the family for picnics.

The week after the picnic, Mark was with another girl, but Mary Case soon returned.

"Is it serious?" Soos asked Mark.

"No," he answered. "I have graduate school to think about."

"What is she going to do?"

"She'll go to school also."

"Where?"

"We might live together." Mark looked at Solome.

Solome had the flu. She felt miserable. Maybe it was a sinus infection. Her cheek ached. She took antibiotics and lay in bed a day and a night. Soos called and said her mother sounded awful. Could she help? No. I don't want you and the girls near me. I'll be all right. It just takes time.

The second night, Solome lay awake. She felt weak again. She read the label. Sleeplessness and nervousness was one of the symptoms.

Somewhere, Solome dreamed she was at a dating service. A rhinoceros was loose in the yard.

Solome went to the St. Paul Grille one evening for dinner with her discussion group. She drove down Summit Avenue lined with mansions. She liked St. Paul and its surroundings. The University Club, the Ordway Concert Hall and Rice Park with its ice sculptures during winter carnival, the Historical Society between the Minnesota Capitol building and the St. Paul Cathedral, the Mississippi River, farmer's market, the warehouse district, the old stockyards, Harriet Island, Mounds Park.

"I watch the birds at the feeder," Solome told her friends, "sparrow after sparrow. They are busy eating, then suddenly fly off for no apparent reason. Their wings sound like tissue paper."

Jane Mead looked at Solome.

"Stephen is going through a fearful phase," Solome explained, "suspicious of everything. Sometimes when I look at him, I see birds in his eyes."

After dinner, she took Selby Avenue back toward her house. She passed the St. Paul Curling Club. She had read about it in the newspaper. Some women had started the new club, or re-started the old club after many years. It was a name Stephen had asked her about— the name of a game he couldn't remember— a game in which a woman rolled a stone shaped like a teapot down a runway of ice. It was one of the first times she noticed his forgetfulness. If only she had known she was starting a slow roll down the ice. What would she have done? What could she do? Just keep going.

There was an opening for curator at the Historical Society, but Solome only had a B.A. in Art History. She wasn't eligible to apply. She wished she had continued graduate school until she had a Masters. She was too old now. She didn't want to go to school. She didn't want to study. It took her longer to read a book for her discussion group than it used to. Her stack of books by the bed weren't read as quickly as they had been. She didn't want to write papers, or take exams. She didn't want to work on a thesis. Yes, a woman had graduated college at the age of 78, but not Solome. She had made that decision early in life, she thought as she listened to the women around the table. She became Stephen's wife and the mother of three children. She was no longer Solome Holfgren, but Solome Savard. It was too late to go back. She would go on with what she had. A bachelor's degree and a need to work.

She would deal with the new winter—her limitations. Maybe they were more like demons.

Solome continued working four days a week at the Historical Society. She visited Stephen in the evenings. Her time seemed to pass quickly. She still had the moments she woke in the night. On Saturday mornings she looked at the ceiling and wondered where she was going. She prayed with her group at the Monday night Bible study.

The Monday night meeting began her week. She would not leave it. One Monday evening Soos needed her help. Brian was out-of-town with his work, and the girls were sick. Solome went to her house, and called the Forman sisters where the meeting was that night. Solome rocked Sarah while she tried to sleep, but continued to wake because her nose was stopped up and she had trouble breathing.

Sarah had started to kindergarten in the afternoons. She would be one of the youngest in her class, and Soos had thought about holding her back, but decided at the last minute to send her. Soos seemed to have some relief. But as soon as Solome thought she was over her depression, she would be depressed again.

Sometimes in the mornings, on her way to work, Solome stopped by Lockwood. Sometimes she stopped by Soos' after Brian left the house. One morning, Soos was sewing a costume for Sarah's dance recital. Sarah would be thunder in a lightning and thunder dance. She stomped her feet on the rug to show Solome how thunder sounded.

"Susanna, you're doing too much," Solome pleaded when Sarah was watching television. "Half notes, dance lessons— "

"I don't do as much as my friends who have boys in little league," Soos answered. "I have to keep moving."

Solome understood. It was what she was doing also, she thought as she drove to work.

Solome worked in the Acquisitions and Curatorial Department. Someone would call to say they had cleaned out their grandparent's attic. There were some artifacts. Would the Historical Society be interested in looking at them? There was a certain amount of tact required. Often the artifacts were brought to the Historical Society. Other times, the curator made a field trip to the site.

Solome had her own cubicle at the Historical Society. She ate lunch with others in the staff lounge with its large glass window and courtyard. There were children at the Historical Society daily. Their noise echoed in the hall. Their tennis shoes squeaked on the floor. Susan and Sarah liked to come to the History Society. They liked to see the other children. They liked to visit the museum and have lunch at Cafe Minnesota. Solome's mother sometimes met them for lunch.

One day, after they finished lunch, Solome walked her mother to her car. Solome turned before she went back into the building, and saw her mother drive up over the curb as she turned into the drive at the ticket booth to leave the parking lot.

After work, Solome shopped at Daynard's in downtown St. Paul. She bought some things for the girls. She ate in the River Room. She thought about her mother and how soon she would be in Lockwood with Stephen. Solome spent as much time as she could in the store that evening because it was hard to go home without Stephen there. Some evenings were harder than others. When the store began to clear of people, Solome made her way to Daynard's parking lot. She drove through downtown St. Paul, usually vacant of an evening, unless there was a concert or some event, and started up the hill to Summit Avenue.

When she turned into the cul-de-sac, she saw her house on Upper St. John Street. She braked and sat a while looking at the house. It was a large, two-story brick and wood house with a new roof. The windows were washed. The landscape was in order. It was a handsome house in which she had lived over 25 years. The Savard house. She remembered when she and Stephen had seen it. She wanted it the moment she saw it. They had taken a Sunday afternoon drive after reading the real estate section of the newspaper. The wood was painted white; she thought of painting it gray, which they did their third year in the house, and had kept it gray through the years. An understated, but substantial house. She remembered the mortgage that had nearly swallowed them. Then, after fifteen years in the house, they began making two payments a month and the mortgage was paid. She had left a small light on in the kitchen, and one upstairs in her bedroom. She pushed the garage opener on her visor and waited until the door lifted. She drove into the garage, turned off the motor, pushed the button, and when the door was down, she got out of the car. Why would she want to sell the house? It was her fortress against the uncertainty and loss.

For some reason, she thought of the cabin at Crane Lake, the little moon floating around the planet of her house in St. Paul. What was the cabin doing up in the cold dark of Crane Lake, the bones of Brown at its side?

Gretchen asked Solome to come to New York. Solome held tickets on her Delta frequent flyer. When she called to confirm the reservation, they needed her pin number. She didn't know it. Couldn't they get it for her? No. It had to come through the mail. It would take two weeks.

"But I'm leaving next week."

"You can go to the airport, but it will cost you $75."

"I have to drive to the airport?"

"Delta doesn't have an office in St. Paul."

Solome looked through Stephen's drawer in which airline information was kept. She could not find the number. She tried to get into the system with numbers they frequently used for password and pin number. Stephen would not know. She remembered the days when Stephen's secretary, Janet, took care of their plane and hotel reservations. Now Solome was on her own.

Solome drove to the airport, drove into the long term parking by mistake. What happened? She'd taken the wrong entry gate somehow. It was all the construction. She drove around and around, looking for a place. Finally, she found a place and went into the airport. She could only use the escalator for one floor, then ran into more construction. She took the elevator down another floor and walked through the underpass into the airport.

"I don't know why they told you to come to the airport," the clerk said.

"I don't know my pin number." Solome was annoyed.

They had her where they wanted her. She would pay her $75. She could tell them she wouldn't fly Delta again.

In New York, Gretchen and Solome stopped by a neighborhood market. Gretchen turned away from the grocery cart to look at produce and when she turned back, her purse was gone. In half a minute, it was gone—

Gretchen cried, "My purse— "

She ran to the door to see if anyone was running, but saw no one. She turned back to the store, but everyone was busy shopping.

The manager came.

"It vanished in an instant. I'm always so careful." Gretchen continued to cry. "I watch every move I make. I always carry my purse inside my coat. But just this once—"

There was nothing the manager could do.

The police were called. It didn't take them long to arrive. Gretchen made a report. There was nothing they could do either. It happened too often.

Solome and Gretchen left the cart in the aisle and started back to Gretchen's apartment to cancel credit cards. Already whoever took her purse was loading up with cameras and cash. Gretchen called the VISA number. She called the bank. It was closed, but there was a number to report lost cards.

"Do you want to call Dennis?"

"He feels so helpless when he can't do anything." Gretchen was still in a panic.

"List the cards you carried with you," Solome told her.

"I thought you were at the cart," Gretchen said.

"I was looking at the produce with you."

"You don't know what it feels like," Gretchen said. "— How angry it makes me."

"I do know what it feels like." Solome was irritated with Gretchen. "I lost your father. Don't you think Alzheimer's is a thief? I lost more than my purse."

"Can't you stop harping? He's my father. I know what has happened to him. Stop bothering me with your problems."

"Stop bothering me with yours," Solome said.

Gretchen decided to call Dennis in case he could think of something she hadn't. He told her they only would be responsible for $50 worth of charges on a stolen card.

"At least they didn't get much cash," Gretchen said. "But it's my wallet. My purse. My date book! How will I remember my appointments?"

The next day Solome continued to work with the cancellation of Gretchen's cards. She had an early class, and Solome said she would be glad to help.

It was calmer with Gretchen out of the apartment, though without Gretchen there, Solome had to face the apartment by herself. The kitchen was ugly. Its one window faced the brick wall of the building next to it. There was nothing to look at, nothing in which to have an invested interest. Maybe that's why there was emphasis on studies, on ideas, on something outside the apartment. The plumbing knocked. The faucet leaked. She saw a cockroach on the floor when she had to get up in the night. She and Stephen always had stayed at the Hotel Beacon on Broadway at 75th, or in other neighborhood hotels when they visited Gretchen. Solome felt the shoddy shape of the whole world when she stayed in Gretchen's apartment in New York.

What was memory? Solome thought as she sat with Stephen at Lockwood on Saturday afternoon. It was something she had. Memory was a language, and language was a network. Therefore, memory was a network. Certainly memory was meaning. It was solid as frozen water. Yet it could transform into water again. That's what memory was. A form that could reshape. A retrieval of connections. Two mirrors facing one another at an angle that reflected the same image over and over, making a long tunnel of the same continuous images. Because of memory, Solome had a ship. It was a ship with cargo. Cargo that the pirate ship, Alzheimer's, could not take.

Solome sat beside Stephen in his room. She watched him move his hand against his leg. What was he doing? She thought of Stephen in his chair in their bedroom. Was he remembering Brown sitting beside him? Was he petting Brown?

Solome got up, wiped her eyes, and stood at the window. Stephen was on a journey. He would return to himself in the afterlife. It was the Christian hope.

Memory was a promise of the sea.

Stephen Savard

The lake was   Had we ?   I heard the lap of waves Crane Lake. They not stop. Come to drown. I   take my ax to water to   chop   waves.

Solome Savard

Solome found passages in the Bible for which she could hold God responsible: *You have. . . made all their memory to perish*— Isaiah 26:14 For a moment, she understood another way to look at Stephen's disease. She saw Alzheimer's as a part of heaven: *Their sins and inequities I will remember no more*— Hebrews 10:17. God forgot all the sins of humanity that stretched across the heavens. God himself allowed Alzheimer's into a part of his thinking.

That's what she came to church to hear. To be reminded that when her world broke apart, when towers fell, God remained— and that according to his word, the broken would be whole again. She had to pull that thought from her own forgetfulness.

Alzheimer's dominated everything. Solome saw it every day she visited Lockwood— Saturday, Sunday, Monday— the evenings she sat beside Stephen while he was gone to sea. The times she visited with the family of the man who shared Stephen's room.

If Stephen had words he would ask how Solome knew him. He looked at her puzzled.

"What doing   here this ?" Stephen asked. "Were they   daughter? didn't what he think   what he didn't   mother?"

Solome listened for meaning she could understand. Sometimes she felt she entered Stephen's life before she knew him. She knew, in Alzheimer's, short-term memory went first, then mid-memory, pushing him farther and farther back. They could be childhood friends. She could go into his life where she'd never been. He tried to cover himself with words. He just couldn't think at the moment, but he kept trying.

"What   doing ? I did yes of," he said. "I called Dad."

There— Stephen had connected with a thought.

"What did he say?" Solome asked.

"Let's go   there the   shirt left." Stephen talked as if he was dreaming. "This isn't my house."

Sometimes the things he said were right.

Stephen tried to continue, but his words disappeared as soon as he said them. Alzheimer's was a constant rain. It left splots of water smearing the words on the page. Stephen forgot what he was trying to say. He didn't understand. It made him angry. It made him unpleasant to be with.

Where was he going?

"Only now matters," Solome told him. "Memories depart. You can be yourself without the cargo."

It was something he should know.

What was it like inside Stephen's head? Solome tried to think of his confusion. His thinking had become fluid. It was water that had some sort of containment, some shores, but they were not in sight.

Solome talked to Stephen at Lockwood as though he understood. Susan was now eight, Sarah five.

"Stephen? Do you want to hold one in your hand?" Solome took his fingers in her mouth. She brushed with her tongue, but quickly pulled back. No, that was over between them. She didn't want to stir any remembrance of that in Stephen.

Diane Glancy

Stephen Savard

She   take from sister
      on road   father she cried   go
      and   was there riding   now

Solome Savard

That summer, Solome received a call about her mother. She had taken a walk and could not find her way back to her house. She had knocked on someone's door. Solome could take her mother to Lockwood, but she did not want to go.

"Mother, you can't stay by yourself." Solome was firm.

"I can live with you."

"No, you can't. I want my own life. I don't want to take care of you every day."

"When have you ever taken care of me?" Margret asked. "I take care of myself—just not in my own house anymore."

"I'm gone most days. I would worry about you here by yourself. What would you do? What if you wandered off?"

"I was thinking about something and walked too far without paying attention," Margret answered. "It could happen to anyone. I'll watch television. Read. I'll do what I do at my own house. We can have supper together in the evening. I could help Soos."

"No, mother, you couldn't."

"What would it matter?" Gretchen asked on the phone.

"How can you get rid of her too?" Soos asked.

Imagine a woman opening a box and finding it empty. Imagine an only child saying, the world is mine. Imagine finding out that it wasn't. Imagine not knowing what to do. Imagine Solome doing what she didn't want to do. What nothing in her wanted to do. Imagine facing truth. Solome's mother would live with her. Solome would put her in Gretchen's room. Imagine feeling like an unlikable woman in an unlikable world.

The next week Mark Stephen left the dog with Margret when Solome wasn't home— the dog he had given Solome for Christmas— the dog she didn't want— the dog Mark didn't have time to care for.

"He'll keep me company," Solome's mother said.

Solome had the power of attorney for her mother. She could force her into Lockwood. But she would not. Her mother was in her 80's. She could live into her 90's. What if Solome didn't have money to keep both her mother and Stephen in a home? What if she was destitute? What would she do? Stephen had assured her that wouldn't happen. They had enough savings. But she woke at 3:00 a.m. as though her money was running out and she had no way to cover her debt.

She worked at the Historical Society, she reminded herself. She had a job. She could sell the house and live in a simple apartment. Her recurring worries of money were unfounded.

She was in the bottom of the sky.

She had washed the house.

She had fed the sea.

It would take a dumpster to clean out her mother's house.

Solome told Mark he could begin hauling off his grandmother's magazines. He and his friends could give her a hand. Should Solome save some of the furniture for Gretchen? Mark? Mark had started graduate school at the University of Minnesota. He had wanted to go to one of the universities in the east, but hadn't been accepted. Yes, Mark's apartment was barren. Solome would ask Mary Case what they wanted.

The real estate agent put a *for-sale* sign in the front yard of the Holfgren house. Margret didn't come out of Gretchen's room for an afternoon.

The dog whimpered at her door.

Alzheimer's had battered Solome. Not even her children understood. Stephen's disease separated her from them. Their lives were expanding, while hers was diminishing. Was she experiencing with Stephen what God had experienced with her? Someone there, but not there. Solome wanted to face herself. She didn't know it would be so?— Unlovely. She wanted something real, but not this real. It was her own distant heart she bumped into.

Batter also was a covering for pork chops or chicken. It was something that made something else better.

Solome read another article about China in the newspaper— a country forgetful of its humanitarian responsibility. Solome remembered the handle on her pull luggage had been broken when she returned to St. Paul. She thought of the Chinese workers. She remembered the blank look on the faces she had seen.

Solome took her book on Chinese art, which she had bought at the Minneapolis Institute of Art, when she visited Stephen at Lockwood that afternoon. She talked to him about the art. What was she doing? He didn't understand, but it gave her something to say to him. He didn't mind her talking. He didn't respond, but she felt somewhere he understood the book was about someplace they had been together. No, she knew there was nowhere he understood.

She mentioned the different dynasties: Yuan, Ming and Qing. There had been the Mongols, the Communists, the western influence. Solome liked the leaps she could make when talking to Stephen. He would not question her logic.

"Early painting was not done to make a formal likeness," she told him, "but to say something of what the artist thought."

For a moment, Stephen seemed to look at Solome instead of beyond her.

"Look at the Alzheimer's, Stephen, the austerity of early Chinese art—mountain, rock, tree—the calligraphy written in the corner, saying something we can't read." Solome liked talking to Stephen about the art book. "There was simplicity, clarity, balance. There was the ambiguous use of space. You see," she pointed, "here it is not the rock that is important, but the brush strokes that make the rock."

You see, it is not memory, but the thought of memory—

In the evening, after Solome returned from Lockwood, she worked at her sewing machine making some simple dresses for the girls. She also finished a skirt for Susan which closed with Velcro.

That night, when Solome turned out the light in her bedroom, as her eyes grew accustomed to the dark, she saw a strange dimness from somewhere. What was it? The Ojibway spirits she read about at the Historical Society? She got up from bed, half afraid. Maybe the ghost of Stephen. Her heart pounded as she walked down the hall. What was it? In the other room— the sewing machine light. She had not turned it off.

The next day, Solome received a note from the tour guide of their trip to China. It had been sent to everyone. It was notice that one of the couples who had been on their tour had been killed. It was some sort of accident. Solome hardly remembered them or the trip. She got out the photo album and found the couple. It seemed like years ago. Solome would have liked to ask Stephen if he remembered. Maybe somewhere he did.

Solome received a phone call from Buyck near Crane Lake. Someone had been living in her cabin.

"But it isn't heated for winter," she told the constable who had called. "The electricity is off." Maybe they had figured out a way to turn on the electricity. The man told her the woodstove and fireplace had been used. The beds and couch were turned on their sides to catch the warmth in front of the fireplace. At least, there was no phone they could use.

"Is the birch bark canoe still there?"

"I don't remember."

"It was an antique my father had. It was suspended from the ceiling."

She called back several days later.

"It wasn't there," the constable told her. "Maybe they chopped it for firewood."

Solome had some friends who had bolted their cabin against winter intruders, and the intruders had finally burnt the cabin down.

At least the cabin was still there.

"I'll be up in the spring," Solome said. "Just close it back up. I'll pay for repairs on the lock when I come up."

She thought again of how she lived in a country where she owned properties. She lived in a country where everyone was important. Even old widows and women who were no longer necessary. No one could be dismissed. The individual had a chance. What if she had been born in India? Russia? She would not be in her comfortable house on Upper St. John in St. Paul. What if she had been born into a low caste with no way out? What if she had an alcoholic father who beat her and she had no place to go but had sold into prostitution to support his alcoholism?

It seemed every other week there was an article in the newspaper about the torture and death of thousands in other countries. Solome felt a black wave of possibility cross her. Would she be murdered if she lived in another country? Would she be considered a useful citizen? Worse yet, could Alzheimer's patients be murdered? What third-world economy could sustain or even tolerate the slow and expensive *retrograde* to birth, when patients disappeared into death the same helpless way they had entered life at birth? Solome could see how it would make sense. Were the health care companies already considering it? Weren't patients already secondary to them?

On Friday, as Solome worked at her desk at the Historical Society, Jane Mead called and wanted Solome to go with her to an evening program on Harriet Island on the Mississippi River in downtown St. Paul. Solome had seen it in the newspaper. *Spread your Blanket on the Ground.* Solome turned to it in the paper while Jane was on the phone. *The Compleat Wrks of Wlm Shkspr 37 Plays in 97 Minutes.*

"I've had too much abbreviation," Solome said. "The whole world is abbreviated for Stephen," *for Stph Svrd,* Solome thought. "I can't go, Jane."

How easily Solome had slid through life, as if on a sled, Solome thought as she sat by herself that night. Then she found resistance. Alzheimer's was the wall. How easily she had spilled. How awful it felt to be dumped. She felt the condescension, the pity, the triumph of women in the grocery store she knew whose husbands were still functional. Their lives were still whole as hers had once been. But the women should be careful. One wrong move and it all unraveled. But what had been Solome's wrong move? What had Stephen done to deserve his Alzheimer's? He had educated students to think critically and act on what they believed, to examine what they believed and why. He had looked at hard points overlooked in American history, the mistakes American had made. He wanted students to know the past because it gave them the basis on which to go forward. But now Stephen, the educator, had become un-educated.

If Alzheimer's was un-educating Stephen, it was educating Solome. It was a difficult series of courses. It was about imposing limits on the physical properties of their lives, which also was the process by which those limits were surpassed. It was a two-fold going of more than one way. It could be done by single word, such as "batter." While Stephen was locked in Alzheimer's, he also moved beyond. The crunch of the containment was a process of breaking the imposed limits. Yes, the imposing of limits was a breaking of them both in the object of Alzheimer's.

For some of the husbands of Solome's friends, the mental properties had outlasted the physical. In Stephen, she had his body, but his mind was someplace else.

It was the business of Alzheimer's.

This blasting area.

Solome and her mother were on their way to spend a few days at Crane Lake. The dog that Mark passed on to his grandmother was in the backseat. Solome wondered again how long she would keep the cabin. In the mail, she had received new assessments on her property for sewer lines. But she knew it was pressure from the resorts that wanted the privately-owned properties. It had not done much good to protest before the council in the past. It just delayed the changes for a while. The cabin also needed more repair each year. Would all those summers spent at Crane Lake disappear too?

Solome drove north past the moraine where glaciers had pushed the topsoil to southern Minnesota and uncovered the stony subsoil. The pine forests had been logged. The miners had taken the iron-ore. Just north of Crane Lake, were the boundary waters. Beyond them, was Canada, the Arctic, the frozen outer space of Alzheimer's where Stephen waited. Yes, the spruce trees were missiles pointing up toward God's chair in heaven. This is who she was. No wonder she hadn't known. She was Solome, the empty, who asked for a head on a platter. She was Solome, a child of God, in the family of Christ by faith. She never would have believed it.

In Buyck, Solome and her mother stopped at a small office and had the electricity turned on.

When they got to the cabin, the door was chained and they couldn't open it. They would have to drive back to Buyck and have the constable open it for them.

He returned to the cabin with them, helped Solome turn the furniture upright and move the bed back into the bedroom. The birch bark canoe was gone— probably in the ashes of the fireplace she would sweep out, or sold to an antique store somewhere.

"I never liked it anyway," Margret Holfgren said. "I told Frank I didn't want it up there on the ceiling."

"You should have sold it," Solome told her. You could have taken a vacation with the price it brought.

When the constable left, Solome looked through the cabin for what else was gone. She could not find sheets or towels. There were other things missing. She would have to think.

Solome and her mother slept in the same room that night, the dog at Margret's feet, growling now and then at its new surroundings. Solome reclaimed the cabin from whoever had broken into the cabin mid-winter and stayed there— how long? She thought of Alzheimer's as the intruder.

She wasn't afraid. This was her family's cabin. This was hers. She cried each night as she went to sleep because of the unbearable absence of Stephen. During the day, she and her mother cleaned the cabin. She worked outside pulling weeds, swatting away a swarm of mosquitoes, thinking her way through her downsizing. The dog was tied on a long rope. Once Solome saw him sniffing Brown's grave. In the evening she faced the night with her mother. But sleep became a regenerator that plugged Solome back into life. In the murky sludge of sleep and dream, she floated over the curve of earth and found the curve back into herself.

Her faith was the rope, the cord line that kept her from going adrift. It was what she had chosen to get through the rest of her life. She had one foot on the rope of Stephen's boat out there beyond sight, but she could feel the pull of the rope under her foot. This was the self she had hunted for. A self that could hold all her contradictions and desperation. This was the Solo she was once again.

She blessed the day though she felt the despair of her loss. She remembered when she realized Stephen had had the potential to be a college president. His abilities and the momentum of their lives had moved toward it. She remembered when she watched it pass. Stephen was like the tall, old tree that had been cut down. But its roots still spread under the ground, and she could remember its shade and the sound of the wind high in its leaves.

In the mornings she woke, eyes puffy with tears, but with a resolve to get through the day. She called Soos to ask about the girls.

"Who would have known we would end up like this?" Margret asked her daughter as they sat together of an evening, wrapped in a blanket in deck chairs as if on an ocean voyage. "Two dowagers— though Stephen isn't dead."

Solome felt the diminishing process of life, but she said to her mother, "You've got two great-grandchildren. There will be more. We don't go away with nothing. It just feels that way."

"We're two wives of two kings," Margret said. "We're two wives of two Lazaruses who won't come back from the dead."

"We're two crones who have known grace," Solome told her mother, "though we've been jutted up against one another, cracked apart— other parts have been grafted onto our fractured selves."

"I don't always know what you're talking about, Solome," Margret said, "but I know you do."

"What if we gain our soul, but lose the world?"

The last evening before Solome returned to St. Paul, she stood on the shore at Crane Lake. She looked at the evening pines, the rounded sky above her, the lake glittering over the curve of earth, her consciousness on it like a little mound of sequins.

She saw a pontoon cross the lake in front of her. It was an older couple riding together, enjoying the evening. She could see their gray hair. Solome held that image. She could almost feel Stephen hold her hand. She was on a ride too, with Stephen, out across the watery grave of his Alzheimer's.

Solome caught an idea of something somewhere. *The mind existed outside the brain.* Maybe then, memory existed outside the head that was supposed to hold it. Maybe Stephen was remembering somewhere. Maybe too— language could exist independent of words, and somewhere Stephen was able to talk. Maybe consciousness was a part of the larger universe. A part of God. Stephen was only disconnected from his brain. But his mind existed— somewhere—

Solome was hopeful. Solome was despondent. She felt her contradictions. Her very name was divided between the two appositional Salome's. She was clothed with the struggle of forces. But the journey was more than the destination. It was the *process of the migration* in the Native American history she read at the Historical Society. But in the Bible, where she was at the moment because she had to be, it was outcome that mattered. With faith, she could be a Solo act, a woman whose husband was incapacitated with Alzheimer's. No matter where she would drift— no matter if she would sink, faith and hope were there to lift her. With Stephen she had flown through a mosquito net of demons. They were on their way home. That's what demons were— an absence of truth. An absence of faith to fight the desolation. To resist the destruction. Yes—

Solome had the desire to see truth.

It cut right through to Stephen where she had dreamed his gift, his president's office.

It cut right through the hard core of herself.

www.ingramcontent.com/pod-product-compliance
Lightning Source LLC
Chambersburg PA
CBHW051835020726
47502CB00005B/1804